MY TIRED SHADOW

JOSEPH HIRSCH

Published by Underground Voices
www.undergroundvoices.com
Editor contact: Cetywa Powell

ISBN #: 978-0-9988923-2-0
Printed in the United States of America.

Made in the USA
Lexington, KY
02 February 2018

INTRODUCTION
By James Brown

Glory and tragedy are rarely inseparable in the sport of boxing. Being the "greatest" came at a great cost to Muhammad Ali with Parkinson's disease, which doctors attributed to the many blows he took in the ring. Look at Joe Louis. Once a household name around the world, he spent his last years as a "greeter," a kind of glorified doorman in Vegas, hooked on coke and booze. And what about Mike Tyson's meteoric rise as the youngest heavyweight champion in boxing history, only to end, a few years later, in utter disgrace? This is hardly a fraction of the big men who fell from grace, and there are sixteen other weight divisions in boxing, all of them chockful of similar stories of success and failure, fame and obscurity, and, most often, drug and alcohol addiction. In boxing writer Joey Hirsch's novel, *My Tired Shadow*, we meet the classic "I Coulda Been a Contender" Ritchie Abruzzi, an Italian Stallion, minus the heart of gold. Unlike his Rocky movies counterpart, Ritchie is more cruel than kind, more reckless than wise -- more flawed and real, in short, than white America's unrealistic thirst for a humble white champion.

If there is light at the end of the tunnel for washed-up fighters, you won't find it in Joey Hirsch's harsh depiction of life beyond the ring after the last bell has rung. From the barrios of East L.A. to the trailer-park ghettos of Venice Beach, Ritchie takes fights where he can get them for quick cash under the table. It could be a bare knuckles brawl against a jail bird in a parking lot, or a charity boxing event at the VFW against a former rival, or even accepting an embarrassing role in a B-grade movie as a zombie boxer. Whatever the job, if the money is there, he'll take it. His days of self-respect are long gone, replaced now by booze and self-loathing, hell bent on his own destruction. Even his long lost son, who as an adolescent briefly comes back into his father's life, isn't enough to change the trajectory of Ritchie's downward spiral.

In *My Tired Shadow*, Joey Hirsch has created an unrelentingly bleak portrait of an aging fighter who has nothing left to lose and little to gain. He's at the point of no return, and that makes him unpredictable, dangerous and deadly -- more so, even, than the shady characters and hardcore criminals with whom he surrounds himself. For Ritchie Abruzzi, there is no salvation. There is no redemption. Welcome to the story of a once talented boxer wonderfully captured in the free fall of his brutal descent into a hell of his own making.

MY TIRED SHADOW

"We hate those weak and suppliant gladiators who, hands outstretched, beseech us to live."
— Marcus Tullius Cicero

For James M. Brown

Chapter One: Five for Ritchie

It was morning in L.A. and the sun hit the smog, casting a citrus pall over the valley. Even sporting sunglasses didn't help much, and Ritchie felt like one of those scientists with the big black goggles watching a nuclear detonation go off in the distance.

The call came from Alpo after he'd done four miles of roadwork in Venice.

Ritchie asked him how much. The price was right and he cancelled the shower he was about to take. He got in his car and started the drive from Oakwood to Ramona. He never carried a gun, which might have been a mistake. On the other hand, maybe Alpo was right and he did sort of look like a cop and no one would try him. His black Interceptor screamed 'undercover,' except for two minor details. The first problem was the shag button-tuck interior, which gave the car its cholo-chic vibe. The other thing was even though he wasn't black or Mexican, he was a dark enough Italian to look like maybe he belonged down here and wasn't out to make a bust.

People sometimes came up to him speaking Spanish, and didn't adjust to English until they saw confusion crease the corners of his chiseled face.

His phone vibrated in his pocket and he took it out of his Adidas warmups. He drove over a bridge, a train rushing across ancient tracks below causing everything to rumble as if in an earthquake. He checked the face of the phone. It was Alpo again.

"Yeah."

"Mira, you boys are gonna throw them things in the Oaxaca Food Truck lot. We gonna block it off so nobody who ain't paid can't see. That includes cops."

A housing project appeared on his left. These were low-rise two story buildings, unlike the big boxes they had back east. Poverty was prettier out west, if only because people here knew how to add color to give even the grimmest modular box a bit of subtropical flair. The housing projects in Queensbridge or Canarsie seemed to know only the season of perpetual winter. Things grew in LA, even in the ghetto. The little accents all over the complex made it look less like a project, things like the Spanish red tile roofs here, and the Lady Guadalupe statues praying for Los Angeles behind the barred windows there. The palm trees were dirty but at least they were still vegetation.

New York just killed you up front with no time wasted. L.A. tricked you with its beauty first, with its beaches and its sun, and then it did the job on you.

"Who owns the lot?" Ritchie asked. He didn't want some poor security guard spotting them and then getting killed over his minimum wage gig.

Alpo laughed and Ritchie knew the answer. "Yours truly. I'm an entrepreneur and a man of many talents."

Ancient murals covered the high walls running up and down the blocks, broken by a Korean grocery lit by sickly neon, interrupted by a small auto body shop whose windows were filled with a selection of shining hubcaps.

Ritchie had seen this mural before, and he liked it enough for it to take his mind from the task at hand for a moment. Whoever painted it knew L.A. in their bones, and had somehow summed up the sun-poisoned city with a surreal depiction of skeletons in mariachi outfits shaking maracas to greet a landing flying saucer.

Some asshole gangbangers had already put a tag over the painting, a jagged pitchfork along with the name of the through-street smeared over that. He knew the thug had done it to mark his territory like a pissing animal, but a part of him suspected the unseen tagger did it out of jealousy too, hatred because he would never paint something as beautiful as the mural beneath his graffiti.

"Who's my opponent?" Ritchie made a left toward an Armenian cemetery. From this distance the taller memorial stones blended in with the downtown skyline and assumed the same dimensions. It made it hard to tell the graves apart from the glass-skinned skyscrapers.

"What you worried about?" Alpo laughed, a high effeminate titter that didn't match his face, his tattoos, or anything else about him. "You're Ritchie 'Redrum' Abruzzi."

"I was." Ritchie checked his reflection in the rearview. One of his blackish wavy locks had come loose from the damp strands on his head, a stray curl that made him look like a doo-wop singer crooning for pussy on stage.

"You're still you," Alpo said.

"I don't think so."

"We're about ready to find out."

Ritchie slowed the Crown Vic. Two Mexicans inked down to the last pore of skin stood in front of the chain-link gate to the Oaxaca lot. They pulled the entrance aside for Ritchie and he pulled in.

He spotted Alpo standing between two trucks, looking at a sheet thin as rice paper, working out some scheme in his head. Ritchie wondered if he had graduated from bricks to banks.

"Oh, shit," one of Alpo's crew said. "I seen you on TV way back in the day. You snuffed this dude dead in like three."

"Leave my fighter alone," Alpo said, half-joking. He nodded at Ritchie, not wanting to wave him over since that would require one-handing the master plan he held.

"Where's the other fighter?" Ritchie walked over to Alpo.

"They're on the way. Gridlock. Welcome to the City of Lost Angels. Mira, peep." He handed Ritchie the piece of paper he was holding.

Ritchie took the tracing paper in his hands. It was so thin that he risked tearing it just by holding it. Sunlight broke through the sheet and he saw his fingers on the other side of the paper. On the sheet was a sketch of a concrete arch bridge, with little spiked flourishes like minarets topping the structure.

"You got talent." Ritchie handed the sheet back to Alpo. "You going to get a tat of that or something?"

Alpo beamed, and he nervously touched the razor scar that broke across his eyebrow, traversed both lips, and stopped on the point of his chin. "Nah, it would make a nice backpiece but it ain't about to be a tat and I didn't do it."

Ritchie took off his sweatshirt, peeled down to his own wife-beater. Alpo looked at the sweat stain on his chest. "Did you just get done whooping somebody's ass?"

"I was doing a little roadwork when you called."

Alpo removed his shades, a set of Maybach Diplomats whose gold frames probably cost more than he was dropping on this fight, unless they were knockoffs scored from one of the South L.A. sweatshops. He fixed Ritchie with his cold, green-grey eyes and rubbed his precision-trimmed beard. "You thinking of making a comeback?"

"Only here," Ritchie said, waving at the trucks around them. "And only for some pickup chicken scratch."

That was a hint. Alpo took it, reached into his pocket for a stack of hundreds that could fill a coffee can if unrolled. He pulled off the ivory clip and sanded fifty hundreds to Ritchie, who took the folded stack and put it in his wallet, where the money barely fit.

"You civilians and your wallets." Alpo shook his head and laughed. "I thought you Italians more like Mexicans."

"Wise guys keep their money in rolls like that, back East."

11

Alpo carefully took back his sketch from Ritchie's free hand. "You ain't no wise guy?"

"Nothing stupider than a boxer, except maybe an ex-boxer. And that's before you factor in being punch-drunk." He looked at the sketch he'd just handed back. "So what's the story?"

Alpo's green-gray eyes turned liquid jade for a moment. "Oh, mira, man. There's a contest. The old bridge is built of this shitty-ass concrete that ain't gonna make it much longer. The architects came out and looked at it, right?"

Ritchie nodded. "So everybody loves it cause it's on that historical list of shit nobody wants to tear down, so they're all butt-hurt about razing it. What's the city's solution?"

"What?" Ritchie started doing limbering exercises, spreading his legs and stretching his hamstrings.

"A contest," Alpo said. "Best design gets the bridge and their name on the bridge." He held up the sheet to the light again. "My daughter got the best design."

"Wish her luck," Ritchie said, and stood up straight again. He started doing neckrolls.

"She ain't gonna need it."

A voice came from behind him. "You assed-out, Rocky."

He turned. His opponent was standing there. He was shirtless and bald, his black skin shellacked with sweat, each marbled muscle standing out in the sunlight. He wore a white doo-rag over a head shaped like a pigskin turned on its side for the kick.

Ritchie wasn't impressed with the guy. It was jail muscle, non-moving muscle that came from hitting the weight pile too hard. It wasn't punching muscle. The fighter's sponsor stood behind him. He was shorter than his fighter but his height didn't alter the fact that he exuded the air of a shot-caller. He wore a blue suede puma tracksuit and old school white K-Swiss sneakers. He seemed more focused on grooming his hair than the fight, flattening the three-sixty waves to his scalp with a wood-handled brush that was the same burnished ebony tone as his skin.

The crowd was now about fifteen deep. The engines on a couple of the food trucks started up and the sooty smell of exhaust hit the air. Voices rose and faded over the growl of the engines. Hundreds shifted hands in side-bets and fistfuls of green Benjamins caught Ritchie's eye as he tried to concentrate on the man before him.

He didn't recognize the guy from his pro days or from the gym, but there were gyms in LA like there were swap meets. The guy started shadowboxing, throwing quick shoeshine punches at an invisible enemy in front of him. His overdeveloped trap muscles wouldn't let his arms stray too far, and the effect of watching him try to jab air was like watching a tyrannosaurus rex try to wipe its ass. Ritchie tried not to smile.

The guy was sufficiently amped up now and he looked at Ritchie, grinning and exposing a gold tooth. Gold was soft and neither of them were wearing mouthpieces. "Don't take this shit personal, man." The guy started doing shoulder-rolls. "But I just got done doing a bid in Quentin and you look like the white bulls that used to shake me down and tear up all the pictures my kids sent me."

"That's all right." Ritchie took up his stance, left out front and right clutched to the side of his face like a cellphone. "You look like the black kid who stole my bike when I was little."

The smile dropped from his opponent's face, the gold tooth disappeared. His crew laughed behind him though, clowning. Ritchie thought there was a good chance he would get out of here alive. They'd made him as Italian, or at least not Mexican, which would keep the tribal tension from getting out of control and turning into gunplay.

The engines on the food trucks died, and the drivers got out. Ritchie glanced over at one of the vehicles that had been staggered in a herringbones formation to give them cover from everything but the L.A. county copters. On the trucks were little hand-painted jalapenos with bandoliers crossed across their chests and six-shooters in hand, Pancho Villa-style.

"Bet," Alpo said, stepping between both men. "No kicking, no biting, no spitting, no elbows, no maricon shit, all right?"

He looked at Ritchie, who nodded. "Bet?" He looked at the black guy, who shrugged. "Come out swinging at the bell."

Someone honked the horn on one of the converted ice cream trucks. The dude came forward trying to take Ritchie's head off with roundhouse shots wide enough to make Ritchie's shirt billow from the wind.

Ritchie weaved and punished the man twice for his mistake, ducking down and digging to that body-beautiful with a liver and kidney shot. The man was about to discover that he could armor his soft organs with a layer of muscle, but the organs themselves would cry out when hit as the vibration carried through the muscle. Ritchie stepped back, and punched off the backfoot, digging his fist toward the softness of the man's solar plexus and twisting his knuckles on connecting.

The man grunted as if constipated and sagged onto Ritchie with all his dead weight. He almost toppled as the man leaned on him. Ritchie took two steps back and let the concrete greet the guy. The man's chin touched the pavement with a thunk loud enough to earn a sympathy groan from the fans.

"Oh shit."

Ritchie stepped back two or three paces, used the side-view mirrors of the trucks around him to see how far he could back up without getting pinned against the side of the truck. These trucks weren't as forgiving as ropes or turnbuckles.

"Shit …" The guy stood up, trailing a thread of mucus-like blood from his chin. He wiped that away and exposed the new cleft he'd picked up courtesy of his fall. A loose flap of skin dangled over a blood-covered bit of exposed bone. The man turned around to his promoter.

"This nigga's cheating." He looked back at Ritchie, who didn't say anything or change stance. 'This nigga fouled me."

"Fight," Alpo said.

Ritchie knew objects in the mirror might not always be trustworthy, but he thought he had a good idea of about how much distance there was between him and the Pancho Villa decal behind him now. If Goldie was going to bum-rush him again, he had something for him.

"You okay?" Ritchie asked. It pissed the other man off worse than a straightforward taunt would have.

"I'm fin to make you get on your knees." The man came forward, no jab, no head movement, just wading forward in blind rage. He threw all his force into his next left, his planted foot leaving the ground and taking his hooked punch with it, all the torque from that T-Rex arm sailing for Ritchie's head.

Ritchie ducked, and the man's hand went into the side of the truck, crumpling its tin side. That wouldn't have been a problem, except that one of his knuckles caught a riveted bolt joining two sheets of metal over the skin of the truck. The knuckle had grazed steel with a shearing speed.

"Ah!" The man held up his right hand, the third finger dangling by sinews of whitish fat. "Help, man." The guy turned with pleading, stricken eyes. His skin was ashen from shock.

"The fuck we look like?" Someone shouted. "EMTs?" Ritchie turned to him and squared up his shoulders now that there was no chance of receiving return fire, at least not from that one useless hand. He targeted the bridge of the guy's nose with the second and third knuckles, keeping his punches short enough so that if the man sidestepped or fell he wouldn't hurt his own hand too bad against the side of the truck.

There was a crack and a squish as blood and cartilage switched places in the man's nose and red beads spurted from a newly-deviated septum. The man shelled up, curling into a fetal yet-still standing ball.

"Go down," one of his boys shouted.

Ritchie continued to unload, adrenaline spilling from his veins, the ghost of a cheering crowd summoned in his skull, the natural cocaine high that came from violence causing him to throw harder. He landed shots between the man's arms covering his head and body, a left dug to the ribs and bouncing off with a thunk, the feel of fist on rib something like punching a canteen filled to the brim with water. He delivered a clubbing shot to the back of the head after that, a sneaky paralyzing rabbit punch. The fight would have been called by now in the ring, ruled a TKO victory, or at the very least there would have been a pause to deduct a point for that last shot. But there was no ref, just a pack of dogs watching a dog fight.

The man crumpled to the ground.

"Get up!" Ritchie shouted. He didn't know the guy and didn't have anything against him, but this was one of those moments when he didn't know himself, either. All he knew was that where before there was some fear and sadness there was now only hate and rage. He wanted to hurt and be hurt and the only person who could give him what he wanted was now folded on the ground. He liked to feel like he had been in a fight even when he won. Now nothing would be sore in the morning except for his fists.

He turned around, saw Alpo's cold lupine eyes fixed on his, a smile of near-sexual satisfaction on his face. He glanced over the other Mexicans nearby, some sitting in the trucks, others leaning against their metal sides, one crouched down in that pose they always made when throwing up their sets or taking group photos on the yard in prison to send back home. The black guy with the hair brush was cheesing from ear to ear, still tending his wooly black waves with his wooden brush. Ritchie Abruzzi had earned his five large.

Chapter Two: Perillo Breaks the News

The block was crawling with cops when he got home, but that didn't mean anything since there was always a gang of cops in this section of Venice. If they weren't here for him, he would find out why they'd been here from Kerouac in the morning. It sounded like his semi-transient neighbor was having too much fun in his Airstream camper right now for Ritchie to go bother him. Besides that, he wanted to ice his right mitt and maybe soak it in brine.

He parked in the space next to the Craftsman bungalow where he lived, behind a Benz whose owner he knew had already let himself into his house.

Kerouac stopped humming along with Manzarek's keyboard solo, and his face appeared from behind a beaded gypsy curtain over the window of his aluminum camper. "You got a visitor."

"I know," Ritchie said, and turned back to his front porch.

His neighbor closed the window on his Globetrotter, sealing himself back inside his hotbox of sage, marijuana smoke, and hotplate cooking smells.

Ritchie opened the front door, and spotted Perillo sitting in a dusty settee that had been in this place since he had moved in more than a decade ago. If Perillo would let him, he could probably take the thing down to one of the hipster vintage shops on Abbott-Kinney and make a grip off it.

The old man was sweating more than usual, wiping his bootblack-quality dye job to the top of his head, and then softening down the grey splashes on the sides. He looked up at Ritchie, a pained expression on his face.

"You don't have a TV?" Perillo had any number of chins (Ritchie had never bothered to count them), and they wobbled now.

"Don't need the distractions."

"You should watch it sometime." Perillo reached inside his jacket for his pills.

Ritchie walked into the kitchen and opened the fridge, took out some one-percent milk he'd gotten from Ralphs. He listened to Perillo from the other room. "I was on TV."

"Yeah, I know your boy had an eliminator at Oracle." Ritchie burped and put the milk away. Then he opened the freezer, took out an icepack, and cradled his fist in it.

"Title fight at Staples," Perillo corrected him on both counts. "Not that it matters because I was the star of the show."

Ritchie walked back into the living room and sat down in a rattan chair that creaked as it accommodated him. "What happened?"

Perillo glanced out the window behind him, toward the fading sun. "Little post-fight brawl. That Deidrick Derrell punched my boy after the bell and I jumped in the ring."

"Your vagina act up?"

Perillo shot him the finger. "Comedian, it's angina." A pile of letters was scattered on Perillo's egg-shaped paunch. He picked them up and fanned them toward Ritchie. "You ever get your mail out of the box?"

Ritchie stood, sighed, and moved over to Perillo like a truant student on his way to the principal's office. He took the mail, patted his old promoter on the shoulder, and then walked back to his chair. "Seriously, did your pacemaker kick in?"

"Nah, but I think I've had enough excitement for one lifetime. I'm about to retire, maybe go back into something less stressful than boxing. Maybe I'll go back to driving trucks in Hackensack or bail bonding again."

"You gonna sell Top Billing?"

"Ritch, we're Italian. I ain't selling shit if I got a choice. If my son don't want it, I'll look for nephews who want it."

"What about your daughter? She isn't dumb and this isn't the nineteen-fifties or something."

"I got nothing against broads in boxing," Don said, "at least not on the business side of things. I don't like to watch them punch each other up. I ain't no massage … massage." He gave up on trying to say the word "misogynist" and studied Ritchie a little closer now. "What did you do to your paw, Big Time?"

Ritchie held up his right hand. "I was hitting the heavy bag, trying to do one of those old Floyd Patterson kangaroo punches and caught the chains when I punched a little too high."

"You still train down at Azteca?"

Ritchie nodded.

"How's Bam-Bam?"

"I haven't been to see him in a while."

Don sighed and his belly rose in time with his breathing. "Your father came along at just the right time. Frankie Carbo had just gotten sent up for twenty-five when 'Bam-Bam' Abruzzi was going through the ranks like Mexican water through a tourist." He chuckled. "If he'd started a decade earlier, he'd have never gotten his title shot. He was too proud to take a swan dive for the combine."

Ritchie shook his head. He didn't want to be bitter, but it couldn't be avoided. "A lot of good his integrity did him." He nodded in the direction of Hollywood. "Former world champion living in a crummy apartment."

"At least he's got Denise."

As if on cue, Kerouac started singing along with Jefferson Airplane's Somebody to Love, warbling like Grace Slick. Don laughed at that.

"I wish there were more people like him around here," Ritchie said, nodding toward the caravan, "from the old days."

"Beatniks beat bullets. Hippies didn't hurt nobody, except for Charlie Manson and his crew."

Ritchie was still thinking about his dad. "If I had the ducats, I'd put him in one of those nice retirement homes."

"They got a good one in San Pedro."

Ritchie slowly took the icepack off his right hand and walked it back into the kitchen. "The old Santa Fe hospital's been redone. They're turning it into senior apartments and big lofts."

He set the icepack back in the freezer and returned to the living room. Don looked up him. "So what's stopping you?"

Ritchie sanded his fingers together. "Money. It ain't complicated."

Don's voice was a seductive whisper now. "The comeback trail is calling, kid. You were a popular fighter. You keep yourself in condition." He looked at Ritchie's reddish right hand. "When you ain't punching chains like a momo."

Ritchie paused, thought about it. "What kind of money are we talking?"

Don's tongue flicked out of his mouth and wet his lower lip. He grunted. "You were a popular fighter, all action, not one of these huggers or pretty boys."

"I was a throwback."

"What did you run your record to?"

"A respectable eighteen wins, two losses, one no-decision."

"No decision?" Don squinted. He'd managed Ritchie from the beginning all the way to his ill-fated title shot, but that ND was down the memory hole. "Against who?"

"Braehmer," Ritchie said, and immediately regretted bringing it up. "At Max Schmelling Hall."

Don snapped his fingers, the cobwebs cleared. "Oh, that's right. That's where you met Anna. She was one of the ring-card girls. How is the little Fraulein?"

"We've been divorced for a few years."

"How's Matteo?"

"Calls himself Matt now. Haven't seen him in years."

"'Calls himself Matt.'" Don made a face like he'd been served a shot of pickle juice. "Is he ashamed of being Italian?"

Ritchie shrugged. Don let it go. Ritchie sifted through the letters his old promoter had given him. He returned to the subject at hand, the only subject ever really at hand. "If I get back in the ring, what kind of money can you get me?"

Don shifted his humpty-dumpty girth on the settee, breathed like he was two gasps away from a heart attack. "We do one club fight for peanuts, like five grand, to see where you're at."

"Five grand!"

Don held up his hands. "You'll clear a hundred per. I'm making enough with my other fighters not to take anything away for myself, cut man, corner."

That calmed Ritchie enough for him to keep listening. "We won't overmatch you. We'll find a journeyman with more losses than wins. See where you're at. If you look good, and you're confident, I've got the juice to get you a TV date on an undercard. It won't be on American TV, probably Telefutura, but I can get you twenty-five large for that."

That sounded better. Ritchie had an ego like anyone else, and a bruised one at that, so the idea of being on TV again was pleasing. Plus, Mexicans appreciated his style, hard to the body, good work inside, cripplers to the kidneys like Chavez.

He'd fought in Mexico before too, against Yaqui Pomona at the Estadio Tomás Oroz Gaytán in Ciudad Obrego. He liked Mexican food and women almost as much as he liked Italian food and women.

He was risking his life for five large here and there, entertaining Alpo and a cluster fuck of drug dealers. He was also risking his hands in these bareknuckle brawls, and playing with his life just by going to the bowels of East Los and fighting.

"Maybe" Ritchie said.

Don's head sagged until his chin touched the protruding orb of his belly. He knew that "maybe" meant "no" and he knew why Ritchie was turning down the money and the fights. Losing in the streets concealed by food trucks in front of fifteen people was one thing. Losing under hot lights in front of a crowd and cameras was another. Cameras remembered. The footage would live forever. His bloody face after the Fulton and Giachetti affairs, back-to-back losses, were defeats recorded and remembered. They were replayed now on ESPN Classic from time to time, and on the internet. He didn't watch TV or surf the web, but word got back to him and it still hurt. He'd had his chance for the brass ring and he'd missed it. No sense in going back, getting his hopes up, trying again, and losing one more time. That chapter was done. He'd made a play for the world championship and had to settle for the NABF belt, a paperweight compared to the crown jewels his father had picked up.

"Think about it at least," Don said.

Ritchie nodded, playing along. Think about it. He wouldn't think about ugatz. He turned his attention to the pile of mail in his lap. It was the usual, a bombardment of leaflets encouraging him to consider selling his house to real estate sharks who'd just discovered the beach, who saw sugar-white sand concealed beneath the bumper crop of heroin needles and used condoms heavy at the reservoir tips scattered throughout Venice. There was only one letter personally addressed to him and he didn't have time to open it right now.

"Again with this shit," he said.

Don lowered his eyes, softened his tone. "Ritchie …" Ritchie didn't like it.

"What's up?"

"That's why I come by here." He pointed at the postcards and flyers on Ritchie's laps.

Ritchie's heart dropped to his knees. He didn't show it, any more than he showed the fear that he might lose if he went back into the ring. "You want to sell?" Ritchie asked.

"I got to sell," Don said, pleading. Ritchie didn't like that either. He knew Don was a proud man, and that this was as painful for him as it was for Ritchie. But this moment was inevitable. He held out his hands to reason with Ritchie. "I bought this place for forty grand thirty years ago, when it was nothing but bums and girls growing reefer out in front of their lawns." He smiled for the ghost of Venice, and then the smile disappeared and it was back to business.

Don stood up from the settee and took one of the realtor's ads. The photo on the glossy card showed an Italianate masterpiece draped in pinkish bougainvillea and bookended with Mexican fan palms, standing in place of Ritchie's bungalow with the gables corroded to seaweed-green after years of battering from saltwater spray.

"I can get one-point two mil, minimum," Don said. Ritchie fought the rising rage, wishing again that the guy he'd beaten had fought back more before folding.

"It's all right," Ritchie said. "Just give me a week or two to clear my shit out of here and find another place."

Don placed a hand on Ritchie's shoulder. "Take a month."

"Okay." That solved that. "Anything else?" Ritchie could feel his face getting hot, his ears stinging like he'd been cuffed with a looping hook.

"Don't be like that," Don said. "I didn't come by just for that. I come by to see how you were doing."

"I'm doing."

Maybe he would sell his meager possessions, head down toward the pier, and learn how to be a bum. He could sift through the garbage cans, go to Hollywood and dumpster dive, and find stuff to sell in the Free Speech Zone with the rest of the knuckleheads. He'd smoke weed and join drum circles, let his hair grow long and uncombed until he was unrecognizable. He'd forget he'd ever been a boxer, or even an ex-boxer.

"Hey," Don tapped his leg, tried to bring him out of the black hole he was sinking into. Ritchie preferred to keep sinking, and didn't respond.

"There's a little smoker coming up, a benefit for breast cancer thing. Five-hundred dollars for you. The fight would be off the books."

"I don't need your charity, Don."

"Hey, you momo." Don reached his hand behind Ritchie's neck, holding him the way Ali used to steady opponents to set them up for the jab when the ref would let him get away with it. "It ain't charity for you. It's charity for the broads with breast cancer. And if you still don't want my money, donate your purse to the foundation."

Ritchie smiled. He felt like a teenaged prospect again, being doted on and buttered up by Don Perillo. He loved the old guy. He smiled. "All right."

"Yeah?"

"Yeah."

This way he could fight again, not in front of a handful of sadists and felons on the street, but in a real venue, and with a real crowd. It wouldn't be the Trump Taj Mahal and it would be for pennies, but a VFW hall or an armory would remind him of the good old days. At least he wouldn't have to feel guilty about it, slink around like he did for these pickups he'd been doing occasionally for Alpo.

"I'll send you the details." Don stood. He headed for the front door, stopped, and turned back to Ritchie. "You might even get some tail out of it. You donate your money to save these broads' titties and they'll look at you like 'hey, maybe this is a nice guy.'"

"No thanks," Ritchie said, and stood to walk his guest out. "I stuck my dick in a bear trap once and I'm still paying alimony on it."

"She was something, though," Don said, as they walked out onto the sagging porch. Soft buttery light illumined the windows of the Airstream up the block. Kerouac was jamming so hard to Watts Prophets and their bongo accompaniment that the globetrotter shook from side to side.

Both men laughed. "That can't be good for the shocks," Ritchie said.

"Looks like he's having an acid flashback."

The window to the trailer slid open, and Kerouac stuck his head out. He was wearing a Greek fisherman's hat with a captain's yellow scrambled eggs braids laced around the brim. "Night settles on Venice." He closed the window again and disappeared back in the camper.

Don looked at Ritchie, happy that now thanks to the poet's intercession the night might not end on a sour note. The air was muggy and Don was sweating marbles.

"He might be a Vietnam vet," Ritchie said.

"The gangbangers better watch out. Those boys shoot back. The agent orange is a mother." Don nodded at the house. "Let me give you five-grand when you leave."

"I told you I don't want charity."

"It ain't," Don said. "You sat on this place for a decade and kept up maintenance. Yeah, everybody and their mother wants to buy it now, but you stuck it out when there wasn't another white face out here besides a process server or a cop. And you kept it in order."

"I'll sleep on it," Ritchie said. "Just out of curiosity, why didn't you use the house for your fighters when they were actually training?"

"Tried." Don wagged his head from side to side. "This was Casa de Weak Legs, though." He folded his arms across his gut, like a genie about to grant a wish. "You can't have a camp worth a shit this close to the beach. Guys try to do roadwork and see nothing but girls in bikinis, and they break camp. I'd rather send them up to Big Bear where there's no distractions. Venice is nothing but distractions."

Ritchie did a Burgess Meredith growl. "Women make weak legs, Rock!"

Don walked toward his Benz. The fucker wasn't hurting financially, Ritchie knew, no matter what he said. "You ever think about acting?" Don said. He hit a button on his keychain fob and hidden headlamps awoke in the Mercedes.

"Nah, I got offered a modeling job once for some underwear company. The money was right, but the dude kept hitting on me."

"It might be something you should look into," Don said. "You got a tough guy look, but you're pretty too. Ain't as pretty as a pair of titties, though. Speaking of which …" Don opened the door on his Benz. Ritchie waited. "You mind wearing pink gloves? They want all the fighters wearing pink gloves for the breast cancer thing. Raise awareness and all that."

Ritchie shrugged. "A fight's a fight. I don't care what color the gloves are."

Don winked. "That's the right attitude." He got into the Benz, started the whispering motor, and pulled out. Ritchie watched as the old man drove off, away from the fading sun and the creeping surf, back in the direction of the city.

Chapter Three: I've watched you kill my Father Many Times

They called him Kerouac or Kumbayah, with more than a trace of sarcasm, and while he claimed it didn't bother him, Ritchie always made it a point to call him by his real name, Lawrence. The man seemed to appreciate it.

Lawrence Kramb was a remnant of the old Venice scene, before Jim Morrison had roamed the beaches and the bikers had roared through the streets on their choppers. He was old enough to remember when gangs used switchblades and a man could get years in prison for being caught with a couple of joints. He had to at least be in his sixties, though he was preserved by sunshine, Buddhism, and his own inner light. He moved spryly when he walked. He occasionally smoked a cigar but there was no rough edge to his voice when he spoke. When he sang, his voice had the tremulous quality of a talented but nervous young man trying his chops for the first time in front of a crowd.

Ritchie knocked on his door with the hand not holding the letter he'd opened last night. He didn't hear the shower running, and figured now would be a good time to talk to the old man. "Permission to come aboard?"

"Granted!"

Ritchie opened the front door. The old man was sitting in front of a table covered in blue Formica, laboring on some delicate piecework. Sometimes he worked on ships in bottles. Today he was painting little skulls made of Mexican sugar.

"Sit," he said, without taking his eyes off the skull.

Ritchie plopped down on a couch that ran the length of the trailer's far wall. The couch was covered in tartan plaid. It reminded him of the shorts worn by the Scottish boxer Ken Buchanan.

"How are you, my friend?" Lawrence dabbed a bit of red paint onto the crown of the Dia de los muertos skull.

"Good, good." Ritchie looked around nervously for a moment. The walls were wood-paneled and the oatmeal shag at his feet was deep enough for it to feel like his feet might disappear in it. "How are you?"

Lawrence pointed his brush tip toward the kitchenette of his trailer, where a stack of stapled pamphlets lay. "Just got my contributor's copies for a new anthology."

"Can I get one?" Ritchie stood. Outside of the trailer a dog barked and an argument started in Spanish.

"Help yourself."

Ritchie walked into the kitchen. He took the topmost copy in his hand. The cover featured a black and white photo of a streetwalker in torn hose and a satin nightie. She glared at the photographer snapping her picture, her face a mask of paint and bruises. Skin Row: Sex and Love on Skid Row.

"This a short story or poems?"

"Poetry. I only write poetry."

The chapbook had a cottony weight to it, and felt as if it was printed on recycled paper. "I'm not a big reader, but I'll give it a whirl." He flipped through the mimeographed pages, walked back over to the couch, and sat again. "Here," Ritchie said, digging a hundred from his wallet. He handed the bill to Lawrence.

"You don't have to pay me for the book. We're part of a socialist collective and we printed it with grant money, anyway." The hundred sat on the edge of the table where Lawrence painted, the c-note catching a couple of dabs of red acrylic. Ritchie feared the bill was going to get ruined.

"Nah, that's just a fee I owe you for monthly maintenance."

Lawrence stopped painting, looked over at Ritchie. He arched his eyebrow until it pointed like an inverted version of his Vandyke beard. "Don't patronize me."

Ritchie held up his hands. "Before you parked this bad boy on this block, I used to have to go outside every morning and clean shit off the sidewalk. And not dog shit, either." He could have gone on about how people rummaged through his trash and left TV antennae used as crack pipes laying around, but he decided to leave it alone.

"I see."

"Also, I might need your translation services."

Ritchie held the letter between his hands and Lawrence set his skull to dry on a crumpled section of the Free Venice Beachhead.

"You can speak a bunch of languages, right?"

"I'm a polyglot."

"Your sex life is none of my business."

Lawrence shot him a withering stare.

"What all languages do you speak?"

The old man stood and walked toward the sink in his kitchenette. His bushy King Henry beard was flecked with blue, yellow, and red paint. "Well, Spanish is de rigeur if one wants to navigate Los Angeles. And my favorite poets are Russian, like Lermontov for instance."

"I read Crime and Punishment in high-school."

"Did you enjoy it?" Lawrence finished wiping his hands on a paint-encrusted rag and walked back toward Ritchie.

"Yeah, it's one of the only books I've ever read. That must mean something, but I don't know anything about Russian poetry."

The ancient poet donned his reading glasses and held out his hand for the letter. "Poetry was once serious business in Russia. There was a time when poets could fill city squares, stadiums even."

"Any good poets out here in Cali?"

"Robinson Jeffers was the last poet from here to acquit himself well, but he also turned Big Sur into a damned tourist trap." His eyes scanned the page. "Bukowski has his defenders but I am not among them, except for some of the early stuff."

"What language is that?" Ritchie asked.

"It's Russian."

Ritchie leaned forward. "What does it say?" He braced for the worst.

Lawrence looked up at him, the glasses inching their way down his thin nose. "It says, 'You killed my father years ago, and now I'm coming to see you.'"

Ritchie clenched his jaws together and masked the fear swelling in him. It was something he had learned to do a long time ago, on walks to the ring when surrounded by hostile crowds booing him during bouts away from home. Fear could cause a man's heart to beat until he would swear the muscle was pushing through his chest, but if the eyes and the mouth remained fixed, other men couldn't see the fear. Women could, Ritchie had noticed, and he even knew a bookie who used his girlfriend to watch weigh-ins and faceoffs with him because she could detect imperceptible twitches and breaks in eye-contact between two stony-faced fighters putting up fronts, little tics and gestures that men missed.

"What's the name of the person who wrote the letter?" Ritchie finally asked.

"Konstantin Kro …"

"Kroekel," Ritchie said. He put his head down and stared at his hands.

"He says he watches your fight with his father online all the time, and he can even see the second when the life leaves his father's eyes. He says his mother doesn't …" The poet's voice faltered. He looked up from the letter, at Ritchie, deciding not to continue even though he'd been asked to translate.

"Thank you," Ritchie said as he accepted the letter back. He crumpled it up into a ball, but didn't throw it away.

"Was this a pugilistic thing?"

Ritchie looked up at the ceiling of the caravan, where Lawrence had painted seagulls in flight piercing gray thunderheads.

"Yeah, Vasily Kroekel in Pyatigorsk, Russia. He came in a ten-to-one dog and I beat him from pillar to post for ten straight rounds. I didn't know he was going to die afterwards. It's the ref's fault for not halting the action sooner."

"These things happen." The poet's voice was soft. "You know, I never understood the fascination with boxing, even though it has produced some great literature, from the likes of Norman Mailer, George Plimpton, Ernest Hemingway."

Ritchie shook his head. "I don't understand it, either. If these writers love boxing so much, why not put down the pen and fight?"

"Some of them tried," Lawrence said, and resumed his seat in front of the table where his little sugar skulls were drying. "Believe it or not, they envy men like you, see you as gods even."

"There isn't much to envy." Ritchie wanted to unburden himself, let the dam break, tell Lawrence about his old punch-drunk father living in a Hollywood apartment one step up from an SRO. He wanted to tell the man about how he was a month away from getting evicted, and how he would be lucky if he managed to end up with an old vintage camper of his own when it was all said and done. Maybe he wouldn't even have his life a month from now. He looked down at the crumpled ball of paper in his right fist. Then he looked at Lawrence. "He said he was coming here to see me?"

"That's what the letter said." Lawrence leaned right in his chair, selected a maroon beret from a pegboard where he kept his hats, scarves, and small tools for minor repairs.

"Could you tell if it sounded like a threat?"

Lawrence placed the beret on his head and adjusted it until it achieved the correct slant, casting a shadow over his eyes. "There's no way to discern tone from that letter. It is affectless, matter-of-fact."

"I don't want to be looking over my shoulder every day." Ritchie shook his head. "I got enough on my plate."

"I'll keep an eye out for you." Lawrence winked and then picked up one of the unpainted sugar skulls in his hand. He cradled it between thumb and forefinger, as if ready to recite the soliloquy from Hamlet. "The Regent of Rose Avenue shan't let his fellow Dane down. I know all, see all, hear all."

"Speaking of which, what the hell was going on last night with all the cops around here?" Ritchie stood up from the plaid couch. He didn't want to waste the poet's whole day. He knew the old man treasured time as precious, especially the early morning hours before the noise from the boardwalk drowned everything else out.

"Yes, yesterday evening I intended to go to Ralphs for some tuna for the strays around here, but they had the street blocked off. They busted up a bicycle chop shop in Oakwood."

"Oh."

"They carried out about five-hundred bikes from the house, from what I heard. All expensive carbon fiber jobs stolen from Dogtown and Marina Del Rey."

"That explains that." Ritchie walked toward the door, stopped. "You sure you should be feeding the strays, though?"

"I'm weaving a tangled web to at first deceive, and then, once I have them ensnared, I'm taking them to the clinic to have them spayed and neutered." He waved his paintbrush like a conductor's thin baton. "I usually remain as neutral as a Swiss banker in such matters, but I'm being paid per cat and they are a nuisance."

"What about the ducks?" Ritchie asked. "My friend Stitch told me they spread diseases and the Canal Council is trying to crush their eggs."

"Ducks are a different matter." Lawrence flipped his paintbrush around in a petri-sized tray, stirring the tempura paint with the wooden handle. "I have no idea if waterfowl enteritis is communicable between ducks and humans, but I do know that duck, if prepared correctly, is delicious."

"You been to New Panda yet? Over in Baldwin?"

Lawrence shook his head, flipped his brush back around and swirled the horsehair bristles in sunshine yellow paint. "No, but if you bring me some takeout from there, you will have earned my undying loyalty for a lifetime."

"Next time I'm there." Ritchie opened the door to the trailer, stepped outside. He immediately expected a bullet from the man whose father he'd killed with his hands all those years ago in the dead of winter, in some Russian town whose name he could barely pronounce. No one was there to kill him yet, though, and he wondered how long the gods were going to let him dangle like this.

Chapter Four: The Spider's Basement

Hemp threads were strung from one side of the room to the other. They were laced in crossing patterns that forced him to duck and weave when he came anywhere near the rubber dummy in the center of the room. Don had come down here once and called it the spider web, and the name had stuck.

Ritchie walked around the web surrounding the scuffed rubber torso in the middle of the room. He headed toward the far wall of the basement covered in coral backsplashes.

At the base of the wall was a fireproof safe made of welded plate metal. Ritchie worked the combo on the safe and opened the heavy door. He pushed aside his NABF belt, and wrapped twenty Benjamins on the outside of the thickening paper wad. He'd save the rest of the money for groceries, rent, and to make his monthly child support nut. The bank was up to forty grand, which would have meant something twenty years ago and in a city other than L.A.

He pushed aside the money and fumbled around until his hands landed on the Colt Python. The barrel of that bad boy was as cold, long, and hard as the cock on a robot porn star. Ritchie had a hell of a grip, and strong hands, but even his wrist wobbled when he took the thing up for a moment and hefted its checkered grip in his palm.

His mind's eye conjured up Vasily Kroekel back from the dead. He saw the man running toward him with revenge on his mind. He hadn't seen the man's son, and he was hoping he never would. The last thing he wanted to do was blast him with a gun, especially one that was more for show than shooting. Not that it wouldn't shoot, though, if the time came.

Someone had given the piece to his father, Ritchie "Bam-Bam" Abruzzi, the real champ, not some interim seat-warmer who got lucky due to the alphabet soup of sanctioning bodies and proliferation of regional titles. They'd also dedicated a statue to the old man in the Abruzzi highlands of Italy, to commemorate the boxer who'd done justice to the town from which his immigrant father took his name.

The gun was a gift, a lavish offering to a demigod to whom Ritchie could never compare. He studied the gold inlays, the Italian cameo carvings of the Madonna on either side of the trigger guard. The blue steel was engraved with scrollwork, fleurs, and paisleys covering every inch of the shooting iron down to the hammer. Ritchie knew dick about guns, but he knew the thing must have taken quite a bit of work to make, and that it would probably be a shame to have to even fire it. What if gun smoke stained those cameo virgins?

He threw the piece back in the safe with the money and his belt and then closed the metal door. Then he peeled off his t-shirt and stripped down now to his gray drawstring sweats. After that he walked to the corner of the room, reached down into the bucket of briny saltwater he'd picked up from the beach earlier this morning. He soaked both of his fists in the water, letting the salt work its way over his leathery skin while whistling Sinatra's Summer Wind.

When the song was done, he walked over to the pull-up bar and stooped to get the roll of duct tape on the ground. He placed the roll against his incisor, tore it with his teeth to get it started, and then uncoiled the tape around the layers of old tape already cocooning the steel pull-up bar that had disappeared a long time ago. He unwound the duct tape around the bar twice.

The sound of the ghetto bird roared overhead, the rotors of the police helicopter counterpointed by the whir of the trailing news choppers. Ritchie jumped up and grabbed the taped pull-up bar with his brine-covered hands. He held on in a baseball choke grip, with his hands reversed, one overhand and the other under. His fingers struggled around the new layer of tape he'd just added, his forearm muscles flaring up and the pain going all the way up his shoulders and into the cables of his neck as he pulled, grunted, and gasped. He did ten quick pull-ups in succession and then fell to the floor with his hands behind his head, fingers interlocked on his occipital lobe.

He struggled into the sit-up position, groaning as he lifted himself into a crunch and summoned that little bit of extra will to lift himself from a sit-up into a standing position. If he'd been an insect his thorax would have cracked by now.

"Shuh!" He let go of a nonsensical martial hiss, something to get himself psyched as he bobbed and weaved through the rope strands. He stood sideways, reminded himself not to square up to the target even though it was just a dummy. He kept his chin tucked tight to his shoulder, and once he was through the latticed maze of rope he covered up with a high peekaboo guard, imagining that the armless rubber torso in front of him was trying to punch him. He moved close enough to fight in a phone booth.

Be the firstest with the mostest, he heard his father say. He dug shots to the floating ribs of the rubber man. The punching bag's base was filled with beachside sand, but it still rocked from the force of Ritchie's blows as they lifted him. He peppered the solar plexus with combos, laddering from three, to four, to five punch combinations to the head and body, working upstairs and down, feeling his muscles burn from where he'd done his punishing pull-up regimen followed by the suicide sit-up. The ocean brine dried on his palms and he slipped an errant elbow to the nose, which he disguised behind a short hook. He then returned to his high peekaboo guard.

Always fight on the ref's blind side.

Except there was no ref in a street fight, which was good and bad. Good because he could clear five grand in thirty seconds, and keep one-hundred percent of the profits.

It was good also because he wasn't a counter puncher or the type who liked to feel a guy out for a couple of rounds. He had always been a brawler, not a boxer or a puncher, and he'd always felt shackled by the eight ounce pillows he was forced to wear on his hands in the ring.

The drawback to a bareknuckle encounter was that if he got hit without a gumshield someone could send one of his teeth through his lip and he could be disfigured for life, or at least require surgery that would eat up all the paper he'd made with these pickup matches. Or a shot could scrape his eye and detach a retina, and he could spend the rest of his life being forced to close one eye whenever he parallel parked, like that one old-time pug who forever complained of seeing double. Hell, that could happen even in a sanctioned bout with a ref in the middle of the ring and a doctor waiting on the apron. People died all the time boxing. He couldn't forget that because he had done some of the legal killing, as had his father.

He hooked a left to the liver of the dummy, low on the right with surgical precision. He ducked a phantom return combination from his stunned opponent. Those body shots hurt, but the pain came in a delayed reaction, which meant the other guy was still dangerous before the agony hit him and he dropped to the deck. He flurried four to the breadbasket, punching the latex six-pack, took a half-step to the right and then twisted his body like he was driving a golf ball and his arm was a nine iron. He put his more than two-hundred pounds into a right that contorted the head of the dummy before it returned to position, still and lifeless. Twisting the neck of an opponent with a punch to the side of the jaw usually turned the lights out. It was such a sure thing that they called that point of the jaw the button. Push it and wait.

"Don't take it personal." He patted the dummy on the head, bobbed and weaved his way backwards through the spider web, having memorized where he'd strung the ropes so well now that he could afford to throw punches off the back foot, flicking his stinging jab like a wet towel as he high-stepped through the hemp lines. He still had it.

Everything in him said lay down, sleep it off, champ, but just like doing roadwork at four in the morning in a drizzle, or saying "no" to a glazed donut shining as his hungry stomach ate itself into a knot, he knew that denying himself what he wanted was all that mattered. It was what made him a man and gave his life meaning. It was torture without end, but torture without begging or complaining or crying, or even showing pain from the wounds inflicted by time, by other men, by the giant opponent that was the world.

He went back over to the pull-up bar and gripped the new layer of duct tape, which was dangling and frayed at the edges of the bar like gauze from a poorly-wrapped glove coming free in a fight. "Gah!" He let out another pre-language grunt and hissed, spit dribbling down his mouth onto his chin. His body swam in the air, cheating the fatigued muscles with the other stabilizers coming in to give him some help. A boost of adrenaline came from nowhere and he shot up like a rocket, performing the rest of his ten and dropping to the ground in a quivering mass.

Ritchie rolled like a tortoise from left to right, grunting from the pain of new muscle ripping its way into form. He writhed until he'd accomplished a crunch, and from there stood feeling like he'd just bathed in Icy Hot.

"Okay."

He'd punished himself enough, although it wouldn't hurt to soak the registered weapons in the saltwater for a few more minutes. Then he would do some finger push-ups to protect the soft bones in the hands, the ones meant to tickle the ivory that he still needed to batter bone.

The sound of Sinatra's voice came to him again, and he wondered if through the thundering of his pulse if he might not be hallucinating it, or if there might not be some weird echo that made his whistling ricochet around the haunted confines of this coral-walled basement.

A moment later he realized it was just his cellphone going off upstairs. "Shit." He ran around the spider web and up the stairs, to the kitchen, where a half-consumed protein shake he'd guzzled straight from the blender sat next to his cell.

He picked up the phone. "Hello?"

"You all right?"

It was Alpo. "Yeah, man."

"Did you mean what you said?"

Ritchie could barely hear him over the roar of the ghetto bird, which sounded perilously close like it was getting ready to turn the roof of his bungalow into a helipad. "I don't know, man. It looks like I might be assed-out."

"What do you mean, papi?"

Ritchie wiped the sweat from his free hand against his gray pants. "I mean I'm getting evicted. This area's getting …" He faltered.

"Gentrified." Alpo laughed his high-pitched titter. "Usually it's brown and black folks getting thrown out by y'all, so it's refreshing to see some white-on-white crime."

"It looks like I might need to keep working on a down payment for a house. And the market's on fire right now."

"You mean…?"

Ritchie nodded, so fatigued that it took him more than a couple of seconds to realize Alpo couldn't see him through the phone. He spoke. "Yeah, keep me on standby. I might have to throw them things again to earn my daily bread."

"You're a fan favorite, man. I used to watch you back in the day."

Ritchie grunted.

"I mean it," Alpo said. "I wanted to box."

"Why didn't you?"

"I got mad brittle hands. For real, I broke my metacarpals just slap-boxing this fool outside the Jack-in-the-Box once."

"How the hell did you survive coming up?"

Alpo laughed. "Blue steel, man. It's how the West was won."

The phone vibrated against Ritchie's ear. He looked down at it. "Crap."

"What?"

"I got to roll," Ritchie said. "The ex is on the other line."

"Baby mama drama. What's she look like?"

Ritchie's stomach growled and he used his free hand to pick up the blender and tip it toward his mouth. The cookies and cream sludge made its way down the glass sides of the blender, toward his open mouth. "You don't want none of that," Ritchie said, slurped up some of the protein smoothie, and then set the blender back down with a bang on the table.

"I'm just a squirrel trying to get a nut," Alpo said.

"Nut is right." Ritchie hit the call-waiting button without saying another word to Alpo. He took a deep breath, and figured it was even money that when he was done talking to Anna he might need to go another round or two with the rubber dude in the basement, even though his muscles were long past the point of burnout.

Chapter Five: Headbutt of Love

It wasn't just that he was fighting his first southpaw that night. His timing was off. Ritchie was doing everything he was supposed to do, just a fraction of a second late and a couple of inches wide. But whether a man missed by an inch or a mile, a shot that didn't land didn't do anything but take twice as much out of a fighter as a shot that connected.

"We ain't gonna get a decision on the road," Don was saying as he slapped Ritchie with a drenched loofa between the first and second rounds. He pointed at Der Bulle, sitting on his stool in the blue corner, getting a rubdown from his trainer who slathered Vaseline across the German's brow. "Get out there and do what we worked on in the gym."

The bell rang for the second round, chief seconds and cut-men cleared out of the ring. Ritchie and Ernst Braehmer went back to feeling each other out, tentatively circling, sniping with jabs and straights. They threw potshots that got deflected on the shoulders or caught on the gloves, followed by halfhearted counters.

At some point, they decided to work on the inside at the same time. They ended up jockeying for position, struggling with interlocked elbows and smothering each other's punches, kissing close, and doing a curious dance. The Germans in the stadium booed from their perches in the half-empty concrete seating. The ref broke the boxers at one point and said, "Stop to wrestle."

Ritchie kept backing up to lure Braehmer in. The German was clever and feinted each time before stepping in, drawing Ritchie's lead with the false step, and then circling around him to counter. Ritchie turned with Braehmer, who kept those black hawk eyes trained on the middle distance. The kid had a good look-off, and whenever he threw a shot his eyes didn't go where his punches were aimed.

The crowd kept booing, but Ritchie didn't give a shit. He was still only an up-and-comer and this fight was only an undercard attraction for some domestic fighter. Besides that, he'd already gotten his purse, and whether the crowd knew it or appreciated it, what was going on was high-speed chess.

Ritchie threw an up-jab through Braehmer's tight guard, trying to pierce the leather wall he'd made with his black gloves. The German anticipated the move and picked off Ritchie's jab. Then he threw a shot back that landed high on Ritchie's forehead, snapping his neck back like a Pez dispenser with his fluid catch and shoot.

"Wieder, Ernst!" Braehmer's corner-man shouted.

Ritchie didn't have to speak German to know what Wieder meant. A lot of boxers had a lather, rinse, repeat technique. If something worked once, it might work again. Ritchie was ready this time though, and when Braehmer threw for the same reddened welt on the forehead, Ritchie slipped under the shot and delivered his signature liver punch. His fist landed on the German's defensive elbow block. Nothing was as discouraging as fighting someone who knew what you were going to do before you did.

He wondered where the hell the German had learned the Philly Shell. Germany was a long way from Germantown. Frustration caused Ritchie to throw a five-punch combo. None of the shots even grazed Braehmer, but at least they put him in retreat. Ritchie rushed forward to close the distance he created with his frenzy, and Braehmer practically tripped over his own feet as he scurried away.

Braehmer's back bounced against the ropes, and as he rebounded he moved right into Ritchie's momentum. Ritchie poleaxed the German with a straight right and followed that with mixed jabs and straights to the pecs of the stunned man. He punched as if trying to break through the boxer's chest cavity to reach through to his back and pull out his spine.

"That's it!"

The German was on queer street, but his smarts overruled his pride and rather than trading with Ritchie he jumped in for the clinch. The problem was that since he was a leftie and Ritchie was orthodox, their feet became tangled and their heads clashed.

The deadbeat crowd came to life to moan at the mutual agony of the men who collapsed to the canvas at the same time. Ritchie saw the black lights the old timers talked about, and when he could see again there was an ancient Jewish man with horn-rimmed glasses shining a pen light into his eyes.

"Das was fur heute."

"What?" Ritchie asked.

Vito was holding the cold metal of the End-Swell to the side of the mouse on Ritchie's cheek, while Don clenched a cotton swab in his mouth and rubbed anticoagulant solution into the wound on Ritchie's head with his latex glove. "It means a no-decision. Fight was stopped before the fourth." Don took the swab stick out of his mouth and pressed the cotton end to the fresh wound. "We came all the way here to fuck a dame and you end up kissing your sister."

After the match, Ritchie showered, donned a leather jacket and jeans he'd picked up at KDW Mall in Berlin, and then went ringside to watch the main event.

That was when he saw her.

Anna Sommer was not his type. She had carrot-colored hair (a "ginger" as the kids called them) with a smattering of red freckles and a face as pale as a kabuki mask. He liked his women dark, with Semitic or Italian curls, Mediterranean fig-brown eyes, with noses a bit too big for their faces. He preferred women a little loud, obnoxious, and a bit on the sleazy side. An Italian eight, an around-the-way-chick, was better than Norwegian super model ten in his eyes. Fake tits were okay, especially when shamelessly displayed in bunched, tanning-booth bronzed cleavage bursting from a top.

Something about this girl got to him, though, besides her memorable ring entrance. She had struggled with the card, the oversized "5" that signaled the round number. He watched as she stepped in sparkling metallic heels through the second and third ropes into the ring. She tripped and fell in the center of the ring. The giant card fell over a decal on the canvas, the cardboard concealing some coat of arms advertising a local brewery.

She had rebounded well, kept a frozen smile on her face as she stood. She held the card in her shaky hands, her eyes watering as she bravely pranced with the "5" around the ring. She thawed that coldhearted crowd with her runway-ready strut, her back straight and her chin high. That half-packed hall clapped more for her than they did for the two fighters at the end of their plodding twelve-round snoozer that passed for a main event.

Ritchie saw her on a "grab-and-stab" mission at a local discotheque in town later that night. He hadn't broken camp, and hadn't had an orgasm or a drink in eight weeks, and now he intended to do both. He'd just wasted two months and endured jet lag to get a blemish on his record, after delivering a picture-perfect shot to that guy in the ring. The clash of heads wasn't intentional and Braehmer was a good fighter, but he had the guy doing the funky chicken from his shot. If they hadn't butted heads, it would have been another KO for the resume and he would have built buzz in Europe. What's more was he now had a cut over his eye that might heal improperly and become a scar. Someone who watched footage before prepping for a fight with him might decide to target that wound and open it afresh, and he would get a rep as a bleeder like a lot of white guys.

He had to fuck something, and he had an intro at the ready that was better than a standard pickup line to break the ice with her. He sidled up to the redhead at the bar, where she was nursing a frosted shot of Jägermeister. The bar back was a giant double-exposure of the Berlin Wall painted in random spots in Warhol candy colors. David Bowie was warbling something on the sound system and Ritchie squinted partly from the pain in the cut but also from the strobing lights.

"You got a lot of heart. I like the way you picked yourself up tonight."

"Oh scheisse,' she said, and covered her mouth with her small fingers. She had a complex about her gap apparently. He thought it was sexy. "You saw me?" she asked.

"Yeah." He pointed at his wound. "You see me?"

"Yes, I'm sorry it stopped like that." She pouted and traced the contours of the wound, which gaped like the mouth of fish snagged by an angler's hook.

"It's all right."

He forgot about his dick for the next couple of hours as she told him about her life. Her father was a G.I. stationed at Rammstein Airbase. Her mother was a Catholic schoolgirl from Bavaria who was only sixteen when she got knocked up by a soldier, a lieutenant who lost his commission and ended up in brig for impregnating the young local girl. Anna's mother had wanted an Abtreibung, but abortion would have scandalized the little town where she lived, so she gave birth and worked as a barmaid in a rathskeller to support her baby. Anna eventually ran away to Berlin as a teenager and hung around the train station with junkies and hookers, but never touched dope or sold her body.

There wasn't much to keep her in Germany, and she wanted to use the English she'd learned in school on Americans who weren't drunken soldiers or tourists. She had a passport and used it to leave Deutschland with Ritchie and Team Abruzzi on their return flight to the States. "Well," Don said, "at least this trip wasn't a total wash. You got a broad out of it."

They had three or four good years together. Their salvation was marathon sex sessions when he wasn't sequestered in camp, secret hours in which he let her bring out the bitch in him. She would ride him and he would grip her hips while she slid her pointer finger in and out of his mouth and he sucked it. She was shy even when orgasming, and would cover his face with the fingers not in his mouth as she swiveled her hips and whispered, "Baby, Ich komme. Du bist der beste."

He didn't know why the finger thing got him so hot, but he felt guilty for it. The gindaloons would have dubbed him "half a fag" if they'd known about it. The old Italian guys at the Villa Roma resort where he was a busboy as a teenager even told him never to eat pussy, because that was "also for half-a-fags."

After dispatching Kirk Witherspoon in four rounds at Trump Plaza Hotel, he and Anna celebrated the victory by fucking on every surface in their hotel room with the curtains over the window pulled open onto the view of the craggy moon competing with the neon lights of the strip. Ritchie was on his knees at the foot of the bed, Anna on all fours at the edge of the bed with her back to him as if preparing to be mounted doggy-style. He'd eaten her out from the back, his nose perilously close to her asshole, while she bucked against him as if he were a cornered opponent whose face she battered into submission with her pussy. His nose, which had already been softened up by Witherspoon, broke while she was grinding against him in the throes of one of her multi-orgasmic contractions.

They stopped fucking and started laughing. He walked to the bathroom, stuffed his nostrils with toilet paper, and returned to the king-sized bed to lie with her.

They curled up together for a couple of hours of mindless TV. Half-eaten hot fudge sundaes and shrimp cocktails were arrayed in glass bowls and metal steam trays on a room service cart covered in white linen. He cradled Anna and told her about Randall Cobb, how his nose had been broken so many times that he finally just had the bone removed.

"Schrecklich," Anna said, "Absolutely grauenfall."

"Yeah, nasty."

On their honeymoon, she told him about how she watched him in the ring against Braehmer, and he consoled her with a little story to keep her from reliving the embarrassment of her stumble in the ring later that same night.

"It's Emile Griffith's fault you tripped."

"Wovon laberst du, Schatz?"

He told her about how the bisexual champion had been ridiculed by Benny Paret in the run-up to his fight, called Maricon until he snapped in the ring. He beat his tormentor, pinned and crucified him on those three ropes, where he dangled like a Cuban Christ. He remembered how his father had shown him the fight as a kid, how he watched with horror as Griffith the gentle black lamb turned savage and ripped at Paret's head like a panther felling a zebra.

"They put in that fourth rung after Griffith killed Paret."

"And your father showed you this?"

His tears had caught him by surprise, and she held him. Then they made love, her finger in his mouth unburdening him of the manhood he'd inherited from his father. Later she discovered he'd also unfortunately inherited his father's temper.

True, he had never hit her and never would strike her. That meant he was better with women than his old man, but that wasn't much of a bar to hurdle. He shouted often, and she trembled when he did it, until she got used to it and started snapping back at him. Eventually she no longer feared his rages, and only got scared and grew mute when his shouts were accompanied by him slapping himself in the face until he was steaming, or putting his fist through a plaster wall or wooden cabinet fixture. Then she would blanch, turn so pale that he could see veins beneath her translucent skin. She would cry and he would beg forgiveness for scaring her and hurting himself, destroying the furniture of their new home.

He was bad for himself and for her. The difference was that he couldn't escape himself, but she could escape him. Near the end of their relationship his tantrums were his way of trying to drive her toward safety and sanity, toward a life away from him and his fists. She loved him and while he loved her, he discovered he loved punching men more than anything else. He was incapable of raising a family or being a husband and he couldn't even fake it and go through the motions, but he only figured this out after Matteo was born and they were both sporting gold wedding bands.

Her voice on the cellphone broke through the fog of his memories. Reminiscences of love were finito now.

"He's coming out there," she said. He noticed she'd lost all her accent, that cute Bayern sound of long vowels and umlauts that hung in the air so that even her statements sounded like the questions of a curious child when she spoke. Italian certainly had a reputation as being a romantic tongue, but there was nothing that equaled her furious whispers auf Deutsch when she was about to come back in the days when they were together.

"What do you mean?" Ritchie asked. His right hand was starting to act up again from where he'd hammered the guy the other day. He should have confined himself to body work, since the body was always a softer target. The crowds liked headhunters, though.

"Your son."

"Matteo?"

"Matt," Anna said.

"I don't know," Ritchie said, and reached in the freezer for the icepack. He draped the blue latex bag around his right fist like a hand wrap.

"What don't you know? He has his own money."

"From where?" Ritchie walked into the living room. Lemon-colored sunlight was filtering in through the windows of his bungalow, and sparkling clusters of dust motes flitted in beams of light like packs of fireflies.

"He has a job at Villa Roma."

Ritchie couldn't suppress the smile. He hoped Anna wouldn't detect the happiness in his voice, or at least that it wouldn't irritate her. "Just like his old man."

"Let's hope not."

He paused, stowed the urge to tell her to go fuck herself. "You know," he said, "in boxing that's called a draw."

"What is?"

There was a pause on her end, followed by the flicker of a lighter starting to life. She was smoking now. Maybe that had done something to change her voice. "What you just did," he said. "Saying you hope he doesn't end up like his father. In boxing, when you try to lure somebody into throwing a shot, it's called a draw. You're trying to start a fight with me."

She inhaled a draught of smoke and spoke as she exhaled. "Do you want him to be like you?"

"What's wrong with me?" Ritchie asked. He knew there was something wrong with him, but that was his business, not hers. He walked over to the settee where the impression of Don's fat ass was still there, imprinted with the force of a fossil in a creek bed.

"You're a boxer. Do you want your son to be a boxer?"

"Hell no." That was an easy enough question to answer. She was right, which made him angrier. She didn't have a problem with his vocation when it put them a hair's breadth away from the good life.

After the Mayfield fight he was in line for a mandatory shot at Travis Fulton's WBC strap. Don had faith in him, and he'd given the young newlyweds one of his properties, a modern house as square as a giant shoebox, built on a knoll where a former orange grove sat. There were glass curtain walls. A myrtle hedge surrounded the property, and they had a nice inner courtyard where, after Matteo was born, Anna would go with the baby and soak her feet in the kidney-shaped wading pool while breastfeeding.

There was a bamboo bartender's station by the pool, displaying Witco wood sculpture with Olmec heads and frowning Tiki god faces carved into it. Neither of them drank, not at first at least. That bar saw nightly service after Ritchie took that "L" to Fulton and then followed it up with an ass-whipping upset to Giachetti.

Ritchie got more solace from the surly wooden gods carved into the bar than he did from that bloodsucking shrink, or from his wife, who grew increasingly tired of massaging his wounds as they accumulated with the losses and finally hardened into unconcealable scar tissue.

She hated him for losing those fights. She had never tried to steer his career, but she'd been eavesdropping when Don told Ritchie what was within reach if he took Fulton out and made a couple defenses as lineal champ, as the "man who beat the motherfucking man."

"I know somebody who's going to let this one place go for a song," Don said. Ritchie would use his fists to punch a path for him and his family up to the hills of the promised land. The house was a mere 1.2 million dollars and located in the Platinum Triangle, in the heart of Holmby Hills. Matteo would be going to school with the children of movie stars and they would live like lords in a manor. All Ritchie had to do was beat Fulton, and then HBO was prepared to ink a four-fight contract for $2.5 million.

But Ritchie had lost and everything fell apart. They sold the small house where they lived when Ritchie was a contender. Anna moved back east to upstate New York, to Callicoon with their son, where they'd started out their life together.

"Are you listening?" Anna said.

"Yeah," Ritchie said. "What do you want me to do?"

"I want you to try to talk Matt into getting on the next flight home. Can you afford a plane ticket?"

Ritchie bit his lip, thought about countering her question with his own query: Can you fit a marinated braciola in your ass? He didn't have the heart to fight, either, though, and settled for sarcasm. "I usually collect about ten-thousand cans in my shopping cart at the beach per week. If I step my game up, I might be able to get him a coach ticket. I still got a few frequent flyer miles left from when I was a professional punching bag."

"No Don, either," she said.

"What's the matter with Don?"

"I don't want my son hanging around mafia types."

Ritchie lay the icepack across his face like a beauty mask. "Anna, the RICO Act took care of the mob. You're in New York. You should know that. The party ended when John Gotti got pinched."

"No Don."

"Fine, no Don," he said. "I'll do what I can, but Venice is a deathtrap. If Matty wants to get into trouble, it's everywhere." He knew she bridled at him calling his son "Matteo" so hopefully "Matty" would be a serviceable compromise between the boy's given name and the waspy "Matt." At least "Matty" ended in a vowel.

"What kind of trouble can he get into out there?"

Ritchie sat up on the settee. "Heroin, gunplay, AIDS, it's all here. Kids boost cars, bikes, anything that's not nailed down in the shops on the boardwalk, sunglasses, hats, shirts."

"Matt is a good kid. He likes skateboarding."

"He can do that here, too," Ritchie said. "They've got a good park."

"Good," Anna said. "Just keep an eye out for him."

"All right." Ritchie's thumb drifted over the "End" button on the cellphone. He wanted to press it more than a president yearning to mash the nuclear red button in his apocalyptic dreams. A part of him hated her and that was the only part he was willing to show her. Another part of him missed her finger in his mouth.

Anna, he wanted to say, and his heart hurt. He hung up.

Chapter Six: Bam-Bam and Redrum

No one was home at the crummy apartment where his father lived, so Ritchie drove to the stucco box Denise called home. Her place was in a palm-shaded cul-de-sac of similar dingbat houses in a development called the Aloha Mermaids.

Ritchie parked behind Denise's dirty red Honda in the carport next to the mailbox with the atomic starburst on it. He wondered as he got out of the car if her mailbox wasn't also getting stuffed with offers from real estate developers. This area had a nice vintage Polynesian feel that the young six-figure hipsters would eat up, like an old Lester Baxter luau come to life. It was hard not to notice how everything old became new again, especially in L.A. Some of the Mexicans he'd seen while driving to pick-up fights were rolling around in old-school American steel monsters with white-wall wheels and tailfins, the chicas wearing carnations behind their ears and looking like pachucas while their dates sported greased ducktails.

He walked up the stairs to the beige house above the carport. The front door was open, with a heavy grilled meat smell carrying through the entryway. "Ritchie?"

Denise had ears like a bat. "It's me. Just stopping by."

She came from the back of the house. "Come on in. The champ just woke up." She smiled. "He's watching one of his old fights on tape."

The place was built on an open floor plan, the accordion wall between kitchen and living room bunched to one side. The house reminded him a little of the place where he'd lived with Anna on his way up the ranks. He suddenly felt sadness tinged with a dull pain.

"You want something to nosh?" Denise walked over to the glass coffee table where a grease-stained brown paper bag sat next to two large Styrofoam drink cups.

"It smells good."

Ritchie sat on a camel-brown Naugahyde couch beneath a framed photo of Charles Atlas, flexing his greased muscles for the belles while wearing a cheetah-print speedo. He was grateful the photo was on the wall behind him and he wouldn't have to look at the beefcake while he ate.

"This looks good," he said, opening the bag. Inside was grilled lamb sprinkled with dill and a layer of something yogurt-based drizzled over it. "Where'd you get this?"

Denise walked through the room, to the doorway. She took a Virginia slim out of a gold case. "Raffi's over in Little Armenia."

"You guys go to church?" Ritchie tore into the sandwich. It was damn good and probably would have been just as delicious if he wasn't starving.

"We found a good place. Got a painting of a saint I got to show you, too." She lit her smoke with a zippo that featured a girl in a grass skirt dancing.

"How is he?" Ritchie asked.

She shook her head. He set down the remaining half of the sandwich in the greasy tinfoil and dug a thousand dollars from his pocket. Denise watched him and said, "Doctors are useless. You know what this last one said?"

"No." Ritchie stood and walked the money over to Denise. Her bottle blonde job was a bit more obvious at this distance. She took the money and he watched her stuff the bills in her cleavage. Due to the botox and the plastic surgery there was a twenty-year age difference between her face and the sun-wrinkled skin that started at her neck.

She patted Ritchie on the shoulder and tried to blow the smoke away from his face, into the muggy air. "He said you can't really know what's going on with the brain of somebody who's got this punching dementia until they do an autopsy." She shook her head and flicked the growing ash from the end of her long cigarette. "They can't tell us what's wrong with the brain 'til he's gone. Some of the lesions don't show up on CAT scan."

Ritchie walked back over to the couch and sat down. He loved his father and cared about his health, but right now priority one was finishing the job on that sandwich. "I wish there was something I could do," he said with a full mouth.

"Maybe it's just dementia, like regular age."

"Nah," Ritchie said. "He ate some major bombs in the ring." The crowd roaring from the TV in the back bedroom could attest to that. Ritchie had watched his father's old fights so much as a youngster on the projector that he could tell which bout it was with his eyes closed, guided only by the noise. This one sounded like Abruzzi-Bonaventure. Howard Cosell's Brooklyn-inflected blow-by-blow gave it away.

Her frown disappeared and her glassy brown eyes shined like preserved amber. "A fan came by the other day."

That made Ritchie smile. "No shit?"

They shared a smile now. Ritchie wasn't sure what her angle was, but it couldn't be money because the man didn't have much. Love was possible, but both she and his father had been divorced three times before they met, which made love a proposition with diminishing returns. Maybe she was just lonely.

"He came all the way from Australia."

"Boxing is weird like that," Ritchie said. The sandwich was done. He carefully wrapped the foil into a ball and placed it back in the paper bag. "You go to a gym and see a guy with a mop bucket and he could be an ex-world champ. Maybe he looks like a nobody to most people, but for the hardcore heads he's like a god."

"That fan love is still important to him."

"It helps make you think the lumps were worth it," Ritchie acknowledged. He sometimes got letters from people who weren't even born when his career started, who saw his old matches on the internet or on ESPN Classic. He also got requests for autographs on gloves or old glossy eight-by-tens. There were some good memories and some victories mixed in with the humbles. Then again, sometimes people sent him death threats in Cyrillic.

"How's the memorabilia thing coming along?" Ritchie hated to touch on a sore subject, when the afternoon was pleasant enough thus far, but it mattered. If Denise got some traction in a court of law, Ritchie might not have to throw her a grand here and there to help keep his father off Skid Row.

"Oh," she said, and snubbed the Slim against the wooden handrail of the staircase. "Let me show you."

She coughed once, adjusted a gold crucifix dangling above the grand she'd stuffed there. She crossed the room, walked into the kitchen. "Come here."

Ritchie stood. She popped her head out from the kitchen, nodded toward the Styrofoam cups next to the paper bag. "You can have one of those."

"What are they?" He looked down at the glass coffee table.

"Rosewater and strawberry milkshakes."

"That sounds good as hell." Ritchie burped, his chest scorched from acid reflux, "but I got to watch my weight."

"What for?" Her maternal instinct to feed and fatten was triggered. He'd never asked her if she'd had kids. "You ain't training no more. Why torture yourself?"

He couldn't tell her it was because he wanted to keep on top of his game because he didn't want to get beaten to death in an East L.A. bareknuckle brawl, so he pointed at the monitor of the computer on the kitchen counter.

"What's going on?"

"Oh," Denise said. Her breath smelled from the cigarette, so Ritchie didn't get too close. "Someone was selling your father's old boxing license for two hundred dollars. Then there's this." She clicked the mouse and scrolled down. The jangle of Giardiello's tags rattled behind them, and the Pomeranian with the orange coat weaved between Ritchie's legs.

"The greatest himself," Denise said, "Muhammad Ali signed a photo for your father. It says…" She paused to read the item description on eBay. "'To the toughest dumb white bastard not named George Chuvalo.'"

Ritchie laughed. That was high praise, since Ali had already gone full-blown in his adherence to the Nation of Islam when he signed the photo, and had always been sparing in his praise of most whites aside from Gorgeous George even before he figured out the white man was the devil.

"How much?" Ritchie asked.

"Authenticated by Sports Memorabilia Unlimited of Fort Lauderdale. The bid's up to twelve hundred."

"Too rich for my blood."

Denise pointed down to her cleavage. "I can use the money you give me from time to time to buy it. Then we take it to an attorney. After that we prove that bastard Youngman is behind this."

His father's voice carried from the bedroom. "I gave that prick everything to hold for me, for sentimental value, in a storage locker."

"I don't think there was a market for this stuff back in those days, but Bam-Bam still wanted it kept for you kids. Now Youngman's selling it all off online."

Ritchie flushed, turned red from anger. It pissed him off to think his father's manager had not only fleeced him while he was fighting, giving him peanuts for title shots and bleeding him with chicken-shit deductions that looked good in the ledgers but still were shady. The guy was now also taking advantage of his father's dementia to sell off his legacy piece by piece. Bam-Bam's mind was a fog and the only real memories he had left were being slowly sold off one by one from a storage locker in upstate New York.

"Cocksucker," Ritchie said.

"You think we got a case?"

He shrugged. "If I knew anything about the law I'd have been a lawyer. I'm just a dumb fighter."

"You're not dumb." She reached her hand out toward him, and stroked his cheek with a flamingo-pink cracked nail.

Ritchie walked out of the kitchen, toward the bedroom. The lights were off in this part of the house, the only illumination the cold blue of the boob tube's rays. "Hey, Pops." Ritchie paused on the threshold of the bedroom. His father was half-supine in a Craftmatic adjustable bed aimed toward a TV where his former glory beamed. The walls of the room were covered in rich Kodachrome centerfolds of all the great Italian stallions, hairy-chested and burly Rocky Marciano wearing a smile with that mixture of malice for most and love for mama that defined so many Italian men. The background behind Marciano in the photo was emerald, a deep technicolor so rich it looked like an edible mint frosting. Next to Marciano was Graziano, his features a bit smoother, with matinee idol looks and a dangling black curl not unlike the one Ritchie had. It was easy to see how James Dean was slated to play him in the film adaptation of the book about his life, but the poor rebel without a cause had crashed his sports car and Paul Newman stepped up to the plate.

Ritchie liked the photo of Joey Giardello the most. His father must have had a soft spot for him too, since his orange Pomeranian namesake was scurrying around here now. Joey had black eyes, black hair, with a perma-scowl on his face and nothing but distrust and violence to offer to anyone who made eye contact with his ghost on the wall. He was dead and it was only a photo, but Ritchie feared him even now. The other photos looked like modeling shoots, like the cameramen buttered the boxers up beforehand, stroking the vanity of the fighters who smiled as if they'd just been told a dirty joke before the snapshot. Giardello looked like he was getting booked on armed robbery and wouldn't rat on his crime partner if threatened with 50,000 volts in Sing Sing. He knew life was out to fuck him, especially boxing, but he was going to spit in the eye of whoever ran the game. He would not allow his pain to provide them amusement.

"I didn't try no fancy Dan stuff in there," his father wheezed, pointed toward the screen. Ritchie didn't look at the fight. He'd seem Bam-Bam take enough of a beating before.

"How you doing, Pop?" Ritchie walked over to the side of the bed and set his hand on his father's frail shoulder. The bones felt brittle as dry twigs.

"Been screwed out of millions probably, losing all my memories, can't really see shit, can't shit without help from Denise. Getting ready to die, but I don't believe in God no more. Got nothing to keep me here and nothing to look forward to on the other side."

Denise entered the room, holding a religious icon painted on lacquered wood. "You got me," she said.

"I'm a burden on you, baby. A man ain't a man if he can't wipe his own ass."

"Shush!" She covered his mouth with her hand and he playfully bit her. She pulled her hand free and smacked him lightly on the nose. He liked that, and even snuck a peek at her cleavage. He reached his hand around back of her and pinched his fourth wife's ass.

"I guess life's still worth living if there's some good tail around."

"Don't be a pig." She slapped his hand away like a nurse making her rounds in a ward of horn dogs.

He smiled, looked at Ritchie. "I'm like Jerry Lee Lewis, the killer. Robbing the cradle." He glanced up at Denise. "And she's robbing the grave."

"Look Ritchie," she said, clearly wanting to move on.

He studied the religious painting. It was a saint in paladin armor ramming his lance into the scaled belly of a dragon, whose forked tongue lolled out of its mouth as blood poured from the wound. The saint in this depiction wore a frog joisting helmet, but Ritchie had been to church enough as a young man to know who he was looking at. He admired the gold leaf background, especially the radiant specks meant to symbolize stars against the blue sky done in egg tempura.

"Where'd you get that?"

"Armenian Apostolic in East Los," she said. "Same neighborhood I got the food."

Bam-Bam spoke up from behind them. "I'm gonna finish that strawberry shake if it costs me a foot."

Denise lowered the portrait slightly and whispered to Ritchie, "His diabetes is under control, but if he finishes that shake he'll have to take more insulin and he still doesn't like needles."

The Craftmatic whined as Bam-Bam brought himself into an upright position. "You think back then when old Georgie slayed that dragon, that the pope took fifty percent of his purse?"

"Bam-Bam!" Denise lowered the icon, afraid of the sacrilege she was hearing. "You shouldn't joke about this stuff. Your soul is serious."

"I sold my soul to Youngman, that prick."

She looked at Ritchie. "Your son and I are on the case."

"I'd a been better off going with the combine. I could a taken a dive and gotten my shot earlier."

61

"We're gonna get your money," Denise assured him, and then glanced at Ritchie. "I'm gonna find a place to hang this up."

He nodded, walked back over to his father's side, and leaned down. This was his first good look at his father today, since the room was so dark. Ritchie's jaw was square, but his father's whole head was as cubical as a cinderblock. An old rule of thumb had it that a guy whose jaw tapered in a triangle shape was chinnier and easier to KO than a guy who had a square jaw. Looking at the man it was easy to understand how he'd never been beaten to the deck. His jaw was like cast-iron and when he rushed a guy in his low Dempsey crouch and the hapless boxer decided to punch the top of his head, they often winced and broke something fragile in their hand. His father's eyes had been smoldering black pits in his youth, but now they were stained by cataracts to a shade closer to Grillo grapes.

There was a frozen expression on the man's face, partly the paralysis of whatever was going on in his brain, partly the effect of him being locked in thoughts of a past he regretted and couldn't change. His mouth was always open, curled in such a way that his thick Brooklyn accent could be sensed even before he said a word. Because of how he had been raised and how his life had turned out, he was in the strange position of having every reason to feel sorry for himself but not the ability to do so. Time, ageing, and disease would kill him before they broke him.

He ignored his son's appraisal now, fidgeted with the controls of his bed, and adjusted until he was half-prone again. "I fought in Madison Square Garden, the Mecca of Boxing, seven times. Sold out each time. Nobody put duffs in the seat like Bam-Bam, except Ali and he was the Greatest except for Robinson."

"Your grandson is coming out here."

Bam-Bam looked away from his old fight on the TV. He fumbled around for the remote, mistook the

Craftmatic control for it, and pressed a button, bringing himself up until he was ramrod straight.

Ritchie rummaged around on the end table until he found the remote, hit the "Mute" button on the TV, and said, "Matteo is coming out here."

"When?" His father was lucid for the first time in Ritchie couldn't remember how long.

"His mom didn't say."

"For how long?"

Ritchie shook his head. "She didn't say that either. She doesn't know."

His father grinned. "She probably can't control him. Kid's probably headstrong." The grin dropped from his face. "Don't let him box."

"I doubt he wants to box."

"Make him go to college, be a lawyer. Do the screwing." Bam-Bam shook his head, grabbed the Craftmatic control again, this time intentionally. He drifted backwards like a vampire returning to his coffin after a long night of feeding. "Being on the receiving end of a screw job ain't no fun."

"I know."

In the other room, Denise had turned on the vintage hi-fi and was singing along with Barry Manilow's Sweet Life while using the electric can opener to unseal Giardello's can of wet food.

The smile returned to his father's face. He slapped his son with a frail hand. "Hey, they're inducting me."

"No shit?" Ritchie reached out a hand and smoothed his father's gray hair to his scalp. The hair was thin as corn silk, though not as soft.

His father's mouth puckered like a fat Mafioso speaking around a wet cigar stub. "They're gonna open the books for me. I'll be a made man."

"You going to the Hall of Fame for the ceremony?"

"Nah, I'll let some jamook journalist talk about me. I want people to remember me as I was, not as I am." He held out his liver-spotted hands toward the adjustable bed draped with a white afghan Denise had knit for him.

"How far's Canastota from Villa Roma?" Ritchie asked.

"I don't know, but if I think about all that good Jew food they got in the Catskills, I might make the trip. Not for the induction, just for the lox and the capers and that pickled herring and that challah. Minga shalom!" He surprised Ritchie with his speed and power, reaching out his hand and latching onto his son's cheek before he could shy away, and pinching until Ritchie was sure a new dimple would be on his face when his father finally let go.

The effort of the gesture had cost the old man, though, and he sighed as if it was his death rattle, the sound truncating in a watery groan. He folded his arms across his chest and closed his eyes. He didn't move, and Ritchie didn't know if he was dead or just asleep, until he spoke one last time.

"Don't let the kid box."

Chapter Seven: Preparing for the Night

Ritchie had seen a newer Venice transplant come into the Azteca thinking they were going to do "boxing for fitness" only one time. They quickly got the message that this was a fighter's gym. The individual in question was a woman with a yoga mat rolled up under one arm and a latte in her other hand. She was trying to get Stitch's attention to ask him about rates, but he was busy chewing out a fighter who'd tried to give him lip.

"You don't like the roaches, that's your problem. I ain't an exterminator. If you're scared of a bug crawling on you, how the hell you gonna man up against someone trying to take your head off in the ring?" She was out of the door before he could finish his spiel about how when he was a kid growing up in Philly, if he didn't find a roach in his cereal box in the morning he got worried and figured the asbestos situation was out of control and someone had better call the super. "Free protein anyway."

The Azteca was always loud, with the competing sound of two ancient Honeywell fans chugging on their groaning circuits from side to side in separate corners of the room, pushing hot air from one part of the gym to the other. Hardcore rap was always on the stereo, a ghetto blaster like the type guys would try walking with down the pier until the cops on their bicycles followed them and cited them. Because there was an age spread among the boxers in the gym, the men had to compromise on early to mid-nineties fare, so they listened to everything from Scarface to Nas, but that was as diverse as selection got. They might tolerate or even enjoy the odd "white boy shit," like AC/DC or Led Zeppelin that Ritchie or Zherik tried to slip on there. Eventually, though, one of the black regulars would get around to making a face like someone farted and then go over to the boom-box, take one disc out, and replace it with another. Training would resume after that.

The exposed brick walls featured a virtual U.N. of flags that billowed only slightly from the muggy draft from the fans, but the French and Ghanaian and Israeli banners were only there for show and the membership wasn't very international in flavor.

Ritchie was the only guy who wasn't black or Hispanic who trained there, aside from Zherik, a Khazak nicknamed "Wolfman" with a bushy unibrow and back hair that made him the main suspect when someone didn't wipe their sweat from the padding after training somewhere in the gym. The name of the place along with the giant Incan sun god painted on the sign out front caused passersby to assume the place was a mainstay for south Cali Mexican and Mexican-American fighters, but Stitch only settled on the name and the signage after the Mexican beer company Azteca offered to buy the old warehouse space. They gave it to him gratis, as long as he agreed to cover the ring apron and various wall space with their decals. Stitch obliged, bombarding every free inch with stickers like a kid handing out flyers for his garage band to anyone who would listen. He was a rich man on account of getting his 10 percent trainer's cut from three boys he'd guided from the ghetto to Olympic gold and then on to world titles, but if someone else was going to foot the bill he wasn't going to stop them.

He stood outside of one of the sparring rings in the gym with his arms folded across his chest, watching two men tag each other as they traded shots at close quarters.

Ritchie came into the gym with his practice wraps already laced on his hands, with his mesh-netting gym bag in tow. His feet groaned as he stepped across the polished wood over to a wall where a cubbyhole filled with gear in various shelves stood. He sat on the padded bench and listened to the sounds of skipping ropes flicking against the ground in staccato, counterpointed by the three-minute timer gonging. Someone was punishing an old-school heavy bag and the chains clamored and twisted around, scraping the steel finish of the rafter from which they dangled.

Ritchie saw Stitch in the mirrored far wall of the room. They made eye contact but didn't acknowledge each other beyond that. Ritchie opened his bag, settled his Reyes gloves over his wraps, and pulled the Velcro tight. He preferred the lace-up models since he could achieve a tighter fit with the drawstring, but he didn't like to ask for help tying his gloves.

"You want a couple dates?" Stitch croaked. The man moved like a spider and he was on Ritchie before he saw him.

Ritchie shook his head. "You and Don Perillo with this comeback shit."

"Why you here then?" Stitch smiled, the mahogany creases in his face deepening, the black papulose dots on his face moving a bit as he sucked his teeth. He adjusted his backwards black leather Kangol a bit so that the white kangaroo logo sat a little lower on his head. Now the white tufts of hair on the side of his head that looked like popped corn kernels were more visible.

"What kind of money?" Ritchie asked. He wondered how long this idea had been percolating in the little evil genius's braincase.

Stitch smiled. He could tell Ritchie was thinking about it.

"Ten grand per for some casino dates. That includes free rooms and comped meals at Tunica and a couple other resorts."

Ritchie tugged at the Velcro strap of his glove with his tooth for a tighter fit. "It's a stretch to call anything in Mississippi a resort."

"You want the dates or not?"

"Maybe."

Ritchie stood. Stitch asked, "How's your license status?"

"Got to get a physical at some point, but the board should pass me."

"You get that piece of paper saying I can put you in the ring, and we'll put this train back on the tracks. I'll only take ten percent. Do the do."

"Do nothing," Ritchie said, banged his gloves together, and walked off toward the teardrop bag. He feinted his way in, moved the heavy vinyl bag with his shoulder as if it was an opponent he was trying to steer with his body weight. Once the bag was out of position, he backed off and let it come toward him, unloading a fusillade of punches before stepping around and throwing a looping hook to the bag so that it made a sound like an ass getting spanked.

"That hook looks like stir-fried shit," Stitch said, walking away. "Other than that, I don't see why you can't at least be a contender again."

Ritchie could have thrown some words at Stitch's back, something wiseass about his one-way ticket to Palookaville already being punched. The truth was he wanted to go for the title again. If he couldn't school these youngsters, there wasn't any point in starting on the comeback trail. He didn't want to be a gatekeeper or a trial horse, someone promoters used to test their kids to see if they were ready to go to the next level. He wanted to be that next level. He'd already been a contender, and a regional champ. He wanted a belt he could flaunt in Anna's face, a belt that came with a payday that could put his father in a rest home.

He'd learned his lesson the first time, too. He wouldn't be one of boxing's quiet men. He would run his mouth, create a character, make the world hate him. He would treat boxing like pro wrestling. People would fill stadiums in the hope of watching someone button his shitheel lip, but they would pay for the privilege to watch and pray for his downfall. There were too many good fighters no one cared to see because they didn't make themselves bigger than the sport.

He'd always had knockout power, and power was the last thing to go. He still had it, and he made the bag feel it. He thumped the leather and holstered his hands next to his head after each combo. His leg and shoulder muscles were now trained by the spider web in the basement and he bobbed, weaved, and shuffled each time he came in. He also backed out at an angle without having to think about it.

After three rounds against the bag he was gassing a bit, and he realized his cardio had gone to shit. Those street fights never lasted more than two or three minutes. He had to get his endurance back, recover his stamina. If he couldn't go the distance with a damn heavy bag for three rounds without wheezing, it was a safe bet that he couldn't handle a prelim with a live opponent for six rounds or so.

He'd given in to Denise's pleading the other day to put away those two strawberry milkshakes, and he hadn't done any roadwork since then. Now he was waterlogged with milk and sugar, and it was time to pay penance. He stripped the gloves from his hands, the Velcro making a ripping sound as he pulled the vinyl-covered straps free with his teeth.

His hands were sweaty beneath their wraps, smelling like fungus. On the stereo Scarface shouted, "My psychiatrist talks but I don't listen. A victim of society fucked by the system!"

He set the gloves back in his bag, zipped it up, and headed toward the bathroom. He had to walk past Stitch's office, where the old man played dominoes against himself at his desk. The cracked plaster wall behind the ancient trainer was covered with a poster shrine to boxers like the one in his father's bedroom, only this pantheon was to black fighters instead of Italians. There was Marvin Hagler, a chiseled specimen of raw muscle with his bald head shining, wearing purple gloves and shorts. Ritchie was convinced God had pulled some kind of switcharoo when "Marvelous" was formed, breathed an Italian soul into a black body. Hagler was from the same town as the Brockton Blockbuster, which only confirmed his theory. Plus he'd moved to Italy after he got robbed against Leonard.

Joe Louis was up on the wall, looking more sepia than black in the old yellowing poster. The Brown Bomber's forehead was creased in perpetual confusion that whites of the time probably mistook for a scowl. Like Sonny Liston, there was a look on his face that said How come I'm a god who's allowed to knock white men out but I'm also a boy who's not allowed to use a drinking fountain? The shit didn't make any sense to Ritchie. At least the racists in the days of Charley Burley and those guys built a color line and kept both life and fighting segregated. You couldn't let a guy beat you in the ring where only heart and skill mattered and then tell him he was less than you. The lie wouldn't hold at that point.

"Hey," Stich said. He looked up from his game of bones, through the crack in the doorway.

"What?" Ritchie stopped with his bag in his hand.

"You still live in Oakwood?"

Ritchie nodded.

Stich smiled. "You dumb guinea."

"That ain't nice. I'm not insulting you."

Stich took his hands off his dominoes. "Insult me. Everyone else does. I bet you call us moolies when we're not around."

"What are you talking about?" Ritchie didn't know everyone, but he thought Stich commanded respect wherever he went. He was tiny, but he was like an ebony Napoleon, a little black wizard-cum-dictator who controlled his fiefdom with tiny gestures, expressing displeasure or approval with slight changes in stance or little nods.

"I'm a Man-Tan Moreland negro according to the youngsters around here, all because I go to those community meetings. They want me to side with the pushers against the cops. They call it keeping it real. You know what I heard from one of those white police at the rec center?"

Ritchie shook his head. Stitch looked down at the array of dominoes, concentrating on the interlocked black squares like a chess master. He didn't look up from his game as he spoke. "Pacific Task says twenty black and Hispanic young men capped in ten months."

"Jesus," Ritchie said. He heard the shots sometimes, even heard the mothers wailing along with the sound of the birds circling in the sky, but he never had the numbers quoted to him.

"Them boys need Jesus. Those numbers ain't even counting injured, something like more than fifty caught lead and lived to tell the tale. That's about seventy in a half-mile worth a neighborhood." He looked up at Ritchie. "Right where your house is."

Ritchie shrugged. "Somebody should tell the realtors that. They want to pay a cool mil for a spot there. They must know something you and I don't."

"They'll take that motherfucker back block by block, I guess. You thinking of selling?"

He checked himself before he could mention the place actually belonged to Don, and that he was getting the boot. A man was supposed to keep his problems to himself. Still a date at Horseshoe wasn't begging if he took it. Work was work.

"I'm going to go to the doctor here soon," Ritchie said, "work on getting licensed."

Stitch beamed, the ancient mahogany skin creasing as the smile breached ear to ear. "You making one last go for the brass ring?"

"We'll see."

71

Ritchie walked off and headed to the locker room. One of Stitch's army of roaches worked its way over a wooden bench, feelers dowsing the air as it scurried across the sanded wood. Ritchie lifted his foot onto the bench, squashed the roach, and undid his shoelaces. After he took off one shoe, he pulled the other one off. He peeled off his polyester sweats and removed his white cotton tee. Next, he reached into the bag for his jar of Albolene and unscrewed the top. His hand swirled inside, scooping up a chunk of the jelly. He rubbed it across his belly, furiously working the stuff into his stomach like a Pentecostal preacher doing the laying on of hands and trying to drive out the fat as if it was demonic spirits. The smell was strong, but it wasn't potent enough to overcome the odor of mildew and stagnant water that ruled the locker room.

Still slicked with the stuff, Ritchie reached inside the bag for his sliced garbage bag and wrapped it tightly around his waist. Sinatra sang about his "fickle friend" from inside of the gym bag. Ritchie furiously wiped the grease from his palms onto his legs to make his hands less greasy so that he could grip his cellphone without ruining it.

He picked the phone up in a tentative, loose grip. "All right," Don said, "I got the address. It's a PAL gym."

That made Ritchie smile. The Police Athletic Leagues always reminded him of his short amateur career, those off-the-books smokers his father took him to in Poughkeepsie, the cigar-smoke-poisoned VFW halls and armories that smelled like a mixture of votive candles and sweat socks. He'd always pray for a "bye" in the amateurs, his stomach a mass of butterflies before each fight. His nerves calmed after he knocked a few guys out. He'd captured gold at the Gloves, still had the little jeweled bauble of boxing gloves on a beaded dog tag chain dangling from the rearview mirror of his Interceptor, interlaced with a Saint Christopher medallion. He missed being part of a team, eight to ten kids shuttled around in a van farting and singing Sabbath songs, sneaking joints in the bathroom before matches (no piss tests in those days) and scarfing down hotdogs and guzzling cokes after their matches (you didn't worry about weight as much when you were still going through puberty).

"You'll never believe who your opponent is," Don said.

"Who?"

Another cockroach appeared to check on his comrade, crawling toward the insect corpse like a roach marine trying to retrieve a downed battle buddy. "Clarence Howes."

"No shit?" Ritchie had fought him in the Gloves. Howes had captured gold at the junior Olympics but a Cuban in the real games had his number and used his ring generalship to box his way to a comfortable decision. Howes turned pro about the same time as Ritchie. They'd almost made a catch-weight fight between them when Ritchie had the NABF belt, but Howes had gone out clubbing one night a few weeks before talks of a purse bid were to start, and the evening had ended with rape charges. He'd pleaded down to sexual assault. It was his first offense and the trial lasted a long time, so he ended up getting time-served and doing a baby bid at Rikers back when it was still known as a place where guys sliced each other with razor blades for cutting in line to use the phone.

"Don," Ritchie said, just now comprehending the insanity of what was planned for the night, "You the one doing the matchmaking for this … benefit or whatever?"

"Yeah?" Don's voice lilted, his back up a bit.

"And you decide to raise money for breast cancer by getting a rapist to box me?"

"They don't know about his past," Don said. "Plus, he took a plea, and he's turned his life around. He paid his debt to society. People change. Look at Tyson."

"All right." Ritchie shrugged. "Listen, I got to get togged up now."

"You at the gym?"

"Yeah."

"Ritchie …" Don's voice hung in the air. Ritchie saw, much to his chagrin, that a bit of the Albolene grease had still gotten smudged onto the cell phone despite his best efforts to clean his hands before palming the phone.

"What?"

"This is just three rounds for shits and giggles, but Hammering Howes is in peak form, man, and he's already on the comeback trail."

"How's he doing?"

"Kid's on the war path. Rattled off four in a row. It was against subpar opposition, guys who got a combined record of about forty wins and sixty losses, but he's serious about coming back."

"I see where this is going." Ritchie closed his bag, got ready to return to the gym proper. He might do some stair runs outside in Venice a little later. L.A. was filled with stairs.

"It's a benefit, but it's also a crossroads fight. You look good tonight, and you might want to think about getting licensed again. At least look into it."

"Truth be told, I wouldn't mind boxing in a ballroom or two again. At the very least it's a free hotel room."

"That's the spirit," Don said, and hung up.

Ritchie killed his phone, uncinched the gym bag just enough to stow it inside, and then closed the bag again. The Albolene was working through his pores, inducing rosewater-scented sweats. The thump of leather gloves popping against double-end bags rang out, and jump rope whistling filled the air. The interval timer lamp pulsed red for a rest cycle, and on the ghetto blaster Tupac assured his mother that even as a crack fiend she always was a black queen.

Ritchie didn't feel so much out of place as he felt invisible. There were worse things than being ignored, and being a ghost wasn't painful. He hoped for every man's sake but especially for his father that dying didn't hurt too much, either.

Chapter Eight: Wheelchairs and Wallflowers

The dressing room was packed with people he didn't want to see. First there was the state athletic commission joker checking his hand-wraps like this was a real fight and he might try to mix some plaster of Paris in there. Then there was his opponent, Clarence "Hammering" Howes, as well as his chief second, Larry Naseem, a blast from the past Ritchie didn't need right now. On top of that Denise had come down here for some reason. She was tailed by a blond dandy in a bespoke suit and striped tie, who looked like he should be talking about stocks on TV right now, not up in Ritchie's grille.

He looked past Naseem, slumping in his prayer hat and dashiki, and spoke to Howes. "Hey man, a fight's like a wedding. We're not supposed to see each other beforehand."

"You act like I forgot." Howes grinned.

"What are you talking about?" Ritchie watched Don cocoon his hands in tape, his fingers disappearing in swaddled white layers.

Howes placed his own wrapped hand on Naseem's shoulder. The old boxer sat up in his wheelchair. "You went up into my man's house and beat him in his last fight, before the warden revoked a brother's privileges."

Naseem gazed off into the ether, looking too much like a black version of Bam-Bam for Ritchie's taste. He didn't need any extra guilt right now. He had done what he had been paid to do, gone to Rahway Prison and fought the former IBF titleholder. He hadn't told the man to pull the armed robbery that put him behind bars and he hadn't told him to go to a pool hall in Detroit a week after parole at one in the morning, which earned him the bullet (fragments of which were still lodged in his spine) and landed him in the wheelchair.

The state official signed Ritchie's wraps in black sharpie, and Don slid the pink sixteen ounce Reyes over his hands. "You lucky we're wearing these bitch-made gloves. I'd take your ass apart with some regulation mitts."

Ritchie was almost grateful for Howes and his bull right now, if it kept him from having to make eye contact with his old opponent sitting there paraplegic a couple of feet away. The man rubbed his Prussian amber prayer beads serenely, with his eyes closed.

"You know I got your number, and you know why." Howes pointed a finger at Ritchie.

"Because it's in the Yellow Pages?"

"Who was your main sparring partner for the Naseem fight?" Howes was speaking about the man in the wheelchair as if he wasn't there. "Washed up motherfucker blew your shot with Fulton and only got it because you're a great white hype living off his daddy's name. If my black ass had your connections, I would—"

"All right," the official said, holding up his hands and walking toward Howes. A couple of off-duty cops here to see the fights came to see what the fuss was about. Don turned to Howes and said, "I got to do some focus-pad work with my kid, and the ref's got to give you the same set of instructions he gave us."

Clarence Howes disappeared behind a wall of men, his voice trailing down the hall. Naseem was still sitting there, and Denise and the chap behind her crowded their way farther into the cramped space of the dressing room. The man with Denise walked between Naseem and Ritchie. He looked at the two boxers with the awe of a history major who'd somehow time-travelled to meet the founding fathers.

The guy scrutinized Ritchie, who noticed he had a chestnut-colored walleye to go with his sandy-blond hair. "You're Ritchie Abruzzi."

"Don't remind me."

A leather slapping noise came from behind Ritchie, and he saw Don with the focus pads on his hands, little concentric circles painted onto their insides ending in bullseye centers. "Let's go, champ!"

"You got to be shitting me," Ritchie said, and shook his head while looking at the Englishman. "You believe this guy? I thought he was just saying that to get Howes out of the room."

"Nope." Don held his hands out for a combo. "One-one-six."

"Go fuck yourself." Ritchie looked at Denise, while jerking his head toward the Englishman in the suit. "This the lawyer you got for Pops?"

She shook her head, took a pack of smokes from her faux alligator purse. "No, this guy won't stop bothering Bam-Bam."

"I came all the way from England. My name is Mitchell Dix." He stuck out his hand for a shake. Ritchie held up his gloved paws, grateful that they were sheathed and he had an excuse to avoid pressing the flesh.

Mitchell Dix withdrew his hand, slightly embarrassed. "Ritchie," Denise said, "do something with this guy." She lit her smoke with a match from book she got at a cocktail lounge.

Ritchie looked at the blond youngster before him. "Mitchell, is it?"

"Yeah."

"I'm going to have to ask you nicely to leave my father alone."

The air smelled sulfurous from Denise's match. Don coughed and waved the smoke from the air with one of the focus pads on his hand. "Jesus, you're going to set off the fire alarm."

"Haw!" She squinted, one of her eyes closing as she drew in smoke. "You think this place has any alarms? It's a miracle the lights even work!" She pointed her Slim toward the corridor. "They're covering up exposed wiring in the walls with posters out there. I'll be surprised if this place doesn't burn on its own before the night's through. Goddamn fire hazard is what it is."

"I apologize," Mitchell said, turning to both Ritchie and Denise. His eyes settled for a moment on Naseem, who groaned as if slowly sinking into catatonia. Ritchie wondered if the ex-champ was punch drunk. The Englishman looked down at him in his wheelchair. "You're Larry Naseem."

"Yes sir," Naseem said, without looking up.

"Born Larry Beckman, former IBF title holder, first man to make a title defense from within prison, with the institution's consent."

Naseem's eyes lit up, and he looked at the kid. A smile cracked across his face, and Ritchie thought Mitchell Dix might be all right. "I was too good to be denied. I didn't just make one defense when I was in the can, neither."

The boy's walleye searched, roamed in the repository of his skull as he thought about it. "You made eight consecutive defenses."

Naseem's tongue snuck from his mouth, so imperceptibly that it looked like his lower lip for a moment, before it drew back in his mouth. "Shysters robbed me on a split decision against Woodson, broke my streak, killed my mojo."

"Wallace 'World-Class' Woodson," Mitchell said.

Naseem jerked a thumb at the kid but made eye-contact with Ritchie "You believe this guy?"

Ritchie felt relief wash over him. Naseem was not only making eye contact with him now, but he was actually talking to him. They hadn't exchanged two words in the run-up to their fight, and not a word afterwards.

"I watched that fight three or four times on YouTube," Mitch said. Naseem was hanging on his every word, as were the other three people in the tiny dressing room. "You won that fight," Mitch said. Naseem looked like a faith healer had touched him, as if he might stand and walk again.

"I wish you was one of the official judges."

"Press row had it for you, too," Ritchie said, "I think the Sportswriters' Association of America had it down as the 'Robbery of the Year.'"

"So did Ring," Naseem said, a bit sternly. "I cut that article out and hung it on my wall next to the calendar in my cell. Felt vindicated by it."

The ref came to the room, stood outside the doorway in his dress shirt and bowtie. He spoke to Naseem. "Champ, your boy can't receive instructions in his dressing room without you."

Naseem looked over his shoulder once. "I'll be on by directly." He glanced at Ritchie, smiled at Mitch Dixon, and shot all in attendance the peace sign. "Salam then." He rolled himself backwards out of the room and cut the wheels on a dime as he exited.

"Where in England you from?" Ritchie asked.

Denise walked around the room searching for something to ash in. Don tapped Ritchie on the shoulder, cueing him to stand up. "Sheffield," the kid said.

"I've been there," Ritchie said.

Don wrapped the groin protector around Ritchie and cinched the Velcro in the back. "I know," Mitch said. "You destroyed the Pride of Sheffield that night."

"Literally," Ritchie said. Don fitted the headgear on him. It was already slicked with Vaseline. "That was his nickname, wasn't it?"

"Matthew 'Pride of Sheffield' Stone," Mitch said, nodding.

Denise had given up on finding an ashtray and tamped her cigarette end onto the concrete floor. "They got to sweep up anyway afterwards." She tapped Mitch on the pinstripes of his charcoal blazer. "I didn't mean to run you off. Bam-Bam loves fans, but he's not feeling too good."

"I understand. I apologize." He looked back at Ritchie. "I already feel like I stepped into a time machine and travelled back into another era."

Ritchie wasn't sure he liked the sound of that. He didn't want to play dinosaur bones to the kid's archeologist. "If Redrum lets me interview him, I'll feel like the trip was worth it." Mitch's eye twinkled and Ritchie saw he was a true diehard. The only kind of person who could wholly believe in boxing was someone who had never done it and never would. Ritchie didn't believe in the sport, and he had given it his life and blood. Now he had nothing, or very little, except some scar tissue already being irritated by the sparring helmet, some trinkets in a safe at home, and people like this kid who believed in him. Life had kicked his ass and made him bitter, but not so bitter that he didn't recognize that the kid in front of him, as annoying as he was, was also the only thing that really gave his life any meaning.

"I'll do an interview with you after the fight," Ritchie said.

Don's hand performed a reach-around and Ritch opened his mouth for the gumshield. He bit down on it and smiled, slammed his gloves together, hopping from foot to foot. Adrenaline was rushing through him as if leaking from a spigot in his heart.

"I'd be most grateful."

Denise mouthed the words "Thank you" but Mitch was too over-the-moon to note that she regarded him as a nuisance to be palmed off on Ritchie.

Mitch nodded toward the corridor. "Are you nervous?"

"What for?" Ritchie asked. "I'm not a woman. He's not gonna rape me."

"Ritchie Abruzzi!" Denise hissed. "How can you say something like that?"

"It's true."

Don smacked him on the back of his headgear. "Sorry," Ritchie said. "I don't want to get sued for libel when this kid writes his piece." He looked at Mitch. "It was only sexual assault."

"Wise guy," Don said, and hoisted his bucket of supplies. He tapped Ritchie on the shoulder. "Let's go, kid." He started a massage on the back of Ritchie's neck, which made all the muscles in the boxer's upper-back loosen.

"Nah, the kid's got a cute style, and he fights scary as hell, so I might not lay a glove on him all night, but he doesn't have much power to speak of. Ali floated like a butterfly. This kid punches like one. At least that's the way I remember it from sparring with him."

Ritchie walked forward with Don Perillo while the Englishman walked backwards in front of them to keep the conversation going on the march to the ring. Denise quickly snubbed her cigarette against the wall.

"It's unusual for a Philly fighter to use that cute style, isn't it?" Mitch asked. "'Scary', as you called it?"

Ritchie shook his head, continued bopping and banging his fists as Don massaged his neck with the hand not holding the bucket. "He's not from Philly. Naseem is from Philly." They entered the corridor of the old converted shul, made from earthquake-tested adobe. "Howes just claims Philly. He grew up in Mount Airy, right outside Chestnut Hill. It's middle-class."

Ritchie hoped the kid wrote for a journal with a large circulation, or at least that he spread the word among his mates back at the pub. He wanted everyone to know the tough guy image that Clarence Howes created of himself was a myth, or a lie. Tough guys didn't rape women anyway, except Tony Ayala and Ike Ibeaubuchi.

Ritchie emerged from the tunnel with his motley entourage, a spotlight worthy of a strip club following them to the stairs leading toward the blue corner. Applause and whistles erupted in the small venue, the sound like the din of a well-attended high school basketball game.

"Redrum!" Someone shouted. It felt good to hear that. The air smelled like stale peanut shells soaked in beer foam. It was the odor of being working-class on a Friday night. His legs trembled beneath him, oodles of noodles-style, like this was his first pro fight instead of a minor non-event in the annals of fistic history. He felt like puking, but forced himself forward, his peripheral vision screwed by the amateur headgear. Hopefully wearing the headgear screwed up Howes' lateral movement as well.

"Coming to the arena right now, a second-generation champion, former NABF titlist, and generously donating his time and his purse to the effort to eradicate breast cancer in the twenty-first century, Ritchie ... Redrum ... Abruzzi!"

The man in the center of the ring was an oily type in a checkered jacket that looked like it was made from shagreened speckled trout scales. His cheekbones and forehead were so pronounced he looked like a gargoyle. He smiled and exposed ionized teeth.

Ritchie climbed up into the ring. Howes was already in his corner, doing knee-bends while leaning against the foam-padded turnbuckle.

The houselights dimmed and the spotlight fixed on the emcee in the center of the ring. Ritchie slid in between the second and third rungs, and stepped through the ropes.

"Sponsored by Slauson's Dent Removal, here is your main event, three rounds of action. Fight fans are you ready?"

Ritchie couldn't hear anything but the blood rushing in his ears. He glanced around at the walls of the old shul, the lime plaster cracked and exposing bits of copper insulation. Denise wasn't kidding. The last thing he needed was for an electrical fire to break out and a stampede to start for the exits. Being in the center of the ring would make it hard to get out of the building. He could see the tragedy making the news tomorrow night, in between a drug bust in East Los and some TV star getting a DUI, two deep-fried, crispy pugilists grafted to the ring.

The mat groaned beneath his feet, the hastily assembled ring a bit lopsided, so that he could feel the grooves between each sheet of the plywood lain beneath the canvas. He looked down, lifted his shoes, and saw the soft soles were flecked with blue resin that had come free from the mat.

He'd gotten some of that stuff in his eyes before and it burnt like hell. He had felt like Ali in his first fight with Liston, just walking blindly for three minutes until his vision cleared. If he were truly a dirty bastard, he would let Howes send him to the deck, rub some of that crap on his fists while taking an eight-count, and then he'd get up and thumb the stuff into the sexual predator's eyes.

"Gentlemen," the ref said, looking toward both corners. He was a bald Hispanic man with crescent-shaped bags under his eyes. Ritchie could tell he'd been a prizefighter, using the same sixth sense war vets and convicts used to ferret out members of their own respective brotherhoods.

"All right." He touched the white band around Ritchie's powder-blue trunks. "All punches above here are good." The ref looked at Howes, who was mean-mugging Ritchie with the intensity of a hypnotist. "Clarence, your trunks are a little high, so I'm going to let Ritchie work in here." The ref karate chopped Howes' navel, where his royal purple trunks rode up. Not only were the trunks pulled high, but they tapered well below the knee, as if they were especially baggy pants that had overheated in the drier and shrunk.

"Touch gloves and come out swinging at the bell."

Ritchie pounded Clarence's gloves before Howes could try some unsporting crap on him by avoiding the pre-fight ritual. He walked back to his corner, felt Don's hands reach in for a final massage like a heat-seeking missile. "Let's go, kid. Knock this sack of shit on his ass."

The timekeeper hit the bell, which rang with a dull thud.

They ran straight for each other, knowing there were only nine minutes to bang and neither their records nor money was on the line. The hot lights made Ritchie squint. Howes dropped his hands low and planted his head directly in Ritchie's chest.

"Hit him!"

Ritchie was afraid to throw, afraid to be embarrassed. Howes opened his mouth, revealing a gumshield that was tricolored, displaying the colors of the Motherland. "Let's find out what your bitch ass had for lunch." Howes slipped a hook to the body that landed on Ritchie's abs with a hollow thud.

He saw disappointment flash in Howes' eyes. Howes had expected Ritchie's middle to be softer. Ritchie threw a counter, sweeping left to the body and followed it up with a mirror image shot on the right, harrowing with his hooks like a reaper with a scythe.

Howes saw both shots before Ritchie threw them, seemingly before Ritch thought about throwing them. Clarence backed up and danced as he did so, winning over those in the crowd who liked a hotdog and stirring the hate of the fans who didn't like a showboat. Ritchie rushed in and Clarence brought those hands up seemingly from the floor, tagging Ritchie on either temple and dancing away, tapering his combo with a jab that just missed Ritchie, who ran forward as fast as he could and threw his right. It was a looping overhand with no finesse that still managed to tag Clarence on the bridge of the nose. Howes kissed canvas.

It was a flash knockdown, more the result of showboating gone awry than anything Ritchie had done, but it was a landed punch. The fucker used the occasion to do a

85

tumbling backflip after the knockdown, and as he got up even those in the crowd who hated him now had a grudging respect for him. He was making the night exciting. His mouth opened again and he stuck his tongue out.

The ref dusted off his gloves, usually a formality but probably needed since the resin was scraping from the canvas.

If something worked once, it might work again, so Ritchie rushed forward one more time, born on the wings of his own adrenaline and the roar of what crowd there was. This fight shouldn't have meant anything but it suddenly meant everything, and there was no good reason for it except that they were animals and this is what animals did.

Howes was ready this time and broke beautifully at the waist as Ritchie threw, making it look as if Ritch was throwing his punches underwater and in slow-motion as Clarence weaved, countered with two punches, weaved again and got out of harm's way.

The two men circled each other, neither committing to an attack or retreat, walking around until the momentum they built died at the bell. The fickle crowd forgot the excitement of the first two minutes and booed to protest the last minute, where the men simply felt each other out and let their nerves settle.

"Sit down," Don said.

Ritchie sat on the stool.

Don leaned over him. "How you feel?"

"Angry."

"Controlled aggression's the name of the game. I want you landing with bad intentions, but he's got you too pissed and you're missing."

Ritchie wondered if his reflexes were shot, or if it was just nerves. Howes was so much faster than him that it felt like trying to fight someone who had telepathy, like he knew what Ritchie was going to do before he did it. The first thing he learned from a trainer was to protect himself at all times and keep his hands tucked to his chin. But the first thing he noticed about the real world of professional prizefighting was that the best boxers kept their hands low and punched from the hips, like Howes.

"Target the body at least," Don said. "His head movement's too good."

The bell dinged and Ritchie stood just a fraction of a second before Don pulled the stool out. That would have been all he needed, to take some kind of vaudeville pratfall to compliment the mockery Howes was already making of him.

Ritchie went into the peekaboo stance, cruised forward and accepted that he might take some shots to get inside. Howes let him get close, then turned on an angle and squared himself to Ritchie's side, drubbing Ritchie's body with five shots. Ritchie turned and Howes backed up, holding his hands behind his back as if waiting to be handcuffed.

The crowd lost it. "Quit fucking around!" Naseem shouted from ringside. He couldn't be in the corner due to the wheelchair, so his son was in the corner.

"I got this," Howes shouted back.

"No talking," the ref said, and then waved to both men. "Let's go. Fight, fellas."

Ritchie walked in with his chin tucked behind his left shoulder. There was no way he could out-slick this kid, but maybe he could school him with fundamentals. Howes stung him with a three-punch combination to the face that stopped Ritchie in his tracks.

Panic set in and Ritchie clinched, telling himself that when they broke he was going to unload to the body. "Let go of him, Ritch!"

Howes lifted his arms and looked to the ref to show that he wasn't responsible for the hug that led to the lull in action. The crowd seemed to side with Howes, and picked up the chant, "Hammer him! Hammer him!" Ritchie wouldn't be surprised if the only people rooting for him were Don and that English kid. Denise was probably outside smoking a cigarette.

"Let him out," the ref said.

They broke and Ritchie used the newly-created space to daisy-chain a flurry of punches to the body. Howes deflected all but one that only grazed him but at least got through. Howes jackhammered Ritchie, skewered him with the torque of an uppercut he brought up from the floor.

The crowd moaned and sparks exploded behind Ritchie's eyes. Ritchie flurried again to the body, a broken record of moves and combination that hadn't worked up until now and wouldn't work in the next few minutes against this guy, but they were all he had. Most were deflected, one or two got through. When he leaned in for the clinch again Howes pushed Ritchie's head down and Ritchie stumbled forward, both of them conjoined and staggering to the ropes, which hadn't been tightened correctly.

Ritchie found his face planted in Clarence's crotch, and Howes responded with a simulated grinding of the pelvis and swivel of hips meant to let everyone know he was face-fucking this loser. The gesture probably looked most convincing to those who were seated behind the action currently going on.

"Hey." The ref pulled them apart, and Ritchie reached around the man to throw an illegal blow at Howes. The crowd booed. Howes stuck his tongue out again. The ref pulled Ritchie aside and pointed a hand at him, wagging his finger. "You do that shit one more time and it's a DQ."

Ritchie shook his head. "What the hell am I even doing here?"

"One more time," the ref said again.

The bell rang. Howes flashed his behind and patted the gluts, telling Ritchie to kiss it. He had the crowd eating out of the palm of his hand as he returned to his corner.

Don had the stool out for Ritchie when he got there. "Give me your mouthpiece, kid." Ritch opened his mouth, let Don squeeze some water on his tongue. Ritchie swirled the cool water around in his mouth while the old man cleaned the mouth piece.

"Spit," Don said.

Ritchie swallowed the water, gulped, and said, "Fuck you, I'm thirsty."

Don shook his head. "You don't look that bad out there."

"You owe me."

"We're fighting breast cancer."

Ritchie opened his mouth for the gumshield, spoke with the wettened rubber clinging to the roof of his mouth. "You might be fighting breast cancer. I'm fighting that asshole." He pointed his heavy pink glove at Howes, who hadn't bothered to sit on his stool between rounds and was smiling at Ritchie from across the ring.

The timekeeper hit the bell. Howes did the Ali shuffle, scissoring his legs as he came forward and jabbing as he circled Ritchie. Some of the impact of the straight shots was caught on the headgear, but it still stung. Ritchie got into a low crouch, as if ready to charge, but secretly stealing a glance at his opponent's feet. He saw those pigeon-toes shifting like Clarence was getting ready to recoil from a trampoline jump, and Ritchie knew that uppercut was coming again.

His opponent wasn't the only one that could read minds. Ritchie took a falling step and swooped with a check hook to catch Howes as he leapt in with the uppercut. The punch connected on Howes with the force of a SWAT battering ram crumpling a drug dealer's door. The piston-force of Ritchie's shot pushed the skin of the man's face from one side of his jaw to the other for only a split second. Howes stepped back, genuinely chastened for the first time in the fight, smile wiped off his face. He nodded to acknowledge Ritchie had actually tagged him.

"Fucking A, Ritch," an Italian booster in the crowd shouted.

"Nice," Howes said, and feinted as if he was going to repeat the shot and then stepped around, the fake-out making Ritchie overcommit with a punch that caught only air and sent him off-balance. Howes made him pay with two chopping blows to the head followed by a clubbing left to the ear that landed solid. Ritchie pursued him, desperate to get even before that final gong. Howes slapped him, a backhanded shot of contempt meant to insult more than hurt.

"Hey." The ref stepped between them. Now it was Clarence's turn to get read the riot act. The glove and the damn rig over his crotch made the gesture hard, but Ritchie tapped the space where the Italian sausage was hidden and let Howes know it was there for his mother any time she wanted to eat it.

Howes nodded to the ref, who waved them back together. "Keep it clean, boys." Howes held out his hand for a sportsmanlike touch, boxing's version of the apology. Ritchie would have trusted it coming from someone else but he swatted the hand away with a straight right and followed with a jab that missed its mark and put him out of position. Howes tried for the uppercut again and landed it so hard Ritchie felt like he was being forced to adjust to the gravity of another planet with each step he took after the bomb connected.

His mouthpiece flew out and hit the canvas, knees-first. The crowd was one hive of chirping locusts feeding on his corpse. His hands and knees were on the deck. Not only had he been throwing like he was underwater, but it now sounded like he was submerged, too.

"Five," the ref said.

Ritchie studied the man saying the numbers as if he were a baby trying to learn how to count.

"Seven."

He got up on unsteady legs, feeling like he held dumbbells in either of his hands. "Are you okay?" He nodded at the ref. "Do you want to continue?"

Ritchie nodded again, opened his arms to show he wasn't hurt, inviting Howes in for another volley of fun and games. Rather than be baited, Howes raised his own arms to Ritchie right back, entreating him to come in and eat some more shots. They both had one knockdown, which made them even as far as the scorecard was concerned, but Ritchie hadn't forgotten that his potshot was a little flash affair whereas Howes landed like a howitzer. The crowd hadn't forgotten either.

"Cut this bullshit out. Fight now." The ref waved the action on, and the final bell dinged. Howes turned to the crowd, raised his arm as if he had Ritchie's heart in his right hand, and for all it mattered to Ritchie, he may as well have.

Chapter Nine: Mike Tyson punched Sheetrock

They presented Ritchie with an oversized novelty check in the ring after the match. He stood holding the thing awkwardly, while Howes stood next to him and clapped with his wrapped hands. "I would have donated my half," Clarence said, through clenched teeth. "But I got restitution to pay."

His opponent surprised him after the exhibition by embracing him. Ritchie shouldn't have been thrown off-guard. He'd seen matches where guys who'd acted like assholes before the fight remained steadfast pricks to the end, but as often as not the fight took some of that out of them and they behaved like gentlemen when it was over.

"You got in a couple shots on me there," Howes said, tousling Ritchie's sweat-dampened curls.

"You put me on ass," Ritchie said in reply.

The second Don sliced the wraps off Ritchie's hands he was in the shower. He quickly toweled off in the locker room and slipped into a green Italia jersey and golf joggers he'd brought with him. A mixture of sweat and water was still beading off his forehead when he made his way to the Interceptor in the parking lot afterwards.

He thanked a couple of well-wishers and fans as they shouted his name and then he got into the car.

Mitchell Dixon rapped the passenger-side window with his knuckles before Ritchie could start the engine.

He cursed under his breath and unlocked the car. He'd forgotten about the English kid.

"Great fight, champ." Dixon slid into the passenger seat.

"Thank you," Ritchie said, a bit robotically. He didn't want praise right now. He needed alcohol, something strong and punishing.

He turned up the volume on his stereo and hoped the pipes of Ole Blue Eyes would be enough to keep Mitchell quiet. "Regrets," Sinatra sang, "I've had a few."

"Any regrets, Ritchie?" Mitch looked at him, the afterglow from the fight still written on his face.

"More than a few, but nothing a drink or seven can't help."

He pulled out, tires screeching. Mitchell slipped his seatbelt on. Ritchie didn't bother.

"So tell me about your debut," Mitch said. He looked out the window at the Mexican palms arrayed in the darkness at the sides of the road. L.A. had him spellbound.

"Let's see," Ritchie said, and turned left. "I fought Tyrone Rivers at Saint Stanislaus Hall, in Nashua. It was my debut and his tenth loss in as many fights."

"Were you nervous?"

"Of course." Ritchie looked in the rearview, saw nothing but empty night. He pressed the pedal down to the floor and the engine roared. "Nothing like those three steps to the ring."

A nauseous look washed across Mitch's face and he braced himself against the dashboard. As his hands reached out, he noticed the golden boxing gloves trinket dangling from the rearview. "Golden Gloves, huh?"

"I still got the Daily News article somewhere around the house."

"Is that where we're heading?"

"Nah," Ritchie said. "We're going to the park."

He eased the ride into a space in front of the Liquor Locker. Two kids in hooded sweatshirts with backpacks stood in front of the ice chest at the store.

"What do you think they have in the bags?" Mitch asked.

Ritchie shrugged. "Bolt-cutters, cans of spray paint." He did his best Tupac impression over the sound of Sinatra. "Inglewood is always up to no good."

He got out of the car and walked toward the store, which was ramshackle and paneled with sagging whitewashed wooden planks. It didn't look like it belonged in L.A. It looked like a bait and tackle shop in Mississippi. Mitchell watched Ritchie disappear inside the store bathed in glowing fluorescence. He appeared again at the counter and handed some money to the Pakistani working the register, and emerged from the shop with a pint of something hidden in a brown paper bag.

"What you got there?"

"It ain't what I got," Ritchie said, and handed the liquor off to Mitch as he started the car. "It's what we got."

Mitchell unsheathed the booze from its brown package as they pulled out, to see what exactly they had on their hands.

"Popov."

Ritchie cut the wheel. "You don't got to drink, but you've got to drink if you hang with me."

"Why?"

"Because I don't want you studying me like a bug under a microscope all night. Just get hammered with me, be my paisan for the next couple hours, then you can wake up in the morning and hammer out whatever you want on your typewriter." Ritchie gunned it again. "Write about how we picked up trannies on Sunset for all I care."

Mitchell smiled so that his eyeteeth showed. "Nobody uses typewriters anymore, I don't think."

"Maybe some of the old-timers," Ritchie said. He reached over, stole the liquor back, unwrapped and uncapped it.

The smile dropped from Mitch's face, replaced by a look of worry. "Isn't that illegal?"

"Nah, we drive on the right side of the road in America." Ritchie tilted the bottle and squeezed its plastic belly, guzzling the contents like he was parched after a long march in the desert and it was water.

"Slow down," Mitchell said.

Ritchie hissed, capped the liquor. "Don't tell me how to drive."

"I meant to slow down with the drinking."

"Don't tell me how to drink." He handed the half-depleted bottle to the boy in the passenger seat and pulled into a darkened lot.

The car was aimed toward some empty picnic tables next to a vacant bandstand. The sweet musk of a recent barbecue was on the air. Mitchell sniffed the liquor, scrunched up his nose, and closed his eyes as he took a sip.

"Don't make a face like that," Ritchie said. He waited for Mitch to finish and then took the bottle back. "You guys pound those pints of bog water on your pub crawls over in England. I've seen you."

Mitchell laughed at that. "Guinness, you mean?"

"Yeah, and then you watch soccer, the most boring sport in the world. No wonder you guys riot."

Ritchie got out of the car, prepared to tilt the bottle to his lips, but Mitchell came around the car and stole it back before he could get another taste. He tilted his head back and Ritchie watched him. Bubbles floated in the bottle as the liquid disappeared. "Now that's a proper pull." Mitch passed it off to him again. Ritchie drank as he walked forward onto the manicured greens of the park.

"Y'all one-time?" A young black man in a green, diamond-quilted bomber jacket approached them, his hands in the pockets of his sagging jeans that covered his unlaced Timberlands.

Ritchie tipped the bottle to his head again, left a final drink in there for his partner. "Nah, we're just here to do some birdwatching."

"Oh, word?" The black kid looked over his shoulder, shot a hand-signal to his backup sitting on a set of benches by the public restrooms. He looked back at the twosome and spoke sotto vocce, hands still in his pockets.

"Y'all keep it moving, then, all right? I can't have y'all fucking up my hustle, so unless you here to buy you got to step."

"We're stepping," Ritchie said, lifting his hands up in peace.

The kid nodded and drifted backwards into the shadows. "Let's move," Ritchie said.

Mitchell finished the bottle, searched for somewhere to pitch it. "Where should I dispose of this?"

Ritchie reached out for the empty container and threw it onto the ground. He slapped Mitchell on the back. "It's roadwork time." Ritchie started jogging and Mitch trailed him.

"You're mad!" Mitch said. "You can't slug that stuff and then run."

"Drunk running's the best running."

He chugged across the open expanse of the greenery. A sprinkler came to life at his approach, and he ran toward the stars on the horizon. He was near the basketball court when he finally stopped running. He hummed the first few bars of the theme from Jaws. Mitchell stood there, looking ready to puke, wondering what came next.

"Just when you thought it was safe to go back in the water …" Ritchie reached into his golf pants for a pint of Grandad he'd bought and pocketed on his way out of the store.

Mitchell burped and leaned over to retch as he contemplated drinking the syrup-colored liquid. Ritchie struggled with the cap. He'd managed to get it off at about the time when Mitchell stopped dry-heaving into a mulched bed of tulips. Ritchie took a slug of the brown stuff.

He held it out to Mitchell, who shook his head and wiped a string of errant post-vomitus spit trailing from his lips before muttering, "I can't."

"You can do anything you want in this life," Ritchie said, drinking for two. He pointed the bottle of liquor toward the benches on the other side of the park, near the concrete pad encircled by a chain-link fence. Because he'd forgotten to screw the top back on the bottle, alcohol spilled out as he pointed the container back in the direction of the dealer whose path they'd crossed. "You just need some crack, first." Ritchie crouched as if on the starting line in a marathon. "I can go get you some crack if you want it. You smoke that stuff and you'll feel like Superman."

Mitch suppressed the bile rising in his stomach and held Ritchie's arm. "I don't want any crack. Thank you for the offer, though. That's quite generous."

"Anything for a fan." He turned, guzzled more booze, and walked to a fruit tree next to a palm. He set the Grandad against the tree and pulled down his sweatpants. He started pissing, looking over his shoulder at Mitchell. "You know what kind of tree this is?"

Mitchell staggered forward. "Orange?"

Ritchie shook his head as he pissed. "That's what I thought, 'til Kerouac set me straight."

"You read his stuff?" the Englishman asked, impressed.

"Sometimes, but only when he asks me to."

That threw Dixon for a loop, but Ritchie spoke before he could ask any more questions. "It's called a loquat. This Mexican dude at the library told me you can make some pretty good pruno with it."

He finished pissing, shook his cock twice, and stuck it back in his pants. "I'm sorry you had to see that."

"Nature called."

"Now," Ritchie said. He staggered a few paces and almost fell, righted himself against the spongy base of a nearby palm tree. The sky was a cloudless purple dome and the air was humid, though cooler than it was farther inland.

"I can't let you leave without showing you at least a trick or two."

"How do you mean?" Mitchell walked over to him, casting a couple of over-the-shoulder glances around them as he walked forward. He'd heard about how dangerous L.A. could be, and they were two white men walking alone in the dark through a strange neighborhood.

"I want to teach you a couple boxing moves." Ritchie took up his stance, and fear spiked in the English lad's chest. The last thing he needed was get KO'd by a drunken former champ.

"Oh, I've tried sparring. I just don't have the skills. I'd rather talk about your life." He giggled nervously. "Trying to teach me to box is a lost cause frankly, mate."

Ritchie lowered his hands, and Mitchell couldn't help but sigh with relief. He was buzzing, but he wasn't drunk enough to slug it out with a pro.

"What do you want to know?"

"Can we talk about your last fight a little," Mitchell said, his knees buckling a bit beneath him.

"Giachetti," Ritchie said, sneering.

"Yes." The Englishman's "s" slurred into an "-sh" sound at the end. He wondered if being punch drunk felt anything like being regular drunk. If so, maybe it wasn't so bad. Mitchell wanted to ask Ritchie how he felt about his father, but he didn't want to wade into some kind of family drama minefield, ask the wrong question, piss the drunken pugilist off, and get coldcocked. Reporters and journalists could afford to get mouthy at press conferences, but if he pissed Ritchie off there was only air and opportunity between them now.

"I don't want to talk about that fight," Ritchie said, shaking his head. He stomped on the ground as if the memory of his second loss was a zombie buried there, trying to pound its way up through the firmament.

"Why?"

Ritchie leaned against the palm, cradled the trunk like the waist of a girl with whom he was slow-dancing at the prom. "I was supposed to lose the Fulton fight. The over-under was around five or six rounds. I didn't get KO'd, so I felt good about myself, even though I didn't win. I was in survival mode, then. Still, I let my wife down. I disappointed my manager ...My father." He pulled himself to the tree and now set his head against the trunk, like it was a pair of maternal breasts against which he could close his eyes and drift off to sleep, consoled by Mama Mexican Palm.

"Giachetti," Ritchie said, "was supposed to be my comeback, a walkover, and it turned into a war."

Mitchell was surprised to hear the fighter sobbing. He was about to apologize for bringing the fight up when Ritchie interrupted him. "The crowd loves blood."

"It's your most popular fight online, most viewed," Mitchell said.

"I don't have a computer. I only know boxing. Speaking of which ..." Ritchie squared himself up to the palm tree. "Let me show you something my father taught me when I was a kid."

"Okay."

A siren wailed and they both turned in the direction of the crimson flash. They watched an ambulance followed by two firetrucks streak through the night. Ritchie quickly crossed himself and muttered some traces of Latin he remembered from his days as an altar boy. His eyes darted around the park, and even though he was drunk he was as alert as a bird of prey swooping down on a field mouse. "Watch out," Ritchie said.

"For what?" Mitchell asked. He held a hand tentatively cupped in front of his mouth and breathed to check his rancid breath.

"There's a Russian coming to kill me soon."

"Say that again?"

Ritchie laughed, and turned to square himself to the palm tree. "All right, now this is called the two-ton okey-doke."

"You're not going to punch that tree, are you?"

"No," Ritchie said. "I'm going to headbutt it." His fist flew for the tree but he pulled the punch as his body rushed forward. His forehead connected with the palm tree hard enough to make a thunk.

"Goddamn!" One of the drug dealers shouted from the benches.

"Hey, go easy on yourself, white boy," his friend replied. Both black men laughed in the darkness.

Ritchie turned to Mitchell, blood streaming down his face, into his eyes and mouth. He licked some of the blood as it trickled and he spoke with its coppery tang on his tongue. "You know about Two-Ton Toney?"

"Yeah," Mitchell said, "Galento." He watched the blood pour from Ritchie's head, transfixed by the beaded flow.

"Shakespeare?" Ritchie spoke around a phantom stogie crammed into his mouth. "Sounds like one of dem unrated Europeans. I ain't ever heard of da bum. I'll murder da bum."

"I think you might need to go to the hospital."

Ritchie's face was awash in blood, thick as raindrops as it poured down. He reached up, felt the reopened scar tissue above his eyes. "This, nah, this is old news. I got this from Braehmer a million years ago." He flinched as he touched the wound. It stung. "Every time it opens it reminds me of my ex-wife."

"You want to go to the ER?"

"Nah." Ritchie waved off his concern. "I could be a licensed cut-man at this point. I got everything I need at home, just in case I get my ass served to me in a pickup fight."

Mitch's ears pricked up. "Pickup?"

"I mean bar fights." He tried to walk back what he'd said, and hoped Mitchell wouldn't remember anything in the morning.

"All right," Mitch said, "we don't have to go to the hospital, but how about we go back to your place, ice that down?" He was still staring at the profusely bleeding wound. He'd seen enough fights to know that, once properly-cleaned, the gash might not look so dreadful. Right now, though his interviewee looked like something out of a horror movie.

"How about something to eat?" Ritchie asked. "I can do some extra roadwork in the morning. I'm gonna pay for this drinking and this." He pointed at the oozing gash. "Might as well pay for a good meal, too."

"Okay," Mitch said, "I'm buying, though."

"My man." Ritchie patted him on the back once, leaving a bloody palm print.

Mitchell took off his suit jacket, bunched it into a ball. "Oh shit," Ritchie said. "I didn't mean to mess your jacket up. I'll pay to have it dry-cleaned. How much?" Ritchie dug into his pocket, produced a wallet bulging with hundreds.

"It's all right," Mitchell said, terrified that one of the shadowy forms in the park would smell the money and he'd have a gun jammed in his mouth a minute or two from now. He gently persuaded Ritchie to stuff the money back in the wallet, to put the wallet back in the pocket of his gray sweatpants, and, most importantly of all, to use Mitch's pinstriped jacket like a bunched rag to staunch the flow of blood streaming from his eye.

"Let's take a different path back," Mitchell said, steering them toward a sidewalk where someone had done a mural on each cement square to commemorate lives lost in the ongoing war over Oakwood turf. They stood on a patch of sidewalk wherein ebony prayer hands were clasped above a black boy named Deonte Crowder. A ray of sun splashing onto the face of the dead concrete-canonized teenager made a chiaroscuro heightened by the neon of the city streets.

"Quite sad," Mitchell said as they walked.

"Yeah, you don't have gunplay like this over in England."

"No, we have our fair share of knife crime, but this is all a bit excessive for my taste."

Ritchie lowered the jacket, already stiff with his dried blood. "Christ, man, I'm sorry for ruining the jacket. Let me get breakfast."

"No worries, mate. Dry-cleaning will set everything right as rain."

"I wish I had no worries."

"We talked a little about regrets earlier. Do you have any?" Mitchell stuffed his hands into his pockets as they walked back in the direction of the car.

"A few."

"For instance?"

"Like tonight," Ritchie said. "You saw Naseem. That's some sad shit."

"But it isn't your fault."

"I didn't need boxing," he said. "I was born into it, but I wasn't a street kid." He waved the blood-stiffened charcoal jacket at the slowly-gentrifying ghetto around them. A light, pleasant breeze picked up force and sent a chill up Ritchie's spine. "These kids from the ghetto, boxing was their way out. And every time I beat one of them, it wasn't like when you beat another guy and just send his ass back to the drawing board. I was sending them back to something a lot worse."

"I see," Mitchell said, hands still in pockets. "But still, they were trying to knock you out."

"Yes," Ritchie said.

"What about your first loss, to Fulton?"

Ritchie smiled at that. Another bracing wind from the coastline reached them and Ritchie put the jacket on over his shoulders as they staggered forward. His dried blood on the jacket gave it the feel of being heavily starched. "No regrets. Fulton was a character. He only has one loss, even now, and that's on paper. They robbed his ass. And he got his third diamond bezel earring after he whooped me."

"That's right," Mitchell said. They were back at the car. "He bought himself another diamond earring whenever he got a new title."

"Yeah, it was only the NABF belt, but I guess it was like a ritual for him. It wasn't like he needed an excuse to splurge on jewelry." Ritchie pulled the keys out of his pocket.

"Can I drive?"

"Sure." Ritchie handed him the keys and clutched his aching skull. "I've got a headache anyway." He walked around to the passenger side of the ride and Mitchell hit the button on the fob to unlock the car.

"He insulted you quite a bit in the run-up to the fight, didn't he?"

"Pulled no punches." Ritchie climbed into the car and fumbled through the glovebox until he found what he needed, one of the white plastic packets with STERILE written on it in all caps. Ritchie started laughing as he tore the package open. "Coagulant granules," he said. "I think the bleeding has stopped, but it never hurts to be careful." He tilted the rearview mirror to his side, and adjusted it as he applied the stuff above his eye as delicately as a woman putting on makeup.

Mitchell turned the key in the ignition, pulled out. "Do you remember some of the things Fulton said to you?"

Ritchie laughed so hard that the precious grains spilled from the packet and into his lap. He picked some of them up and smothered them in the slice in his head. "He said, 'Abruzzi, your mama's got the saggiest titties I've ever seen in my life.'"

103

Mitchell pulled out onto the surface street. The sun was a blood-drenched orb draped with a cotton-thin cover of morning clouds, seagulls floating high above the homeless dozing in sleeping bags on the pier or pushing shopping carts over the tide-soaked sands. "Why is that funny?" Mitchell asked.

"Fucking guy never met my mother." Ritchie turned up the stereo system, lucked into the second verse of Very Good Year.

"You really like Sinatra, eh?"

"Make a left up here," Ritchie said, pointing. Then, "After the pope and my mother, yeah, he's the third part of that holy Italian trinity." He winced as the hemostatic stuff sunk into the wound. "You know, I was pissed after I beat your boy."

"Who? Oh, Stoney?"

"Yeah," Ritchie said. "You asked about regrets, you know?" He looked out the window. "I always wanted one of those belts that you guys have."

"The Lonsdale Belt?"

"That's the one." He nodded his head, dreamily thought of that old-school porcelain and gold belt, some relict from another, misted age. The NABF belt looked like a horse saddle, with a toothpaste-green leather backing. He probably couldn't even pawn the damn thing if he tried.

"I saw that fight on Sky TV," Mitchell said, as he pulled up to a stoplight.

Ritchie yawned and nestled into the comfortable button-tuck job behind him. "It was broadcast domestically on ESPN. Got me a profile in Nat Fleischer's 'Bible of Boxing.'"

"Where are we heading?" Mitchell asked sheepishly. He looked over at Ritchie, worried that the guy might go to sleep on him, lapse into a coma, and die from a concussion. A private, unwanted thought registered. He fought it but it surfaced anyway, and that thought was the idea that maybe Ritchie would be better off dead.

Ritchie shot up in his seat a moment later, as if beating the ref's count at nine. "Well, where we go depends on what you want. The way I see it, we got three options." He turned up the Sinatra and said, "Burgers, pancakes, heroin, or maybe all three if you're really up for some fun."

"Pancakes sound good."

Chapter Ten: Unexpected Beauty

The sun was punishing him for the excesses of last night, coming in coruscating rays that made his temples throb and pulse. Each time his heart beat, the poorly-circulating blood made him feel as if he was being punched. It was a punch per second until around noon when the hangover abated.

Ritchie couldn't remember much about last night, except that his head had started bleeding again, and then he did a face-plant on the concrete outside an In-n-Out Burger. At that point the blood flowed not only from his forehead, but out of his nose.

He was in the bathroom at home now, looking in the mirror and doing triage on his face. He managed to get the Venda Mexicana gauze pad to stick above his eye with a length of surgical tape. The cloth was soft as a duck's bottom, a little something he'd picked up at the South L.A. Supermall. Touching the gauze to the wound caused no pain, and he made a mental note to remain brand-loyal from this point forward.

A car honked outside several times. It could have been for anyone, but something made him suspect it was for him. He ignored the hunch, lifted his face to the glass of the bathroom cabinet over the kitchen sink. Orange blood-boogers were encrusted around the cartilaginous rims of his nostrils. "Shit." He turned on the faucet, adjusted the taps until they were lukewarm, and rinsed his hands. Then he slowly pinched his nose, closed his eyes, and cursed as the warm water dissolved the hardened blood.

Someone knocked on the door. "Hold on!" He flipped the cabinet mirror open and took out two of the STAT! blister packs and snagged a couple of the mini-Kotex tampons from the box he'd picked up at Ralphs last night. Then he walked back through the living room and to the door. There was no keyhole, which was probably an oversight in this neighborhood. There was a glass diamond-shaped pane in the center of the door, but it was made of glazed pebbles and was covered with iron bars, which limited visibility.

He could barely make out someone beautiful, young, and female standing there. He opened the door. "Yeah?"

"I'm Star," she said.

"What can I do for you, Star?"

She stood aside, exposing this year's Mercedes SL 500, black and shining in the morning sun. It was idling. "Would you like to come for a ride with me?"

Ritchie dug into his pocket for his sunglasses with the bamboo frames he'd bought down at the Boardwalk. He put them on, settling them carefully on the bridge of his sore nose. "Star, you said?"

"Star Bella," she said, nodding.

"You'll forgive me for being suspicious. Beautiful young women don't show up at my house, with expensive cars, telling me to come take rides with them."

"I'll give you a thousand dollars, too."

"They also don't do that, either." He looked up and down the block. There were still rows of sagging, paint-chipped bungalows as far as the eye could see, which meant he hadn't died and passed into the hereafter. Kramb's Airstream was still parked where it always was when he wasn't at the Santa Vera Center or the library.

"Someone wants to meet you."

"All right," Ritchie stepped outside, closed and locked the door behind him. "If I'm walking into a hit, who cares? I've seen everything but Jesus anyway. Let's get this show on the road."

She glanced at him as they walked together down the sidewalk to her car. He looked at the idling Benz, the running motor whisper-soft. "You shouldn't leave your keys in there in this neighborhood. I've seen bikes disappear faster than you can blink. People get killed over cars like that."

"It's not my car. He just lets me drive it."

"Who?" Ritchie asked.

"We're going to meet him."

The retractable hardtop was down and Ritchie eased into the car without opening the door. "Nice," he said, sliding into a leather seat set on massage mode. A salty trade wind blew over them.

"You really think I'm beautiful?" she asked, hopping in. She wasn't white enough to blush, but her modesty seemed legit.

He looked her up and down. She had amber eyes flecked with gold speckles, as if some painter had gone over her eyes with the thinnest of brushes covered in honey and used pinpoint precision to fleck her irises. That master painter had also daubed complimentary spots of barely noticeable brown freckles on her butternut-colored skin. She looked like the kind of girl who would resent being called exotic and barraged with endless questions about her parentage, and still her ethnicity was something that made Ritchie curious each time he looked at her. Half Hawaiian and black maybe, or Salvadoran and Armenian? She was some new, perfect mixture humanity had been fucking its way toward for millennia. Ritchie himself felt pretty exotic in a roomful of blond waspy types, but he felt positively white bread in her presence.

"Yes," he said, leaning back and placing his hand on a Birchwood-covered built-in champagne cooler. "You are beautiful."

"Oh," she said, and reached her hand out for his face. "What did you do to your face?"

"I got tagged in a fight last night."

She started the car. "I thought you were retired."

"I didn't know young women followed boxing."

"That's sexist," she said, looking over her shoulder as she backed up. She wore an undercut hairstyle with diamond patterns shaved in her head, a sort of half-mullet, half-Amazonian warrior princess look that made it look like a game of tic-tac-toe was in progress on her scalp. Usually after he stole glances at a woman a few times, he could get used to her beauty. It wasn't working with this one, and every time he saw her he was shocked by her existence. To make matters worse he was old already, especially in LA where youth counted double, and he had put so many miles on his body in the fight game. If he was rich it wouldn't have mattered, but he was poor or at least just getting by.

"I'm sorry," he said. "You're right. You a fight fan?'

"I like female UFC."

"I took enough lumps in the ring. I'm not about to get in a cage."

Kramb opened the window on his Globetrotter to hang a new wind chime strung with dangling metallic skeleton mariachis. He watched the twosome in the Benz, especially the female. The old poet was wearing his Greek fisherman's cap. He leaned halfway out of the window and waxed colorfully, as if he were a conductor announcing the name of a whistle stop. "You are an endless fountain of immortal drink, pouring unto us from heaven's brink."

"Oh," she said, smiling. "Thank you."

"Thank you," he said. He soaked in the morning air buoyed by ocean breeze and listened to his birds entreating one-another to mate, before returning inside of his camper and closing the window.

They drove on. Ritchie felt a trickle of blood leaking from his nose. "Shit."

The car was aimed toward Marina Del Rey's white condos and lofts whose highest stories were visible even from here.

"Who was that guy?"

"Mr. Kramb. He's a poet, been here since way back in the day. He's good people."

"He seems like it. Most guys at the club don't talk to me that way. It's usually just 'I'll give you a hundred bucks if you let me touch your pussy.'"

"Not too romantic," Ritchie allowed. He twisted the tiny Kotex out of its plastic lipstick tube-sized sleeve and created a staunching tamponade with the soft fabric in his nose.

"I could have used some of those things on my last film shoot."

"You an actress?" Ritchie asked. Warm air flew into the convertible as they drove on.

"Aspiring."

"I'm a has-been in a town full of the aspiring."

"Your ride might not be over yet."

"It's looking that way."

She dug a one-hitter disguised as a cigarette from a small hemp purse and held it out to him with a lighter. He shook his head. "Do you mind if I do it?" she asked.

"No, I like the smell."

She steered with her left hand and lit the bat with her right. The sweet evergreen fragrance of weed hit the humid air. Ritchie felt his stomach settle a bit from the secondhand smoke, though it didn't give him the slightest buzz.

"What was the last movie you shot?"

"Oh," she said, blowing smoke out through her nostrils. She inspected the one-hitter to see if there was another hit left in it. They came to a red light and braked. A man in a black Quicksilver wetsuit carried his blue fiberglass surfboard across the street with him. A Mexican woman in a vacant lot wearing an unseasonably warm flannel coat hefted handpicked goods stacked in baskets she took from the bed of her white Datsun.

"It was called Sexy Zombie Sluts." She looked over at Ritchie, expecting him to lob some kind of insult her way.

He shrugged. "Everybody's got to start somewhere."

"Joey made sure to put some empowering dialogue in there. Or rewrite it. I made him."

"Who's Joey?"

She pointed at the woodgrain steering wheel. "This is his car. We're going to see him right now."

"Okay." He could have asked more questions, but decided to roll with the punches.

"Your thousand is in the glovebox."

"Thank you." He pushed the button on the compartment and the catch released. There was a small Manilla envelope with a stack of paper bulging inside. Ritchie took it out, undid the brass hasps on the envelope, and glanced inside. There were the creamy white edges of perfectly aligned bills, crisp and flush as if just drawn from the ATM machine. "Things seem to be in order." He closed the envelope and put it in his pocket. The car was climbing the hill. The higher the house, the higher the income.

"The movie got me my SAG card. It's basically about this woman who gets gang raped and left for dead. The guys who rape her bury her, and she comes back to life and rips their dicks off and stuff. It's a revenge flick, like I spit on your Grave."

"I didn't see that one," Ritchie said. "The only zombie movies I saw were Night of the Living Dead and the one where they're in the mall."

"Dawn of the Dead," she said.

"That one was really good."

He remembered seeing it at a drive-in as a teenager after his squad had collected some scalps in a tourney. Ritchie wasn't the biggest movie buff in the world, but he found that flicks served as good distractions for pre-fight nerves, or as background noise when celebrating wins. He'd caught the other flick, Night of the Living Dead, while working the desk overnight at the Villa Roma resort. Something about it got to him, penetrated the fog that kept a barrier between him and anything that wasn't boxing. The farmhouse where the humans were trapped had a haunted feel that reminded him of upstate New York, of the Catskills and the Poughkeepsie area.

Star sensed he was lost in his own world, and the fact that he wasn't hitting on her made her curious. She spoke if only because she was made uneasy by not commanding a heterosexual male's attention. "I did some adult stuff before this, but it was just girl-girl."

"I'm not judging. Fucking people for a living isn't as bad as punching them."

"Some of them want some violence with their sex. There's a lot of freaks out here."

"You a working girl, too?" He glanced at her arms. She didn't have track marks and there was an aura of health in her honeyed skin and bright eyes.

"No," she said, laughing. "I just dance down at Fantasy Reign. That's where Joey found me."

The Benz continued its steep climb up chalk cliffs, high enough now to be at the same elevation as the Hollywood sign. He hoped she knew to watch out for yahoos trying to take their picture near the thing and standing in the road.

"You like Venice?" she asked.

"Nah."

"How long have you lived there?"

"Fifteen years." He laughed at the absurdity of it.

"How can you live somewhere fifteen years when you don't like it? Don't you want to like your life?"

"It's convenient," he said, and hoped she let it drop. He figured he didn't have a chance with her, figured it was creepy to even consider having a chance with someone who looked so young. The cock wanted what it wanted though, and while he could control what he did with it, he still had too much pride to tell a woman (even one too young for him) that he stayed in Venice because Don let him live there for peanuts.

"I talked to this homeless guy the last time I was on the pier, and he said they shoot so many movies down there these days he could live off the craft services."

"Did you guys shoot Zombie ..." Ritchie trailed off. He couldn't remember the title of the film. He had a post-fight headache.

"Sexy Zombie Sluts," she said, reciting from her CV.

"Sexy Zombie Sluts," he corrected himself. "Did you guys shoot it down here?" He just realized they had already driven far enough that they were no longer in Venice. Venice was back there.

"No," she said. "Joey rented time on soundstages."

"How'd it turn out?"

She shrugged. "We got a distribution deal and a three-picture contract. Horror studios will pick up anything as long as there's enough blood and tits." She gripped the steering wheel between her perfect, blade-like legs as she worked good Cali purple weed into the end of the faux cigarette's mouth. They were moving through curving hills and Ritchie was uneasy. She wasn't wearing her seatbelt and he didn't want to come off like half-a-fag by putting his on.

"Good deal," Ritchie said.

"Jennifer Anniston got her start in Leprechaun. Patricia Arquette was in one of the Nightmare on Elm Street movies."

"Work's work."

"Beats grinding my pussy on old perverts at Fantasy Reign."

"That back in Venice?" Ritchie asked. He hadn't been in a strip club in years.

"You've never been?"

He shook his head.

"I'll give you a couple comps from one of the girls if you want. Just tell them Alecia sent you. That's my real name. Alecia Powell."

"Do you act under the 'Star' name?"

She nodded, lit the one-hitter, inhaled a volute of smoke. She reached out a hand and gently flicked the blood-soaked tampon in his nose, tormenting it like a kid in class smacking the earlobes of the boy in front of her. "Good thing you got a heavy flow pad."

He pulled the tampon free by the string and chucked it into the scrub and chaparral at the side of the road. Picking it up would suck for whichever prison trustee stumbled across it as part of a work detail combing the hills later on.

"Like I said, though, I could have used those for my nose on the movie, because when the Zombie Girl goes to rip open the stomachs of the guys who did her wrong, we used real organ meat and it smelled bad. We put earplugs in our nostrils but I think we could have gotten better coverage with the Kotex."

"If you try Kotex and it works, just make sure to give me credit."

The car slowed down. The air smelled cleaner at this altitude, thinner and free of the smog that plagued the valleys. They were in some pocket of Old World California, something that had escaped the carving knives of the conquistadores and the pens of the city planners. Cali wasn't Massachusetts, and money could only be so old out here, but wherever they were heading was so exclusive that Ritchie couldn't even put a name to the locale. It was perched not only above the South Los favelas and nouveau riche enclaves, but even above the moguls who thought they'd reached the top of the heap.

He felt the ghosts of L.A. around them, silent film stars playing tennis on the grounds of haunted haciendas with Andalusian gardens. The car slowed down to a crawl and then stopped. The wrought-iron gate fronting the estate was framed by two giant arroyo boulders. Trees filled with golden oranges and thick grapes, roses and geraniums masked everything but the briefest glance of a Moresque castle's entry on the other side of the iron. The place was shrouded in paparazzo-proof mystique. It wasn't a rich actor's house. It was a wealthy producer's house.

Alecia hit a button over the sun visor on the driver's side of the Benz and the gate pulled backwards, groaning theatrically like a portcullis allowing them an audience with a king. "Holy shit," Ritchie said.

"I know," she whispered, and looked over at him. "Listen, only call me 'Star' around him. I'm sure he could find out my real name, but I don't use it around guys like him."

"How about Bella?" Ritchie asked. "My Italian's for shit, but even I know that means 'Beautiful.'" She smiled and he had to look away, endure her beauty in small doses like chocolate that was too rich.

"Okay," she said. She drove the gravel wraparound driveway and stopped behind a gunmetal Range Rover and a cherry Audi with black leather interior. The cars were parked around a fountain in which a stone green man folly spit water from his fanged mouth.

Ritchie lightly touched the envelope filled with the g in his pocket, and wondered if whatever they were about to encounter was worth it.

Chapter Eleven: Memories Restored

Being privy to some large negotiations had put Ritchie in the homes of some heavy-hitters, but there was something subdued about this compound that hid wealth more than announced it.

Alecia led him inside through the main door, into a cool main room with walls made of coffee-colored stucco inlaid with swirling starburst patterns. Some of the windows were stained glass, while others gave view onto quiet courtyards where armless statuary watched over reflective pools carpeted with lilies and shaded by overhanging succulents. L.A. had many oases, but this was an Eden.

Ritchie gazed at the ceiling and walls as they walked down the corridor, afraid he might miss something. He pointed at the terracotta tiles. "I got friends back east who'd lose their minds over that grout work." He realized he sounded like a dumb guinea whose imagination didn't extend beyond a good union job in construction, but he couldn't help it.

"Here we are," Alecia said, and then leaned into him, her breath still smelling of good hydro buds. "Remember, it's 'Star' when we're here."

She opened the door on an oak-paneled library. The room was dominated by a couch that looked like a Panzer tank clad in white leather rather than armor, facing a projector screen buttressed by two steel antique statues of Spanish caballeros in visor helmets. Their jousting lances were pointed toward the massive screen, on which a black and white Prohibition-era orgy played out for two men on the couch watching the vintage porno.

Two women in flapper hats, pearls, and nothing else spread the lips on a third woman's vagina, and performed cunnilingus while a man in a cummerbund and monocle smoked a pipe and looked on in clinical, nigh-on Freudian detachment.

One of the two men on the couch, an older black man, spoke of the shrink watching the three lesbians go at it. "I don't know why the doc doesn't want in on that." The man on the couch wore a straw safari hat and a hideous button-up shirt printed with marlins and swordfish. He looked like an ex-vice squad cop enjoying his retirement.

Next to him sat a man with an old camera that Ritchie recognized from his own dysfunctional family's summer vacations. The clockwork, spring-wound whining of the Bolex was comforting as he heard it hum, if only because when the camera was running it reminded him of those times his father was "on," acting like the Bam-Bam the world wanted him to be, rather than beating his wife or his son.

The man turned the camera toward Ritchie and Star Bella, and the ex-boxer shielded his face reflexively with his hand. "Look at him, Lee," the man with the camera said. The black man next to him glanced over, not wanting to be distracted from the antique stag film crackling on the big projector. Lee nodded, doffed his straw hat to Bella, and then returned hid attention to the movie.

"You're everything I could have hoped for," the man with the camera said, his face still obscured by the camera.

Ritchie was ready to throw a punch, held himself in check if only because he had gotten a grand and he didn't want to beat this worm's ass if it would hurt Bella in some way. "Can we turn the camera off?" he asked. He'd matured in the last fifteen years or so, he realized. There was a time way back when, when the camera would already be spilling exposed film and the guy's teeth would be in shattered ruins, like sugary pellets wrested hastily from the string of a candy necklace.

"Sure." The camera stopped running and the man lowered it. He wore a canary-yellow ascot tied around his neck. Ritchie had never seen one of those outside of old films. The guy even had the bearing of a tyrannical director from vintage Hollywood. The only thing missing was the canvas-backed chair, pith helmet and bullhorn.

"Joey Suhne," the man said, extending a hand.

Ritchie took it. The palm was limp and clammy, a dead hand. "Ritchie Abruzzi," Ritchie said.

"Ritchie … Bam-Bam …Abruzzi."

Ritchie winced, stowed the urge to sock the guy in his jaw for the second time in under a minute. He wondered if the black guy on the couch was his bodyguard and if he was packing. "My father is Bam-Bam."

"Oh, that's right." Joey snapped his fingers. "You're Redrum."

"Was."

"Speaking of which …" Joey turned from him, to the man sinking into the contours of the behemoth couch. "Lee, the film …"

"Yassah, boss. I's going." Lee shuffled wide-eyed, doing a hybrid impression of Man-Tan Moreland and Stepin Fetchit as he went to change the reels out on the projector.

Ritchie studied Suhne. The man's face was a mask of frozen arrogance. His eyes sparkled, but it was the glow of a killer in a mugshot who knew his debased act was as close as he would come to fame. Maybe it was just that they were in Southern California in a big house, but the guy reminded Ritchie a bit of Manson, only if his craziness had been backed up by a ton of money. Ritchie knew the kid was swimming in it, unless he was housesitting. The only question was how he got the dough. He definitely didn't do it with Zombie Sluts or whatever it was called.

Lee had finished changing out the reels, and walked across the room to dim the lights. The screen was blank for a moment as the projector ran. Joey Suhne looked at Ritchie and smiled. "I think you'll be pleasantly surprised by what you see."

The Manson comparison was apt as far as it went, but there was something a little less shaggy about Suhne than Charlie, something teenaged and pubescent even though he grew a beard as if to compensate for his perennial boyishness. There was an underdeveloped, stunted quality that kept his ragged beard and long hair from achieving the kind of inverted Jesus quality that Manson attained in his satanic prophethood.

Ritchie wanted to get the hell out and go home. "Why did you want me here, Mr. Suhne?"

"I googled 'Bloody Boxer' and your face came up. I had to track the fight down." He cheesed at Ritchie again with his manic smile. "You're still bloody." He looked over at Lee, who had resumed his place on the couch and was sipping Courvoisier from a crystal lowball glass. "His face is still bleeding, and so's his nose, just like in the fight."

Lee nodded, without looking over.

Ritchie watched the screen with a mounting sense of dread that became full-blown horror as the bell rang for the first round. It felt as if his innermost thoughts were being broadcast on the canvas of the screen.

It was that grimy little Knights of Columbus Hall in Gravesend, Bensonhurst, his final match against that two-bit guido Vito Giachetti.

"Where did you get this?" Ritchie asked, his mouth open as if he was being forced to watch a snuff film. "This fight wasn't broadcast."

Joey Suhne walked around the large, kidney-shaped couch to the end table where Lee had fixed his own cognac. He poured two fingers of liquor into a glass. "This fight wasn't broadcast, but there were a couple of people in the crowd filming, home movies made by family members of Mr. Giachetti."

"Yeah, but where ..." Ritchie was out of breath.

"After I saw you online, I said, 'This man has to be the feature undead in my Zombie Boxer film.' For fight fans who are horror buffs, your participation in this project will be a little Easter egg, an inside joke."

Ritchie looked back at the screen, watched the main event in the "Battalion of the Italian Stallions" card as it unfolded. This was his first fight after a nasty divorce from Anna. The tune-up turned into a war of attrition as they traded leather like cornered rabid dogs trapped in a cage with an uncooked steak between them. He took two shots to land one, connecting with the more powerful but less frequent punches as the younger underdog laddered three and four punch stinging combos that bounced off Ritchie's head as he waded in. Ritchie watched his younger self on the screen land a digging hook to Giachetti's midsection, chastening the younger man and sending him to the canvas, winded and in agony, pulling his knees up to his chest.

"I thought I had him there," Ritchie said, to no one. Lee was engrossed in the fight. Joey Suhne was basking in Ritchie's horror and confusion. Bella didn't know exactly what she was looking at, but she didn't like it.

Joey walked around the couch to stand beside Ritchie and Bella. She patted Ritchie on the shoulder, a consoling tap that sent warmth coursing through him in shockwaves. He thought he'd needed a drink until he felt her touch on his shoulder. Joey's eyes narrowed to slits. He glared at her. "Have you been smoking marijuana in my Benz?"

"It was me," Ritchie said. "I smoke after I work out. It releases lactic acid." He grinned, playing dumber than he was. "You've seen Pumping Iron, with Arnie?"

Joey shot him a fake smile and then his eyes shifted into a momentary glare meant for Bella. She removed her hand from Ritchie's shoulder and Joey relaxed a bit. He watched the fight onscreen. They all did, even Ritchie, who couldn't help it. Joey sipped his cognac and said, "Believe me, I can come up with a better title than Zombie Boxer, but the distributors have a rule for horror movies. The name of the monster must be in the title. It serves as its own elevator pitch. For people just tuning in on cable, they need to know what the movie's about without even bothering to read the summary."

Ritchie watched himself work, throwing unanswered bombs at the young man, on the verge of a stoppage victory when the tape came loose from his glove, unwinding until it looked like he was trying to punch with a roll of toilet paper in his right hand. The ref sent him back to his corner and had his crew work to cut the tape on his gloves. That gave the prick Giachetti a reprieve, a chance to collect his wits.

Ritchie looked at the little string of tape, wincing as he saw it, realizing how much pain God and fate had spared him up until this moment by ensuring that this footage hadn't been shown to him, that he didn't know it existed and that only clandestine bootleg sources for his second loss were floating around until now. If he had to watch himself get ahead, get close to that TKO, or be reminded of how close he came to the promised land every time someone saw the fight replayed on ESPN Classic and wrote him- like they did with some of his other matches- he would have committed suicide by now. The self-destructive binge of last night would have looked like child's play compared to what he would have done to himself on a nightly basis in his quest to forget or at least not to feel. Maybe he would have killed Don Perillo for not wrapping the gloves tight enough. A bit more tape, a little more bandaging, and his attack wouldn't have been stopped. He would have plowed through Giachetti as predicted, and then after that he would have rattled off a string of wins that would have put the word out that Ritchie Abruzzi was back in a big way. He would have gotten another title shot, the second chance that so many men didn't get. In this alternate timeline, he would have won and gotten a few million, invested wisely and not made the mistake that so many fighters did, buying pieces of restaurants that became money pits in six months or less.

His father would be in a rest home right now. And he'd be the one in this mansion, or at least in something bigger than his bungalow in Oakwood. He felt like jumping into the La Brea tar pits. He wanted to punch a hole through the screen canvas and beat the breaks off this punk torturing him with his past here.

"I paid a private detective to find someone with the camcorder footage," Suhne said, and walked back over to his wet bar to make himself another drink. "It was transferred and restored. I think it looks pretty good. Don't you?"

Old Ritchie watched young Ritchie on-screen. The quality of the film still wasn't so good, but the action was of such a high caliber that it didn't matter. Like convenience store footage of a robbery or home movies of skydiving gone wrong, what was happening transcended how it was transmitted, both for him and for the others in the room. He didn't mind the black guy on the couch seeing him get his ass whipped. But he felt like he was being de-balled as the young and beautiful girl who had shown up at his door watched. His younger self returned to the fight with his recently rewrapped glove. The man-child on the screen was full of confidence because he couldn't see into the future. He stuck his chin out and showboated a bit. He did windmills, getting the crowd hyped up as he landed with metronomic regularity. The Compubox machine would have overheated if there'd been one at the small hall, as he beat all his previous records. He was a fluid artist in his prime, painting his masterpiece on Giachetti's face until the young guido landed a game-changing three-piece that opened up Ritchie's old scar tissue, those slices in his head still sore from last night. Scars followed a man like memories.

He was old enough now not to alibi and make excuses, to give the kid credit today for doing good work all those years ago. To give praise where it was due, Giachetti didn't panic when he was in trouble. He got on his bicycle, flurried and targeted that wound until it became a blood faucet, and he followed his work with a check hook with enough torque on it to tighten a lug nut.

"Shit," Lee said, spilling some of his drink as he flinched from the force of the shot. He glanced at Ritchie and said, "You got guts, kid."

"Thank you."

"Where's the other guy now?"

"Giachetti?" Ritchie asked. "He OD'd on heroin. Dead."

"I'll be," Lee said, shook his head, and drank. "Mercy, mercy," he whispered, channeling some black grandma's Christian pity as he savored the taste of cask-aged cognac.

"That's sad," Bella said.

Sad didn't begin to cover it, any of it. She was still young though, so she had time to find out for herself.

Giachetti smelled the blood even as he spilled it, a piranha invigorated by his own devouring frenzy. His own hand wraps had been as white as communion wafers at the start of the fight but were now stained red with his victim's lifeblood. An unanswered volley of at least ten shots came from Giachetti while Ritchie stood there like a blind martyr as he weathered the attack and threw nothing in return. He was beaten into total submission, no answer for the one-way fistic traffic coming his way. The ref waved the fight off, halting the action just a punch or two before things got into that zone where men died. The tiny venue erupted as the referee cradled Ritchie to his chest, hugging him. Redrum was blind, the hematoma beneath his eye swelling like a purple onion sewn under the skin and erupting in a luminous bubble. The other eye was invisible, glued shut in the socket that had been punched closed and sealed by the incoming leather. The ref whispered, "It's all over. It's over."

It was.

From Redrum to just a bum. Ritchie the bloody tomato can, Ritchie from Palookaville, USA. The thoughts and the voices, each a variation on him, a piece of the puzzle that ate him up with self-hate, came alive and spoke now, whispered until all the little mutterings became a screaming crescendo that called him a failure, a loser, until he wanted to perforate his eardrums with his own fingernails. No crowd cheering or booing could be as loud as the circus of his own thoughts now shouting in his head, from this past which he thought he'd outrun or at least learned to hide from. He wished he'd walked into a hit, that Bella the auburn lovechild of California's future that would not include him had at least had the decency to lure him into a more traditional honeypot trap, drawing him with the tractor beam of her fragrance, her soft feminine voice, and her pussy into something like the path of an oncoming bullet or the clubbing fists and stomping feet of some gangbangers who wanted his wallet. Instead she'd brought him into the orbit of something much worse. And still he couldn't hate her because she was too beautiful and he was too weak.

"It was a good fight," Lee said. "You were a true warrior."

"Thank you," Ritchie said.

Joey Suhne spoke to him with alcohol on his breath. "How would you feel about being my zombie boxer?"

"I can't act. I mean, they did a feature a documentary on me, and I played a sparring partner in an independent film about a decade ago, but that was just pickup work as a favor for a friend and a free trip to Canada. I-"

"I don't want you to act. You just have to put on some makeup, some prosthetics, and grunt."

Grunt. Ritchie looked over at Bella. Her eyes were soft, watery either from the cannabis or sympathy or a combination of both, the sandy smattering of freckles on her face glowing in the fading afternoon light. "I can help you with your performance," she said.

"So can I," Lee said, standing. "I've been in the film industry for some three decades. You can learn on the job from the master."

Ritchie grinned. For the first time since he'd wandered into this dark mansion he felt okay, less than humiliated at least. Two out of three of the people he'd just met weren't all bad.

"Who's the master?" Ritchie asked. "You?"

"Me?" Lee Keith took a step back, pointed at the marlins swimming on his chest with the hand not cradling the cognac. "Shit, no. I'm a b-movie guy. Any role calling for an older black man over six foot, from cop to sergeant in the Army, they at least send me the script. I'm a character actor." He shook his head and sipped his drink. "No, I ain't the master. You got me fucked up. I'm talking about Boris Karloff, baby. We got to study Frankenstein so you can get right."

"I don't know." Ritchie looked up at the screen. The fight was over, thankfully. He watched himself, having aged in the ring, as he sank into the folds of his terrycloth robe. Don Perillo massaged his shoulders and shrouded him with a towel. Ritchie hid in the blood-soaked cotton like a bat concealing itself in the folds of its leathery wings.

Joey Suhne stepped between Ritchie and Lee, a smile like another man's frown washing across his face. "I'll pay you fifty thousand dollars for three weeks' work."

"Well, when you put it that way …"

Suhne stuck out his hand for the shake. Ritchie felt his soul slipping away, but it struck him as somehow as inevitable as the sunset, or the unwinding of film once loaded onto the projector. The blood would continue to flow, and the public would continue to pay to see it spill. Zombie, boxer, whatever.

"It's a deal," Ritchie said, and shook, sealing it.

Chapter Twelve: Robinson's Midget

The basin was spread before them like a cyclorama as they whipped down the hill in the Benz. In the rearview Ritchie could see houses on stilts terraced on the downslope of the mountain. Ahead the San Gabriels were in shadow. Griffith Park Observatory glowed like a supervillain's lair, as if the dome might open and a nuclear missile could emerge from the planetarium orb to vaporize L.A.

Ritchie sat in the passenger seat with Bella's legs draped over the leather headrest while she drifted in and out of sleep in the backseat. Lee Keith drove back in the direction of the Valley, while Ritchie pretended having the girl's well-shaped legs draped over him was the most normal thing in the world.

Lee looked over at him, the straw hat pushed up on his brow. "You horny?"

Ritchie glanced in the backseat, toward Bella. "She's too young for me."

"I mean in general." Lee slapped the steering wheel. "I mean, when we drop her off at the club, you want to go in, maybe get fucked?"

"I don't know about that." Ritchie thought about the grand in his pocket. He wanted to get home, sand a few of those bills into the strongbox in the basement, and then sit and wait for the next punch life threw. He wasn't interested in fun. "The only thing they fuck you out of there is money."

Lee nodded toward the backseat. "She'll talk them into giving you a free dance and a couple drinks. I can get it on my own, because I'm a movie star." He shot Ritchie a grin and doffed his straw hat. Ritchie felt like arguing that his minor fame was greater than Lee's, but he let it drop, closed his eyes, and felt the wind whip through the car sans hardtop. This was one of those nights where someone who'd awoken from a coma and hadn't looked at a calendar in years would still be able to tell from just the sounds and smells that it was a Friday night. The weekend was in the air.

"Club will probably be packed," Ritchie said.

"I ain't gonna force you." Lee eased the Benz down a steep hill. Ritchie studied him, tried to remember some of the movies he'd seen the guy in on TV from time to time. Once he was in an airport and saw a much younger Lee Keith in something that had Commandos in the title. He seemed to remember him as the black cop in one of those rote dramas wherein the partner gets shot, grabs his sucking chest wound, and stutters out a speech about how they got to get the Big Boss before the next shipment hits the docks, or all the kids in the city will be hooked on crack.

He shot Ritchie his bracing smile, which was probably the same look he gave when clinching his teeth in rage or wincing in pain. An impish intelligence lit his eyes, but there was also a serene quality to him. He had seen and done things before he'd become an actor.

"That boy don't know shit about filmmaking," Keith said. A couple on a yellow Ninja bike passed them on the left, gunning it through an intersection. A woman with a purple thong sneaking up and out of her jeans shorts was riding bitch. Lee shook his head. "He can keep the rice rocket but that ass looks good." He dug a menthol cigarette from a pack in the breast pocket of his tropical print shirt and lit it with a small Bic. "I'll do anything I can to please a woman, except let her play with my butthole."

Ritchie laughed. Lee smoked and said, "Don't laugh. You get older and these women get bored. They want you try some new shit. I ain't into new shit. I'm old-school." Lee blew smoke into the muggy air and steered one-handed. Smoke poured from his flaring nostrils. "I could tell you wanted to punch that little weasel."

Ritchie didn't say anything. No sense in denying or confirming. "Can't say I blame you. It's a good thing you held off, though. That boy might be your meal ticket."

Bella groaned, started in her sleep from the backseat. Ritchie spoke with his voice lowered. "He's gonna give me fifty large for three weeks, and all I got to do is grunt?" Even with a shortened training camp, Ritchie would have to put in at least a month of work with either Don or Stich to prep for a fight, and that would only net him between five and ten grand.

"See," Lee said, also speaking lower now, "that's what I'm talking about when I say he don't know shit. You don't have to go to motherfucking Julliard or study under Lee Strasberg to know a role where you don't speak is harder than one where you speak." He pointed his half-smoked cigarette at Ritchie. "That's why I'm saying you need to watch Frankenstein. Or I'll do you one better." He pointed at the buildings around them, the Craftsman houses and the weird barnlike condos made of steel and buildings made of corrugated sheet metal. Some of these houses looked like they were built with materials rescued from junkyards, but they had seven figure price tags.

"You go to one of these revival showings they got at the movie palaces. Watch you some Lon Chaney and learn what real acting is. Pre-talkies are good to help you prep for a role where you don't speak. They teach you to communicate with your expressions, your eyes, because they didn't have a choice back then. Check out some of those silent movies."

"I might," Ritchie said. He didn't like the Suhne kid, but he wasn't the kind of person who would take fifty grand from someone without trying to do whatever they paid him to do.

"Once you go through makeup, you'd be surprised at how easy it is to slip into character. First time you look into the mirror and don't recognize yourself, that shit liberates you."

Lee slowed down, cut the wheel, and pulled into a half-filled lot. He spoke with the cigarette in his mouth. "Ain't too crowded, boy. Let's go in there and see what kind of caliber pussy they working with, maybe get our Jimmies wet."

"Gross," Bella said, coming to life from the backseat. She hugged Lee around the neck, kissed him, and he smiled.

"I'm the one your mama warned you about."

She hopped out of the convertible and came around to the passenger side of the car. Ritchie already missed the feel of her legs on his shoulders. He stuck out his hand for a shake.

"I do hugs."

He didn't, and kept his arms lowered awkwardly at his sides as she embraced him with all of her tiny frame. "I might be awhile, so if I don't see you guys in there, have fun."

Ritchie waved absently. Lee looked at him. "Why didn't you hug her back?"

"You think it was rude?"

"Nah, not necessarily." Lee shook his head, asked, "You scared of her?"

"A little," Ritchie said.

Lee held down the button to extend the top back over them. Ritchie spoke as it groaned and moved into place. "He loan you guys this car?"

"Yeah, it's the company car." Lee sat bolt upright to mock the formality of it all. "Super Suhne Productions." He shot a limp salute to some invisible superior officer, maybe Joey Suhne himself. "He ain't got talent, but he's got enough money to pay us all to pretend."

Lee got out of the car and Ritchie got out behind him. "I feel like Sugar Ray's midget," Ritchie said. Alecia had disappeared into an unmarked door at the back of the building, using a key. They were on the sidewalk and heading toward a doorman out front.

"What are you talking about?" Lee asked. "Oh, and don't say 'midget'. You got to say 'little person.'" There was a bit of earnest fear in his eyes. "I worked with one of them on this movie about a dwarf's curse, and he socked an AD in the balls for calling him midget. Ain't that some shit?"

Ritchie laughed, though having been on the receiving end of several low blows, he shouldn't have found it funny. Lee field-stripped his cigarette of the cherry, flicking the embers out and tossing the remaining paper and fiberglass portion between two grates in a storm drain at curbside.

"Hey now!" Lee smiled at the doorman as they approached. He spoke to Ritchie out of the side of his mouth. "This shit is on the house if you let me do the talking."

The doorman was a beefy guy with the physique of a linebacker, but his reddish baby face was loose and fatty, robbing him of any menace he could have conjured with his frame. His voice was high, too. "Hey, I saw you take out Bolo Yeung and Billy Drago in two different movies!"

"In the original script I was gonna whoop Jean-Claude Van Damme's ass, but I felt sorry for him and told them to rewrite it."

The doorman grinned, waved them inside. He spoke into his headset and the thump and boom of music carrying through subwoofers rumbled the ground like a minor quake. Two purple budding jacarandas were potted next to the desk in the lobby where a girl with a spray tan, giant tits, and brown hair stood.

"Hey, I saw you in ..." She stopped, scratched her head. "Don't tell me."

Lee stood there with his hands on his hips, like a VIP waiting for the house staff to apologize for mistaking him for a nobody earlier in the evening. "Brooklyn Ninja!" She finally said, her eyes lighting up as if she had won something.

Lee took up his martial arts stance, karate chopped the air, and then waved Ritchie into the main room.

"Brooklyn Ninja," Ritchie said, trailing behind his famous friend.

"All right, so it ain't fucking Street Car Named Desire. What do you want from me? You still got all your money in your pocket, don't you?"

"Thanks," Ritchie said.

Moonflower lighting shot through the room, dancing through the bar and the main stage, which were both made of glass blocks. The scattered loveseats and leather sofas around the room were covered in bordello-red pillows. Silk curtains were hung between the rooms, giving the place the feel of a Eurotrash fantasy of a Bedouin encampment. They didn't take three steps before two women stood before them.

"Star sent us," the one on the left said. She was a platinum blond in a halter lace body stocking. She wore silver lip gloss that matched her eyeliner. Ritchie could see her dark nipples through her fishnets and he couldn't control his erection. No matter how desperate or depressed he got, his Sicilian blood would always rise for the magic of any woman, from the sleaziest topless dancer to the Princess of Monaco. Life had lost its magic a long time ago, but women never would, not for him.

"You Ritchie?" she asked. He nodded. "Thank God, a real man for a change." She gripped his biceps. "You a fireman or something?"

"He plays one on TV," Lee said. A red light like a laser gunsight flashed over them and then strobed in the direction of the DJ booth.

"You guys actors?" The one on the right asked. She was the kind of black girl who could claim some Cherokee without it being a stretch, a "redbone" as he'd heard Stitch call her type. She didn't bother with wearing a top, and though there was a natural droop to her breasts, Ritchie much preferred that to silicon. Her breasts were tattooed with spider webs that covered everything except her sable-toned nipples. Her blonde pageboy wig was at odds with her even chocolate tone, but the open lie of such flagrant contrast somehow turned Ritchie on more.

"We're about to star in a picture together," Lee said, which may have been true. Ritchie hadn't seen a screen treatment or even a plot summary yet, but he figured Lee must have some part in the thing.

"What's it called?" the black girl asked. She blew a bubble and pulled the wad of gum back into her mouth with a tongue that flexed like a python strangling a mouse.

"We signed a non-disclosure agreement," Lee said, "Total blackout, can't even talk to Variety about it yet."

Ritchie had to hand it to the guy. That was Don King-caliber bullshit, and fast thinking besides. "Shall we?" Ritchie's girl asked.

He nodded. The women walked expertly on their open-toed pumps, one wearing rhinestones and sparkles, the other with jellied heels. Ritchie looked over at Lee, who shrugged and said, "I had to think of something. Pretty sure zombies don't get the pussy wet."

The ladies passed through the curtain and the men followed. The girls sat at opposite ends of a room-length plush-bonded sofa upholstered in leather. It groaned beneath them as they shimmied around on its bulging contours.

"You know," Lee said, walking over to his woman at one end of the couch, "I resent that just because I'm black, Star hooked me up with a black girl."

"You don't like me?" the girl said. She saddled the older man, taking his straw hat off his head, placing it atop her wig, and grinding against him as Bon Jovi came on through the speakers. The music transported Ritchie to the eighties, which he liked, since he'd been young then.

He leaned back against the couch, each mound of the mocha-stained leather feeling like an overinflated silicone breast fashioned by an LA surgeon who didn't know when to stop. He snuck a whiff of the blonde's armpit as she adjusted herself on his lap, savoring the pungency of her sweat.

She grinned at him, ran her fingers covered in manicured nails across his leg until she found his cock, straining against the jeans he'd thrown on this morning. "I can tell you like women, and women like you." She squeezed his cock. "I can see why."

"I got shortchanged on the IQ, but I got the Italian sausage."

She rubbed his ears and he noticed she had palm tree decals on her fingernails. "My Italian Stallion." She pouted, prepping her mouth for baby talk as she inspected the bruises and cuts on his head.

His arms dangled at his sides, all blood rushing to his cock. His right hand touched the strap of her jellied heel, and his hand rubbed the upper side of her foot, so small and well-formed it felt it belonged to a bound geisha girl.

"You like feet?"

"I like it all."

She stroked his cock with one hand, and touched his wounds with the other. The warm female fingers on the wounds were helping more than the fingers on his dick. "This one guy comes in every day around closing time, kind of creepy, but he loves to rub feet and my dogs are killing me so bad by then that I'm always happy to see him. Plus, after this I'm a receptionist at a hotel, which means more standing."

Her girlfriend spoke up. "Paid to get your feet rubbed. This isn't always a bad gig."

Ritchie reached his right hand into his pocket, struggling to open the Manilla envelope. The girl on his lap stopped stroking his bruises and his dick. Her plucked eyebrow arched. "You want to 'b' an 'l.'?"

"What?"

She leaned in and whispered in his ear. "Bust a load. I'll make it worth your while. Two hundred for head. For an extra hundred I'll play with your asshole while I do it. Stick a condom on the end of my finger and shove it up your ass. You've never come so hard."

Ritchie had finally maneuvered the hasps open and pulled one Franklin free of the ten stack. He handed it to her. The smile dropped from her face and her voice was icy. "It's two hundred for head, hon, not one-hundred."

"That's just a tip," he said. "I don't need any head. I'll go home after this and beat off thinking about you."

She segued back into character fast enough to win an Academy Award, gripped his cock as if it were a mole she'd caught wrecking her garden patch. "I think I might suck that cock for free. Generosity makes my pussy wet. Plus," she tousled his hair, "you're hot."

He hadn't touched a woman in years, he realized, not like this. He'd been through so much hell with Anna that during their last year together he envied men in prison and vowed to live out his days as the masturbating Hermit of Venice. Women were magic but they were also expensive and dangerous. They brought painful things, turmoil like love and court dates and children. He wasn't sure that he had enough faith in the future to come inside of a woman without wearing a condom at this point. His seed might grow and land feet-first in a world where people paid to watch men punch each other, and he didn't want to have a son who grew up to be one of those men doing the fighting. Maybe it was better to remain an unborn sperm swimming in his ball sack, or whatever kind of existence those unborn tadpoles had.

His weird thoughts had wilted his erection, and she sensed the change. "Hey, we can just sit here and talk if you want."

Lee's voice came from his left. Double-teaming or running trains was never Ritchie's thing, and even though the couch they were on was large, he was still cramped by having another hard cock in such close proximity to his own. "What did you mean about the midget, anyway?" Lee asked.

"Midget?" The black girl in the blond wig laughed. The DJ played an old Poison song that reminded Ritchie of when the Strip was crawling with hair metal bands and their groupies. "What the hell are you talking about?"

Ritchie's dick was dead, and his fantasy with it. He looked over at Lee while ignoring the waves of hostility radiating from the hard body in front of him. Apparently she didn't want to talk about midgets.

"Yeah, Ray Robinson, when he was world champ …" he trailed off a moment. The stripper on his lap was undaunted, rubbing his balls through the jeans, working their sensitive skin and bringing his cock back to life against his will. "When Ray was champ, he had a whole entourage, blew a grip on paying this midget … little person …to follow him around Europe."

"What's that got to do with us?" Lee asked. His date had switched to reverse cowgirl and was rubbing against his khakis with enough friction to give his dick Indian burns.

"I feel like that," Ritchie said. "Like this Joey Suhne guy is just paying me to trail him, like I'm his toy, his midget in his little entourage."

"It's a job," Lee said, though the way his voice trailed off led Ritchie to suspect he'd been dogged by similar thoughts. Only whatever humiliation Lee felt was probably more complex, since he had to deal with the Uncle Tom thing and whatever extra baggage and complexes came with being black and making it in Hollywood in b-movies.

"Joey Suhne?" The girl in front of Ritchie said. He still hadn't gotten her name and didn't think it was necessary to the proceedings. She'd spoken of Suhne as if his name had superglued her pussy shut. All things erotic were out of the question now, regardless of what kind of instructions Star had given the twosome in telling them to show the men hospitality.

"Yeah," Ritchie said.

"That guy's fucking gross. He called me up into that mansion of his, made me do a bunch of nude photo shoots, and then tried to pull the old casting couch deal on me."

The black girl halted grinding on Lee Keith. He held her by her hips and looked over at the girl relaying her story. "He say he was going to make you a star?"

"No, this was when Suhne was still just shooting pornos, so he didn't even bother to lie about giving me my big break. It was just for money, but ...the kind of stuff he wanted me to do ..." She trailed off, took a deep breath, and stood. "There's not enough money in the world."

"What kind of stuff?" Ritchie asked. He didn't mean to press, but he was curious.

Her eyes watered and she waved her palm-decaled nails in front of her nose as the tears formed in the corners of her eyes. When she blinked, the teardrops rolled down her cheeks. She turned and ran out of the room. The black girl and Lee Keith watched her exit with their mouths open in confusion. The golden curtain partition between the champagne room and the main area was still trembling from her departure, swaying left and right and letting in the glowing lights penetrating clouds of fog from a dry ice machine near the DJ's turntables.

"I don't know if I can do this shit," Ritchie said, "even for fifty grand."

Lee avoided eye contact with him as he spoke. "It's cool. Everything's copasetic. Just ... chill."

Ritchie leaned back in the leather, closed his eyes, and tried to block out the noise of Lee grunting as the black girl grinded reverse cowgirl on him.

"I'm about to come. You gonna make me have to go the drycleaner's after this."

"Bust it," she said, picking up speed and force as she bucked against him. "Bust that nut all over yourself, daddy. Get that dick leaking for mama."

Ritchie stood, needing some fresh air, or at least fresher air, since oxygen could only be so clean this close to sea level in L.A. He walked out of the VIP room, through the main room where a girl announced as "Chardonnay" outfitted with angel wings and a sparkly halo played with her pussy through the thin white gauze of her panties. He barely looked at her, walked past the girl manning the desk who had made Lee as the star of Brooklyn Ninja. Outside the cool night air was infused with carbon monoxide from the buses, meeting the gusts carrying from the Pacific Ocean.

The man-baby linebacker with the headset looked at Ritchie and smiled, his cheeks reddening as if pinched to bring all the blush to the surface of his skin. "Girls so hot in there you had to come outside to cool off, huh?"

Ritchie tried to produce a weak smile, balling his right fist. He wanted to punch something, which was problematic. If he hit something inanimate, like a car window or a brick wall, he might shatter his metacarpals and ruin himself for the only thing he'd ever been good at. And if he swung on someone, preferably a man, he might go to jail or land in some serious trouble, get slapped with a civil suit, all of this of course depending on how high on the hill the man he punched happened to live. He wondered now what he would do, how far he would go, to get a place for himself high up in those hills.

He didn't have to wonder for long, which bothered him. For the first time in a long while, he was scared of himself and what he might do. Something told him he would soon be a millionaire, in jail for life, or dead. He didn't see himself boxing for the slot machine and prime rib crowd in small halls in Biloxi and Tunica for five large here and there, or throwing bare fists for Alpo in the dark corners of Los Angeles and her blind alleys, either. Even less did he see Zombie Boxer opening any doors into the industry for him.

Something had to give, and maybe somebody had to go.

Chapter Thirteen: Over the Wall

The backyard was for sledgehammer work. Some of the best boxers had worked serious snap into their punches by chopping wood, but if he took an axe to anything in California Ritchie had the feeling he might get slapped with a fine or maybe attacked by some conservationist. That left hitting a tire with a sledge to work on his power as the only option.

He'd bought the hammer from a hardware shop in Culver, and had the guy working the desk swap out the fiberglass handle on the twenty-pound head with a wooden replacement. This way when he gripped the sledge, he could toughen his hands and add blisters to the leathery contours of his deeply brined mitts. He got the tire from a scavenger who used to rush him in the parking lot at Ralphs and tell him he could get him anything he wanted on twenty-four hours' notice.

Ritchie gave the guy a sawbuck, his address, and a request. He was surprised to find a monster truck tire with a seventeen-millimeter hex wheel sitting on his sagging porch the next morning. He dragged the thing into the backyard, and started to work pounding on it a day later.

He hit it now, lifting the mallet over his shoulders and dropping the head on the worn rubber that shuddered like a side of beef as it absorbed the blow. He was shirtless, sweating, his muscles a screaming marbled slab crying out as the tissue ripped and his power grew.

Swinging the hammer hurt, which made him angry. He took his rage out on the tire, hacking this time sidearm at an angle, imagining the steel sledge as an extension of his own arms.

Then something came over the wall, a green canvas Army surplus bag. Someone followed the bag over, leaping the keystone retaining blocks in one jump. Ritchie lifted the sledgehammer, gripping it in his raw hands. He drew it back, ready to slam it home and crush the kid's head like a watermelon and spill his brain matter on the overgrown backyard grass patch.

"Dad!"

Matteo held up both hands and Ritchie dropped the hammer. The head of the sledge landed perilously close to his foot. "Shit, man, how did you do that without hurting yourself?" Ritchie pointed at the green glass spikes laid into the wall. They were shards from Azteca beer bottles he'd gotten from Stitch for free. He'd mortared the jagged green bits into the stone himself.

"Parkour," Matteo said. "I got it like that."

Ritchie studied him, didn't see a scratch on his son. "I guess you do." He stood there awkwardly, wondering if he should embrace the kid. He held back, turned, and went to turn the hose on.

Matteo seemed as relieved as his father that the hug had been averted. He walked over to the tire and sledge setup, picked up the hammer by the handle. "Gross." He dropped it immediately and wiped his hands on his skinny jeans. Ritchie wondered why the hell the kids wore their pants so tight these days. A few years ago, they'd worn them too baggy. The young couldn't make up their minds.

"It's slimy," Matteo said.

Ritchie finished drinking from the hose, turned it off, and dropped the snaking line. "I sweat. I'm human."

He turned to go into the house, took the three cinderblock stairs up and held the screen door open for his son. "Come on in."

"Thank you." Matteo walked through the open door lugging his bag.

Ritchie closed the door behind them. "You didn't bring more than that bag?"

"Nah. Just sort of picked up and ran away. I've got everything I need in the bugout bag."

Ritchie held back on asking why the kid had run. Matteo was his son but he was no longer his to raise or even question. He had blown his chance at that a long time ago. "How's your mom?" Ritchie asked. He walked into the bathroom, stripped on the terrazzo tile, and hopped into the shower.

"She hates your guts."

"Yeah, well, I do too sometimes." He turned on the hot and cold taps and took the blast of water in the face. He closed his eyes as the sweat trickled away and the clean water rushed over him. He lathered up with apple-scented soap from a squeeze-bottle, scrubbed down with a loofa and rinsed off. When he was finished, he toweled off and tied the terrycloth bath towel around his waist. He usually walked around the bungalow naked and barefoot after a shower, air drying, but he didn't want to scare the kid.

Matteo sat on the settee. Ritchie walked through the hallway, padding over the hardwood to his bedroom. He selected a polo and some dungarees. He spoke to his son from the other room. "So how long you here?"

"You mean in L.A. or staying with you?"

Ritchie didn't know he had a guest until his son answered his question. He stripped off the towel, dried off, and slipped into his jeans. "You thinking of staying out here?"

"I don't know. I don't know what the hell I'm doing with my life."

"That makes two of us."

Ritchie walked back into the living room, slipped into some well-worn house slippers. He'd go without socks today. He walked back over to Matteo, worked up the nerve to give him a tepid pat on the shoulder. "What do you go by these days?"

"Matt."

Shit. He looked at him. The boy was his father's son. He'd gotten that strong Roman emperor's nose that had chiseled contours and more character than a broken wasp nose. The Italian had broken through those barbarous Deutsch genes. His blood had won out against Anna's. Matt's hair was a dark mass that was wavy until it reached the area around the forehead and ears, at which point it developed a will of its own and curled naturally.

Matt was in fact the perfect likeness of his grandfather when he was in his early twenties, in the black and white photo spread from Look. The kid was only sixteen and probably spent most of his time inside, playing videogames and beating his meat in an air-conditioned bedroom, but his DNA didn't know that. He had the rugged sex appeal of a first-generation Lower East Side tough. His eyebrows were so severe they looked like plucked chevrons, and he had a slightly evil cast to his features that probably not only appealed to girls his own age looking for danger, but would cause grown women to do double-takes before placing him as a kid.

"What are you looking at?" Matt asked.

"You. You look like your grandpa before he messed his face up with boxing."

"I wanted to ask you …" Matt's voice trailed off. Ritchie was thankful for that, as he dreaded what the boy was going to say. "Will you teach me to fight?"

Nerves started in Ritchie's stomach, scattering with the force of a moth trapped beneath a lampshade. "Let's talk about it over lunch. You hungry?"

"Yeah." Matt nodded. "You mad at me?"

"What for? I thought you'd be mad at me."

Matt was confused, shoved a strand of hair away from his eye. The kid was a little damn heartthrob and didn't know it yet. "Why should I be mad at you?"

Ritchie shrugged. He didn't want to do this complicated, messy stuff. "For leaving your mother."

"I can't stand her," Matt said, holding out his hands to the confines of the small bungalow. "Why do you think I'm out here?"

"To see me," Ritchie said. He hadn't expected to catch feelings, but all of a sudden he felt slighted that he wasn't the main reason his son was out here. Maybe the kid just needed a crash pad and Ritchie's place was conveniently by the beach, where the girls and the skate park and the ocean were.

"Come on," Ritchie said. "Putting in work on that tire's got me ready to eat a horse."

"How's pizza?" Matt stood up from the settee and followed his father out the door.

"Sure, but if you put pineapple or some shit on it I'll disown you." Ritchie dug the keys to the car out of his pocket and unlocked the Crown Vic.

"This ride isn't bad," Matt said.

"It gets me from point a to point b."

A girl in a seashell bikini and neon rollerblades flew by them. Matt's eyes followed her as if pulled by a tractor beam. "Yeah, you never get used to it." Ritchie got into the car and his son followed.

Matt rubbed his hand against the velour button-tuck job in admiring patters. "This is nice. Is this shag?"

"Something like that. Got it from some shot caller's stash at a police auction. I left it in, figured people would see it and think I was a dealer and not try to break in and jack the stereo."

"A lot of that going on around here?"

"All kinds of trouble," Ritchie said, nodding as he started the car and pulled out. They drove down the street, with the palms at the sides of the road and the sun hanging in the sky up ahead of them.

"So," Matt said.

"So …"

Matt looked out the window. "Will you teach me to box?" he asked, sheepishly.

Ritchie didn't sigh as much as deflate.

"What's wrong?" Matt asked. He tapped the glass of his window, looked over at his father.

"If you want some self-defense technique, to maybe protect yourself from a bully, sure. If you want to be a pro, let's go out in the backyard and you can let me smash your head in with that sledgehammer. It'll save you a lot of trouble."

"I've seen some of your fights on TV," Matt said. "You're smiling, jumping up and down in the ring after you win. Those ring card girls are hanging all over you. It looks like fun."

"One of those ring card girls got her hooks a little too deep into me," Ritchie said, and winced a moment after the words were out of his mouth. He didn't want to slander the boy's mother too hard in front of him.

"It wasn't fun?" Matt asked.

"It's like cocaine. It's fun for a while and then it stops being fun."

"You've done coke?" Matty asked.

Ritchie shook his head. "No. It was a … metaphor."

Matt shook his head and his shiny black locks flew. "No, it's a simile, not a metaphor."

"See," Ritchie said, turning up the Sinatra a bit. "If you know the difference between a simile and a metaphor at the age of sixteen, you don't need to be taking shots to the head."

"I'll be seventeen next month."

"That's pretty late to start." Ritchie clicked the washer fluid release button and turned on the wipers to kill some of the desert dust that had collected on the windshield. "Most of these kids from the barrio or the projects have been slugging since they were four years old. They'll eat your little white ass alive."

"Thanks for the vote of confidence." Matt resumed looking out his window, sulking.

Ritchie looked over at him. "I'm sorry." He didn't know how to handle the kid. Apologizing like this was something he did with girls, not guys. Guys you punched or told to shut the hell up, but this kid was sensitive, different.

"What's going on out there?" Matt asked, pointing up the street to a tiny white Baptist church with a Spanish-tiled roof.

Bike cops in blue and black spandex stood by on their carbon fiber ten-speeds, wearing Oakley wraparound sunglasses and fingerless gloves. Two police SUVs were parked herringbones style, with their lights flashing but their sirens off. The marque on the tiny church read, "Only God can turn a mess into a message." A black woman in a peplum dress and a massive hat with a funereal organza bow blew her nose into a tissue, while a fatter matronly black woman clutched at a stained walnut casket carried by six black men in Stacy Adams three-piece suits. A deacon with burry gray hair recited something from the New Testament as a light wind worked its way through his purple-striped dalmatic robe.

"It's serious out here," Ritchie said, "You've got to have situational awareness." He pointed at the casket being carried inside the church for services. "You also have to be realistic. If you fight you're going to be fighting kids trying to escape that kind of life. You think you're hungrier than that?"

"You weren't from the ghetto," Matt said.

Ritchie laughed. The kid was right. He could be wrong from time to time and for some reason it felt good to be called on it. "Yeah, but it was in my blood."

Matt held up his arm, displaying the blue veins cabling down his forearm. The kid had good muscle definition. "I got the same blood as you."

"You got half of my Italian blood," Ritchie said, turning left at the intersection. "You can come down to Azteca with me, and we'll see where you're at mentally and physically. Maybe if you're serious, we can think about the Gloves or whatever amateur stuff they got going on out here on the West Coast."

"Golden Gloves?" His son's fingers reached out for the golden trinket dangling from the rearview.

"Yup. I think it's more of an East Coast and Midwest thing. The amateurs out here are geared more toward the Olympics. We can talk about this crap later. Let's grub first."

Ritchie parked between a midnight blue Jeep and a double-decker tour bus from Redondo Beach. "Let's beat these old broads in there," Ritchie whispered.

The door on the tourist bus hissed open, and two women with golf visors and khaki shorts stumbled out at the head of the blue rinse pack. Ritchie walk-jogged up the block and Matt power-walked after him. "Where are we going?"

"You said you wanted pizza, right?" Ritchie asked.

"I'm so hungry I'll eat anything."

Boutique shops stretched as far as the eye could see. Skinny brunettes and Asian girls with vintage outfits and ethically-produced lattes and smoothies covered the ground thickly, ironic wisps of their affectless, unaccented language reaching the ears of the Abruzzi men as they walked up the block.

They passed a couple, the man in a blue Brooks Brothers shirt with the sleeves rolled to the elbow, his date wearing a shirt patterned with golden sequins, both of them walking a black lab with a belled jester hat on its head.

"You like kale?" Ritchie asked.

"What's that?"

"I don't know, but it's like crack for these types of white people."

They stopped in front of a shop with a brick face and a chalkboard menu braced against a cooper's masterpiece of a barrel that looked like it could survive going over the Niagara Falls. "This is it," Ritchie said. "Or maybe not. It's been awhile since I've been in this neighborhood." Truth be told, he avoided this area like the plague, but he wanted to be a good ambassador of Venice for his son. Matt could decide on his own what he did and didn't like about LA, and if he wanted to even stay out here, or remain with his father.

This place had smelled like woodfire pizza the last time he'd been here. Now it smelled like expensive floral bouquets. The ceiling was hung with chandeliers filled with champagne-colored baubles. A "hand-distressed" farm table with a fifteen-hundred-dollar price tag was on Ritchie's left, and two urns brimming with organic lavender soap were on his right, each bar tagged with a fifteen-dollar sticker.

"Dad, this isn't pizza."

"No shit," Ritchie said, under his breath.

A pale woman emerged from the back of the store, her hair pulled so tightly in a bun that she'd achieved the effect of an amateur facelift. She had the body of a twelve-year-old boy and looked like she hadn't laughed or tasted protein in at least a decade. Ritchie thought the dead black man in the casket a few blocks back probably had more life in him.

"Next door," she said.

"Thanks," Ritchie replied. He turned, and they stepped outside.

"How did she know—"

Ritchie put his son in a headlock. "How did she know we weren't there to buy a fifteen-hundred-dollar table that looks like someone beat it with a ball bat? Cause those mooks can smell money and it doesn't smell like me."

They walked in through the glass and steel front of the place next-door. This joint smelled like pizza, but it didn't look like it. Like so much in this neighborhood, the interior had the feel of an installation art exhibit, as if pizza needed some sort of postmodern touch. When Ritchie thought red sauce, he thought a dark, candlelit corner with an exposed brick wall and a port-colored tablecloth, something that would remind an Italian of his great-grandmother's cavernous dwelling in the Abruzzi highlands. This was cold, sterile, a pizza hospital where alien hipsters tried to approximate cuisine for the curious humans who came through their door.

Ritchie tried to keep a game face, walked up to the hostess, who, truth be told, was fine as hell. She had red bangs, multiple piercings including a random gem of some kind on her upper lip, as if her sweat beaded naturally into diamonds. She had greenish feline eyes and a drowsy sex appeal, some princess from the land of surf and sun who would only truly awaken out of her fog for a man who was worthy of her. Ritchie didn't understand who decided who became a famous model or actress and who didn't, or why or how. It was especially confusing out here, where women more beautiful than those gracing the covers of glossy magazines were everywhere and working for minimum wage, and a lot of them didn't even seem all that entitled or pissed about it. She certainly didn't.

"Two?" she said.

"Please," Ritchie said. He caught his son staring at her, and her glancing at Matt. He was jealous, but also happy, accepted that it was over for him, or getting there. Or maybe not.

"Can we sit over there?" Matt asked, pointing to a giant wall-sized mural of a boy in a stovepipe hat skateboarding in a drained pool.

"Yeah," Ritchie said. "You got one of those camera phones to take a picture?"

"I do, but it's in my duffel and I need to charge it." Matt was no longer interested in his father or in the beautiful girl leading them over to their stainless steel-topped table. "I just want to get a closer look."

"Your server will be with you in a moment."

"Thank you," Ritchie said. He pulled two laminated menus from a holder between a parmesan and red pepper shaker.

"You skate?" Ritchie asked. He opened his menu.

"No, but I still think it's cool."

"That's right," Ritchie said. "You parkour." He scanned the menu with his eyes. "What is that, exactly?"

"Oh, it's like ..." His son shrugged into himself. It was the poor posture of all teenagers, but he was also probably shelling up from the industrial strength AC of the uninviting restaurant. "Jumping off buildings and stuff, using physics to walk on walls."

"Why can't you do that?" Ritchie asked. "Instead of boxing?" The Flamenco Pie looked good. It was mozzarella, thyme, fresh bacon, and local organic cherry tomatoes.

"You can't make money doing that," Matt said. "There's no such thing as a pro."

"Only the top guys make anything in boxing, and most of them lose it after they get it."

Matt picked up his menu, glanced at it. Ritchie thought his son was engrossed in searching for his food pick, so he was surprised to hear his son's question, which threw him off-balance. "Did you lose it?"

"I got a little left," Ritchie said.

"So, what are you doing now for money?"

"I'm gonna star in a movie," Ritchie said, and realized he sounded like every other asshole in this town.

"Howdy, guys." A man with a lisp, glasses with black square frames, and gauges the size of champagne corks in his ears stood before them. "Do we know what we want to order or do we still need some time?"

Matt closed his menu, looked at Ritchie. "Your choice."

"We'll have a large Flamenco, and I'll have a water."
Ritchie slid his son's menu to his side, and handed both
cards to the waiter. The waiter impatiently propped the
black placards back into their holder between the seasonings
near the brick wall.

"For you?" the waiter asked Matt.

"Coke, or Cherry Coke."

"Certainly."

The server turned away with his order pad, and Matt
watched Ritchie. "You can be smart and be a boxer, right?
Bruce Lee was interested in boxing. Muhammad Ali was
smart."

Ritchie shook his head. It was heresy to critique the
Greatest, but this hipster pizza joint wasn't as risky an
environment as a gym where black guys saw Ali as one-third
of their triumvirate of black manhood, the other two pieces
being Floyd "Money" Mayweather and Mike Tyson. This
trinity satisfied every criterion needed to surmount the odds
in America, slickness, speed, shrewdness about dollars, a
vicious near-animal fighting instinct, and the mouth to defy
any white man any time he told you to shut up, be humble,
or apologize.

"Ali was smart like a lawyer. Verbal. Mouth-smart,
but he didn't even pass an induction exam to get in the
Army. Even Stitch said you got to be dumb to fail that
mother, and he's got a life-sized poster of Ali in his office."

"Who's Stitch?" Matt asked.

"Guy who runs the Azteca, the gym I train at."

"But there were some smart boxers, right? Guys
who used their brains in the ring?"

"Sure," Ritchie said, "Everyone from Daniel
Mendoza to Gene the 'Fighting Marine' Tunney. Joe Gans
might have been the smartest. Pernell Whitaker had a high
ring IQ. There's a scientific style that some guys use, and
then some guys are maulers like your old man." He paused
and backed up in the upholstered booth to let the waiter set

their drinks down. "Thank you." He took a sip of his water and pointed at his son as he sipped his soft drink through a straw. "You can forget your fucking Cherry Cokes, though, if you're thinking about really training."

"I am."

The kid was stubborn, pigheaded like him. Ritchie knew he deserved this new burden, or maybe seeing it as a challenge would be less self-pitying. "So how are you making money now?" Matt asked. "You're really in movies?"

"Now," Ritchie said. He thought, faltered for lies, decided he couldn't do it to the kid. He wouldn't mention the pickup fights to Matt, but that would mean he'd have to tell his son about the zombie thing. "I'm starring in a movie called Zombie Boxer, a Super Suhne Production." He shook his head, took another drink, and wished the water was vodka.

Chapter Fourteen: The Curse Continues

His phone went off as he was wrapping Matt's hands with the red cotton-elastic bands in the car. "Make sure to wash these things when you're done, and dry them quick or they'll stink and wrinkle."

Ritchie picked up the cellphone. It was a text from Bella, a couple of smiley face Emoji suns wearing sunglasses next to the message, "Just want you to have my number, in case you need it. Nice meeting you the other night."

Matt leaned in and tried to read the screen. "Easy there, killer," Ritchie said, stowing the phone in the Interceptor's glove box.

"You got a lady friend?"

"It ain't what you think." Ritchie finished with the right-hand wrap. "How's that feel?"

He'd already done Matt's left fist. He waited for his son to punch each hand into the other, testing out the soft cotton binding his knuckles. "Good."

"Good. Let's roll."

Ritchie grabbed the door, stopped just as a money-green two-door Italian coupe pulled up next to them. In the passenger seat was a giant Samoan with neck fat like a pack of cooked franks, wearing a leather duster. The driver was a tiny black guy, dwarfed even further by the comparison he suffered to the heavy in the passenger seat. The bodyguard struggled to get out of the car like a child who'd outgrown his big wheel toy.

"Who's that?" Matt asked. He cinched the drawstring on the mesh bag filled with their gear.

"The boxer's Corey 'Chop-Chop' Mathers."

"I've seen him on TV," Matt said.

"You should. He's a world-champion."

Mathers wore a shiny purple and gold throwback Lakers Jersey, numbered "34" with "O'Neal" in white lettering on the back. His hair was in jagged cornrows that zigged and darted across his scalp like the pattern on tire treads.

"If he's a world champ, why's he got a bodyguard? Can't he defend himself?" Matt nodded toward the heavy.

"Because every knucklehead in the street has something to prove, and he doesn't want to punch someone unless he's getting paid." Ritchie opened his door and got out.

Matt waited for the boxer and his bodyguard to precede them into the Azteca before asking any more questions. "What weight class is he?"

"He's a flyweight," Ritchie said. "If he were walking down the street in Manilla or Tokyo, they'd probably be mobbing him. But Americans want everything big."

The mood inside the gym was somber, the slap of leather and skip of plastic rope more sporadic than usual. Ritchie saw why when he got a little farther into the gym.

There was a wicker collection basket with a purple crush velvet lining in which hundred dollar bills floated. Behind the basket was a banner on which a black Jesus painted on polyester canvas billowed from the force of the Honeywell fan groaning in the corner. Next to the basket and the Jesus painting was a stand finished in pecan wood, on which there was a log book and an old story from KO Monthly. The title of the article was "Morehouse vs. Drake: This Time It's Personal."

Ritchie shook his head, spoke low to Matt. "The kid who got bodied used to box in the gym. I've seen him come in here sometimes."

Ritchie reached into his pocket, extracted one of the hundreds, and set it in the purple offertory basket. "Let's go work in the corner." He kept his voice low, and nodded toward Stitch. The tiny old man was wearing a green porkpie hat with a navy band on it. He blew his nose into a tissue, and Ritchie couldn't tell if he just had a seasonal allergy or if the kid's death had him crying.

"Hey Ugly Mug," Stitch said when they got close. "Who you got with you?" The old trainer brightened a bit, the sight of young blood waking him up.

"My son."

"The saga continues. Ain't that about a bitch?" Stitch stuck out his hand. Matt clasped it and was surprised by how powerful the elderly fellow's grip was. Stitch looked at Ritchie. "You gonna put him in the ring?"

"I'm not gonna make him do anything."

Stitch looked at Matt, gave him the onceover. "You want to fight?"

"Yes, sir."

The honorific made Stitch take a half-step back. He would have been less surprised if the kid had thrown a punch. "You got good manners. I guess your daddy ain't raise you." Stitch blew his nose again, and Ritchie saw he had a twill hanky and not a paper tissue. Old-school. "How much you weigh?"

"About one-sixty," Matt said.

Ritchie left the two there and walked across the room to snag a low metal training hurdle. "You think you can boil down to one-fifty-four?"

"Yes, sir."

Stitch folded his handkerchief into a triangle. "All right, I'll talk to someone at Westside, and if you pass a physical you can get a validation sticker for the year and a fight book. How's that sound?"

"Good."

"Smile," Stitch said.

Matt gave a thin-lipped, noncommittal grin. His father was back and patted him on the shoulder. "He means show him your teeth." He looked at Stitch and answered his question so Matt didn't have to show his choppers. "No braces, no bridgework. Kid's gold."

"Fuck it, then. I ain't got to see him cheese."

"Stitch!" Someone shouted from across the room. The three men turned to see the flyweight champ with his Samoan guardian angel in the leather cowboy jacket. They were standing by the door, adjusting some little trinkets "Chop-Chop" had brought with him so that the memorial to the fallen boxer now looked more like a Santeria offering. A lit beeswax candle completed in the effect. "Is it cool if we burn this in here?"

"Yeah," Stitch shouted back. "Just don't burn the fucking joint down." He tapped Matt quickly on the shoulder. "Nice to meet you, son. I'd love to stay and chat, but we got a kind of wake here."

Stitch turned, the thirty-second warning bell dinged, and two men in the sixteen-by-sixteen-foot ring continued trading leather along the ropes.

"Come here," Ritchie said.

Matt set the mesh bag on a bench next to the wall. "What? Oh," he groaned, pointing at the low yellow hurdler. "That thing. I've seen girls using that thing in volleyball practice."

"Don't be a dumbass. Come here."

Ritchie stood to the left of the low metal bar. "Watch me and then do what I do." He kept his feet together and hopped over the bar and back. "Jump this little banana bar fifty times, from right to left." He stopped jumping, and the varnished wood beneath his feet squeaked as his boxing shoes gripped the ground.

"Try it."

"I want to learn how to punch," Matt said, dragging ass over to the steel bar.

"Look, you learn to use your legs, and your waist, and you'll learn how to punch."

Matt hopped from left to right over the bar, his pigeon-toed feet stuck together. He stayed on the balls of his feet without Ritchie having to tell him.

"It's like an earthquake," Ritchie said. "When you see the buildings come down, that's just the end of the thing. It starts deep underground. Same with punches. It's …" He struggled, tried to remember the word the nutritionist had told him, back in the days when Don Perillo had believed in him and had been willing to invest beaucoup bucks in his Great White Hoper, before the downslide.

"Plyometrics," his son said.

Ritchie shook his head. "The student is fast becoming the teacher."

"Mom has a box for this," Matt said. The emphasis he put on Mom wasn't accidental, Ritchie knew. It was meant to be a dig at his father's training regimen, an old-school trick to make him think what he was doing wasn't masculine. It wasn't working. He'd seen guys who did ballet clean the clocks of guys who bunched raw meat in slaughterhouses Rocky-style.

"She work out a lot?" Ritchie asked. He didn't know why, but he secretly hoped his wife had blown up and now spent her days eating ice cream and watching daytime TV, immobile and embittered and laying on the couch on her side like a beached whale.

"Yeah."

He stopped himself from asking if she was seeing anyone. He had to let go, and yet he couldn't. "Your mom told me you were working up at Villa Roma, just like your old man?"

"I was," Matt said, panting. A light glaze of sweat was coating his skin already as he hopped. "But it's only seasonal. All those old Borscht Belt places are dying."

"What did they have you doing?"

"Giving kayak lessons."

"Good," Ritchie said, his hands on his hips like a football coach inspecting his squad in action. "I spent most of my time working the desk during the day and chasing tail at night."

"I was too busy for that." Matt panted as he hopped.

"Well, you obviously built some upper-body strength, but if you want to turn pro, you got to understand …" He glanced around the gym at the guys jumping rope and working the bags. "Most of these guys have to have day jobs. If you've got to work during the day, then it's best your job be something physical. Then once you rack up enough wins you can quit your day job and box fulltime."

"Did you have a day job once you turned pro?"

Ritchie shook his head, took one hand from his hip to scratch an errant itch on the point of his twice-broken nose. "They moved me like a pawn in a game of speed chess."

"How do you mean?" Matt was wincing from the burn radiating up his calves and into his thighs as he hopped from side to side.

"Because of who my dad was, and because I was knocking guys out in headgear, I had investors behind me from the beginning. They fronted living expenses and I got decent-sized purses from the get-go. It won't be like that if you turn pro."

"Why?" Matt walked away from the bar, shaking his head and hissing from the pain.

"Because my name ain't big enough. You can't ride my coattails the way I rode your grandfather's."

Matt leaned down, the agony of burnout causing him to double over. When he came back up he asked, "Can I see him?"

"He wants to see you, but Denise says he's not doing too good."

"She his nurse?"

"Third wife," Ritchie said, "or fourth. I'm not sure if annulments count." He gave Matt a "good game" slap on the backside. "Come over here."

Matt followed his father. Ritchie still hadn't gotten used to the eerie quiet that had settled onto the gym. Usually there was a rapper bragging about how hard he was and cussing up a blue streak about "Nigga" this and "bitch" that. The quiet, along with the ripple of orange light from the candle, gave the place the feel of matins or vespers among an order of fighting monks.

"You think I should keep giving kayak lessons at Villa Roma?" Matt asked.

Ritchie didn't want to say "yes," if only because the selfish part of him was growing used to having his son around, but he didn't want to bullshit the kid either and hurt him. "You got to do something physical. Back in the old days guys were tough as nails. They did shit like pick onions or worked as stevedores."

A wrathful grunt sounded behind them, and Zherik, the Kazakhstani owner of the unibrow and hirsute body, ripped a five-shot combination to the teardrop bag that sent ripples through its rubber hide.

"And when the dude you're fighting isn't getting in shape lifting crates on the docks, he's one of these psychos from one of those countries that ends in 'Stan.'"

"I hear you, my friend," the Wolfman said. "And I want you to know I am proud of my country."

"People are gonna wish the Iron Curtain didn't fall when they get a load of you. You know Vasily Jirov?" Ritchie asked Zherik. The man walked around the bag and threw an educated jab followed by a double hook.

"Yes."

Ritchie looked back at his son. "The guy was trained by someone who would paddle him out to the middle of a river in a boat and throw him overboard and make him swim back."

Matt's eyes widened. Zherik smiled and swung, said, "This is true."

"Or he'd throw Jirov in a room with a pack of attack dogs and lock the door to help the kid deal with his fear."

"This is also true," Zherik said, grunting as he clinched with the bag and saturated it with his sweat.

Ritchie opened his arms to the brick, high-ceilinged converted warehouse around them. "This has to be your new church, and you got to pray every day, all day, because that's what the other guy's doing when he's getting ready to beat you."

"I understand," Matt said.

"Now we're going to work on your stance." Ritchie walked up to Matt and stood alongside him. He made to take up his son's hands, but Matt pulled back. "What?" Ritchie asked, thinking another one of the kid's mercurial whims had struck.

"I want to fight like Roy Jones."

A black fighter across the room laughed, having heard the boy's softly spoken wish as if blessed with echolocation. "Ritch, you might want to tell shorty to look in the mirror. He's having an identity crisis." Laughter rippled through the group of four or five guys who'd entered when Ritchie had been busy instructing his son. They wore black satin jackets with enough patches on them to be eagle scouts. They'd picked up the badges in various all-city tourneys.

"What does he mean?" Matt asked, suddenly self-conscious.

"You're saying you want to fight black, and not too many white guys can do it. It's like having a Bob Dylan voice and thinking you're going to scream like James Brown or blow like Sam Cooke."

Matt's mouth was open, puckering as if he wanted to protest or might even cry. "Here," Ritchie said, and stuck out both of his hands, palms facing up.

"What's this?" Matt said.

"Let's test your quick twitch muscle fibers."

"Patty-cake?" Matt sucked his teeth, looked off with a frown of disgust plastered on his young face.

"Hey, you don't want my help, fine." Ritchie looked over at the steel banana bar, as he called the hurdler. "That little volleyball girl thing broke you off proper, didn't it?"

Matt thought about his still-sore legs, the sharp pain in his glutes like a temporary case of sciatica. "Okay." He acquiesced, stuck his hands on top of his father's.

Ritchie's palms turned and smacked the tops of his son's knuckles before the young man could blink. Laughter came from the group of amateur sluggers by the door, and Matt looked over at them again. Where before he was self-conscious, he was now humiliated, and the red rushed to his cheeks.

"Don't worry about them," Ritchie said. "If you cry about five guys clowning on you, what are you going to do when you fly a couple thousand miles to a country you've never seen before, go into a stadium where people are shouting for your head in a language you don't understand, and you got to knock a guy out because all those corrupt-ass judges in that banana republic are bought off?"

"All right," Matt said, nodding and doing everything in his power not to look over at the black faces, though he couldn't drown out the sounds of their sniping, their clowning as his father called it. "I'm ready this time. You won't tag my hands."

Ritchie turned his palms over and slapped his son's hands faster than the deftest blackjack dealer flipping cards. He followed the slap up with a cuff to his son's ears, clapping him once on each side of the head for good measure before Matt could bob, weave, or even say "Ouch!"

"What the hell?" Matt swung on his father and Ritchie stepped to the side and slapped him again.

"I got taught the same lesson, only I got punched in the face so hard that when I went to blow my nose, my eyes swelled closed. I learned that day your eye sockets and your nose are connected." He paused, asked, "Are you through trying to be Roy Jones? You ready to be Matteo Abruzzi?"

"Matt."

"How about Matty?"

"Matt."

"Okay, killer. Have it your way. You ready to learn the orthodox stance?"

"I want to fight like you did," Matt said, and Ritchie could barely stow the smile.

"The peekaboo isn't for everyone, but if you want to try it."

"I do," Matt said.

"All right. Hold still and let me place your hands and feet." Ritchie kicked his son's legs apart and turned him so that the young man's left shoulder was forward and he wasn't so squared up.

He took his son's hands in his own fists, and felt the resistance there, the mule-stubborn streak he'd inherited from his father and his father before him. It was a curse in the gym, but it could be molded into a blessing in the ring, when intelligence said to quit and preserve pints of blood and millions of brain cells, while pride coursed through the body and made a man willing to trade everything including his life to win, to break the bones and bruise the flesh of the other man who stood before him.

Matt's hands were level with each other, a bit to the front and to the sides of his head.

"Okay," Ritchie said. "We're gonna go so slow that you're going to say it's stupid, like everything else I've tried

162

to teach you today. But just like everything else I've taught you today, it's not stupid."

"It's not stupid," Matt said. He held this position, as if he were a Buckingham Palace guard whose life depended on it. His eyes were serious, and a serene focus had overtaken him. Ritchie remembered the first time someone had taught him in a gym, that knowledge that an adult was imparting something to him that was useful and not patronizing. Matt knew that for the first time in his life he was in a real classroom, one that few saw and only a dwindling number of American men even knew existed.

"Now you're in position to deflect my shots, to block them. But if you catch and then don't shoot, then you're just catching. And this isn't baseball. You understand?"

Matt gave only the slightest of nods, afraid to alter position too much with a flurry of head.

"If I make a mistake, and you don't capitalize on it, then it's like I didn't even make a mistake. And if you don't make me pay, then I'm not going to respect you, and my confidence is going to grow and yours is going to shrink. Confidence in boxing is like the ball in football or basketball. We can fight over it, but only one of us can really have it, all right?"

His son gave the tight little nod again. Ritchie threw up the mirror stance on him, assuming his own counter-peekaboo. "Now, real slowly, I want you to throw a punch for my head, like we're in that one movie."

"The Matrix?"

"Yeah, do it."

Matt led with his right and took a step forward as he did, without even having to be told. Ritchie slowly pushed his son's hand down with his own wrapped fist as his son threw, and then threw his own ultra-slow motion counter. "That was a down parry."

Ritchie switched to southpaw for a moment. "Take up your peekaboo again." Matt assumed the stance, hands superglued in position. Ritchie threw a glacially-paced shot toward his son's body. As the shot was cruising forward, he asked, "Now, some things have to be taught, and some things are just instinct. The really hard things to learn are the ones where someone has to teach you to ignore your instincts in order to perfect your technique. If you always do what your body tells you to do as a reaction, guys can use your instincts against you to play you like a piano."

"Should I be ignoring my instincts now?" Matt asked.

"You tell me," Ritchie said. "Do what your instinct tells you to do, and I'll tell you whether it's right or wrong."

Ritchie's lead left hook to the body was still slowly cruising in at an angle. Matt dropped the right half of his peekaboo guard, blocked with his elbow, and then resumed his stance. "Was that right?" He grinned.

"Half right," Ritchie said. "You dropped your arm to block but you didn't throw anything back." Ritchie mirrored the stance he'd taught his son again. "Next time I throw a hook at your body, and you drop down and block with the elbow, you got to throw something back after you block."

"I caught but I didn't shoot," Matt said.

"Exactly," Ritchie said. "And every time I make a mistake and you don't make me pay, you're making a mistake."

"And the other man," Zherik said, his chest hair matted in sweat, "he will make you pay."

"He'll make you pay by punching you," Ritchie said. "I'm a bit nicer." He looked back toward the steel banana bar on the floor. "I'm just going to make you jump left and right ten times, and then you're going to get your ass back over here and we're going to start over again."

"Okay," Matt said, his hands still clutched to his head. "That's fair enough."

Ritchie's hands were back on his hips. "I don't think you understand."

"What?" Matt said, dread dawning on his young face.

Ritchie jerked his head toward the mini-hurdle again. The Wolfman smiled, placing his own hands sheathed in black sparring gloves on his hips. "You've made your first mistake," Zherik said.

"Give me my jumps and then report back here."

"Shit," Matt said.

More laughter came from the left side of the room, although this was a gentler, croaking sort of cackle. It was Stitch. "You boys are cooking with butter now."

"We're breaking that cherry nice and easy," Ritchie said, which was definitely true. The day he'd hit pugilistic puberty, his father cracked him good in the kisser and started the menstrual flow from his nose.

"One," Matt said, grunting.

"You're gonna be dead-tired tonight," Ritchie said, watching him as the boy hopped from left to right with much grunting but zero complaints. "But don't worry. We're going to go running in the sand in the morning."

The candle continued to burn in the corner of the room, making odd slanting black silhouettes of the men throwing shots at bags, into thin air, or at each other as the timer buzzed again, and the whole thing started over again for the next round.

Chapter Fifteen: A little Roadwork

The Poet Laureate of Oakwood was up before them, and by the time Ritchie and Matt were in sweats and were finished with stretching, Lawrence Kramb was already sitting on a lawn chair in front of his Globetrotter, sketching the sunrise.

"Good morning, Mr. Abruzzi."

"Hey." Ritchie tugged Matt on the arm. He wanted to get a move on before the sun was up, but he didn't want to be rude. "Someone you should meet."

Lawrence set down his charcoal and his sketchpad. "This is the younger Mr. Abruzzi, then?"

"Youngest," Ritchie said. "My son." It felt good to say that.

"Sir," Matt said, and extended his hand.

"Youth," the old man said, "is foolish. And old is the fool." He shook Matt's hand, then took up his pad and charcoal again.

Matt looked at the man, a bit perplexed. He'd rarely met an old person who didn't try to eat up his time with BS and formality. Not only hadn't this guy tried that with him, but he seemed eager to get back to his sketching, as if the kid was an imposition on the secret reclamation of youth he enjoyed each daybreak.

"Let's roll," Ritchie said, tugging Matt's sleeve again. He headed toward an archipelago of purple clouds hovering above. Below the clouds the rising sun tinged the sky's dark edges with veils of red, yellow, and orange laid in bands. The basketball court and skate park were in shadow.

Ritchie ran backwards ahead of his son. "When you run, make sure you run in all different directions, side to side, frontwards and backwards. Know why?"

"No," Matt said, chugging along.

"Because you're going to run every which way in the ring. You train as you fight." Ritchie shadowboxed the air in

166

front of him, and then turned frontwards and kept running. "Keep your eyes open here. You can't outrun bullets."

Matt ran until he was even with his father, wincing from the soreness of yesterday's workout. "What do you mean?"

"I mean we got a thirteen-building gauntlet to run, a certified, bona fide ghetto to hoof it through before we're in the clear."

They ran past buildings covered in chipped coats of paint. There were layers of gang graffiti- crowns, pitchforks, blue names, and red numbers. The tags not only looked like they might not come off with a pressure washer, but looked deeply-engrained enough to resist an exorcism. Pit bulls barked behind fences that barely held the muscled little gargoyle-canine hybrids. The graffitied tags up and down the block alternated from the Shoreline Crips to the Venice Thirteen.

"Why are you taking us through a ghetto?" Matt asked.

"You need to get used to your fear, get used to danger. The deer that isn't afraid to cross the street is the one that gets clipped by the truck. Are you scared?"

"Yes."

"Good," Ritchie said. "Maybe if you stay that way you can avoid getting knocked out." He coughed and hocked up some spit. "Besides, it's not like we're wearing blue or red. And gangbangers are still probably asleep, hungover from last night's partying."

They were in the thick of the Del Mar Houses, a spread of buildings so square they looked like giant cinderblocks laid endwise. They were Spanish Colonial flat-roofed jobs, the wood of their balconies as rotted as pylons submerged in the ocean. They looked more like giant shipwrecked slave galleons than an apartment complex.

"We're going to run on the sand, because your legs got to work more on it than on concrete."

"Dad ..." Matt was already lagging back a few paces. Ritchie turned around again. "I don't want to work my legs anymore. It feels like I got a booster shot in my ass yesterday."

Matt halted, stood in place. Ritchie stopped with him. "What's wrong?"

"I got a cramp."

"Good, use it. Run through the pain."

Ritchie ran in place alongside Matt. "Let's go." He patted Matt on the sweat stain forming in the small of his back.

"I hate you."

They ran out of the ghetto, and neared the beach. A group of homeless men and women lay in old sleeping bags on a grassy mound shaded by a couple of palms. One man with long red hair sat up in his bedroll and made a cigarette from a can of Bugler.

"They always there?" Matt asked. He didn't want to stare, but he'd never seen the homeless so flagrantly using public space or gathered in such a large group.

"Sometimes. Sometimes the police conduct their little sweeps and they scatter. A few might be on the beach." Ritchie's feet touched the sand and he lifted his legs as if doing Iacocca drills through cones. "Try not to step on anybody."

Matt couldn't tell if his father was joking, but he watched the sand at his feet as he ran. He didn't want to make it through the ghetto unscathed only to step on a homeless man and get stuck with a shiv.

The Boardwalk was in the distance. The side of the largest building in sight from here was covered in a painting of a woman with hair waving in red tendrils, a hippie half-shell Venus framed by an angel in a red cloak with her hand outstretched toward a dove with an olive branch in its beak. The gates in front of the Sunglasses Hut and the t-shirt shops and hotdog stands were lifting. The seagulls scattered from the bullnose awnings over the shops as the latticed steel rattled open. A Korean woman in sunglasses swept up in front of her shop and a sprinkler started to life on a nearby grass island.

"How much farther?" Matt asked.

"Just a little bit." Ritchie ran back to him and did circles in the sand around him.

Their run had taken them until they were adjacent to the Free Speech Zone. A woman in a floor-length skirt set out a blanket and started tuning her acoustic guitar, while an Asian man with his calligraphy designs and a black man who did chalk drawings of blues musicians both set up their easels. A juggler oiled his chainsaws while his competition got his fire-swallowing act ready for the day.

Matt's head remained turned in the direction of the Boardwalk until a crick worked its way into his stiff neck, and he was forced to look forward again. The surf crashed against the beach, releasing foam onto the sand as the waves broke against the shore. A barefoot man in a sombrero with a zinc strip on his nose moved farther inland with his metal detector.

They came to a stop next to large piece of driftwood near an abandoned and overturned saltwater-rusted shopping cart. "Here," Ritchie said, and looked around the wood. "Got to check for washed-up jellyfish and heroin needles first." It looked safe and he popped a squat.

"How'd I do?" Matt asked, coming to rest beside him.

"Good." Ritchie looked out to sea. A sailboat was visible in the distance, and the water had a coppery shimmer like a wishing well whose floor was carpeted with pennies.

He patted his son on the back. "It might not seem like it now, but if you keep it up, in a year or two you'll be able to run me ragged on the beach. And you'll probably be able to break me off in the gym."

"I doubt that," Matt said. "You're only in your mid-thirties."

Ritchie tried not to let his laughter come out as bitter. "I would be only in my mid-thirties if I was an English teacher. I'm a fighter."

Matt laughed, without a trace of bitterness. "You're speaking in the present tense."

"Got no choice," Ritchie said. "I screwed up the past and I can't control the future."

"Your future doesn't sound so bad." Matt picked up a handful of wet sand and absently played with it, letting the grains fall through his fingers. "You're gonna be in a movie, right?"

Ritchie had forgotten he'd told his son about his involvement with Super Suhne Productions. "Oh," Matt said, and stood. He beat his hand against his cargo shorts, and the obstinate grains responded like well-oiled breadcrumbs coating a pork chop. After slapping his hand against his shorts a few more times, he finally got his palm clean enough to go in his pocket and bring out his cellphone.

"You kids and your phones," Ritchie said, and shook his head. "That's a no-no. You never bring it with you to train. Leave it in the car if you have to, but you don't bring it on a run, or into the gym, unless you're waiting to hear who they picked as the next pope."

"You'll want to hear this," Matt said. "After you told me about the movie, I googled 'Super Suhne' and found out about the guy who runs it."

"Joey Suhne?" Ritchie asked. His feeling about the director/producer was that the less he thought about the guy, the better. Fights were meant to be left in the ring, and that asshole was meant to be left in his mansion with his dark dreams and the unnamed perversions he'd foisted on that stripper at Fantasy Reign, whatever it was that brought her to tears.

"The guy's grandfather basically got in on the ground floor of L.A. Here." Matt held out the cellphone to Ritchie. He studied the tiny black and white thumbnail photo of the old tycoon, his nose hawkish in profile and his eyes puritanical and grim.

"Shit's too small for me to read, especially with the sun coming up. You read it to me."

Matt put the phone in his pocket. "I'll give you the Cliff's Notes version. Joseph Suhne's grandpa worked for the U.S. Survey Bureau or something like that. He got a five-hundred buck loan and found some oil in Echo Park. You know where that is?"

"Yeah," Ritchie said. "Downtown." He was less than impressed. "Anywhere you got dead dinosaurs I think you got oil. I'm no geologist but you don't have to be one to know that."

"This dude's grandpa had the first real commercial oil well in Southern Cali. He beat the boom."

"That's all good and well," Ritchie said, kicking his feet into the sand. "So his grandson's still got some money left from that oil patch and he's using it to play producer."

"His grandpa was rich, but his parents got hella wealthy."

"Hella wealthy." Ritchie shook his head. The kids and their damn slang. At least his son's shorts weren't super-tight today, like the pants he'd worn yesterday. "What did they do? Buy more oil fields?"

"Nah, check it out." Matt took out the phone, hit the screen to bring the liquid crystal display back to life. He scrolled through the archived webpages to give himself a refresher before providing his father with a breakdown. "The grandad screwed them, divided his ducats between a mistress and a cancer research fund." Matt shrugged. "I think he died from bone cancer and he wanted to search for a cure as his legacy. A wing in a hospital out here is named after him."

Ritchie turned, shifting on the gnarled piece of driftwood. "Why is Suhne sitting up in that big mansion if the grand poohbah gave away the store?"

"Because," Matt said, "one of the kids went into the jewelry business and she started working as an appraiser. She met a guy there and they learned the game, bought up a bunch of estate jewelry and got mega-wealthy, richer than Grandpa."

"And they left it to that little prick?" Ritchie nodded in the direction of the hills rising around the valley.

"They didn't have a choice but to leave it to him," Matt said.

"Why?"

"That's where it gets interesting. They went on some expedition to go buy some super-rare diamonds and they got sick and died. Your boy, their son, got everything."

Ritchie groaned, stood, and rearranged himself as he sat on the sand so that his back was propped against the driftwood. "I wonder how much he's worth?"

"You don't have to wonder," Matt said, smiling. The sea breeze picked up a lock of his black hair and played with it. He closed his left eye and blew hot air from the right corner of his mouth, sending the errant strand away. "I checked it out on Networth.com."

"I hate the internet. Nobody's got any privacy anymore." He was thinking of Suhne googling "Bloody Boxer" and his face coming up in the search results.

A playful smile worked its way across Matt's face. The boat in the distance drifted closer. "Yeah, I guess you want to respect his privacy. I won't tell you what he's worth."

Ritchie balled his right fist. "I know you want to learn about boxing. I can teach you everything I know in three minutes if you want, kiddo."

"Five-hundred million."

Ritchie's fist unclenched, and even though he was parched he managed to whistle. "That's a spicy meatball." He recovered his composure a moment later. "Still ..."

"Still, what?"

Ritchie drew a circle in the sand with his pointer finger, and then elaborated that into a figure-eight. "That doesn't mean much to me. I'm getting fifty grand for this picture, but that's it." He took his hand from the sand and closed his palm. "Rich people are tight-fisted as hell."

He pointed toward a homeless man coming toward them, wearing chocolate-chip fatigue desert camo and pushing a discarded designer baby stroller, its torn canvas panels colored red, white, and blue. The berth of the baby carriage was filled with black garbage bags. Ritchie wondered if the guy was a vet of one of America's sandbox fiascoes, maybe Desert Storm or the more recent Afghanistan or Iraq wars. "If I needed to borrow a dollar, I'd ask that guy before I hit up Joey Suhne. Personally," Ritchie said, "I'm tired of talking about the prick." He lightly touched his son's elbow. "Thanks for the intel, though."

The flesh of Matt's forehead crinkled, and he averted his eyes, his gaze remaining downcast. He didn't say anything, and Ritchie had the feeling that maybe the boy regretted telling his dad all of this, especially the exact dollar amount that Suhne was worth.

An awkward silence hung between them for a moment. Ritchie tried to kill it, forced a smile, and, "You ready for some breakfast?"

"Sure," Matt said, grinning. He paused, and Ritchie grinned back at him. "Can we walk instead of run back?"

"Yes," Ritchie said, "but only because if my old ass keeps it up, I'm going to be in traction here pretty soon. For a boxer, the speed is always the first thing to go." He limped forward, and Matt walked beside him. "That's why it's actually a good thing you're learning to fight with your hands up. The guys who fight the best in their prime are usually the best athletes. They don't have a bag of tricks, though, to help them when they get older. They've got great reflexes, but once those go, they're assed-out. The guys with solid fundamentals have more to fall back on when they're older."

Ritchie made a muscle, flexed like a strongman from back in the days when the Slum by the Sea was still beautiful, and a musclebound man with a mallet could earn his gal a stuffed toy by hitting the high striker until the machine lit up and he was king of the arcade. "Step right up!" Ritchie said, doing his best impression of a barker from those bygone days. "Let's find out who are the men and who are the boys!"

He was smiling, but a voice was dogging him, nesting like a gnawing rat in the back of his mind, something Anna and more than a couple of women he'd dated had said about him being a boy rather than a man. Ritchie knew muscle wouldn't change that, and that punching couldn't solve anything, either. He just wished he could get Matt to understand. Hopefully, the kid would get hit a few times in the ring, decide it wasn't for him, and then he would hang up the gloves, thereby sparing himself no end of heartache.

Chapter Sixteen: Red Car Resurrected

The Benz was waiting for him in front of the bungalow in Oakwood early the next morning. Matt was still beat from yesterday's workout, and Ritchie let him keep sleeping in his bed. He'd crashed out on his settee, using a thin sheet as a cover.

He opened the door to see Lee Keith standing there in a green Bundeswehr field jacket. "Shit, don't act like you ain't happy to see me." He took a drag on his clove cigarette and smiled.

"Morning," Ritchie said.

"You ready to roll?" He looked Ritchie up and down, saw he was dressed for the day.

"Yeah," he whispered, and then grabbed his keys and headed out the door.

"You got a girl in there?" Lee asked. The Benz was gleaming like it had recently undergone a turtle wax.

"It's my son."

Lee ditched his cigarette, pointed at the Globetrotter as he got in on the driver's side of the Mercedes. "That's a nice old camper."

"The owner's a nice guy, too."

"Most of them motherfuckers are parked over on Rose."

"I know it," Ritchie said and got in.

Lee pulled out of the space in front of Ritchie's house and headed for the highway. Ritchie couldn't remember the exact route they'd taken to Suhne's adobe castle, but this didn't feel like it.

"Where are we going?"

Lee ignored him, scanned through the stations on the radio. "No country, no rap, no new shit." He lucked into some Lou Rawls. "I saw him at the Palladium about a million years ago."

Ritchie leaned the seat back and relaxed. He figured that if Lee didn't want to tell him where they were going, he'd find out when they got there. "Alecia tell you Suhne uses real organs in these damn movies, like chicken livers and cow hearts and pig intestines and shit?"

"Man, I don't know if I can hang." Ritchie's stomach somersaulted. Even something as moderate as chorizo and tripe played havoc with his stomach.

Lee pulled a robusto-sized cigar from a pocket on his army jacket, and chomped it in his jaws. "I'd light this motherfucker up, but I don't want Alecia to catch hell from Joey."

"What ever happened to special effects?" Ritchie asked. "Why do they have to use real organs?" He made a mental note to stop by Ralphs and pick up a bunch of tampons before production started. Maybe he'd get credit for implementing an industry-wide standard.

"See, you can do that," Lee said. "Like on this one war movie I shot where my character jumped on a grenade. We used these gel-filled silicone pieces. They were super clean. Easy to get on and easy to get off, vacuformed."

"Why can't we use those on …Zombie Boxer?" He could barely get the title out of his mouth. Hopefully they didn't expect him to do a bunch of promo for the movie, at least not domestically. He could stand humiliating himself abroad, but he didn't want word getting back to his countrymen, especially those like Don who would break his balls, or his ex-wife.

"The real reason," Lee said, chewing his stogie on the left side of his mouth as he spoke out of the right side. "Real meats cheaper than the appliances and Suhne knows nobody likes the smell. He's a cheap, sadistic motherfucker." He shrugged and shifted the cigar from one side of his mouth to the other.

They merged onto the highway, the horizon ahead of them shimmering from smog and heat, the lanes packed with fast-moving cars. "Ain't shit new to Alecia, though," Lee said. "Did she ever tell you about when she worked at ...what's the restaurant where the girls got to have big titties to put in an application?"

Ritchie laughed. "Hooters."

Someone passed them on the left and honked. Lee turned in his seat and stuck up his middle finger to the guy in the golden Porsche. "Fuck you, too, motherfucker."

"She used to work there?" Ritchie asked.

Lee nodded his head, pressed the pedal down to the floor. The speed indicator needle drifted upward. "On the last movie we did, the fucking meat smelled so bad that someone got the bright idea to soak the organs in a big-ass garbage bag of bleach between takes."

Ritchie was about ready to puke. "That means you guys were biting meat covered in bleach?"

"Spoiled meat," Lee said, "soaking in bleach." He shook his head again. "The things a man has to do to make money." He stuck the stogie back in his pocket and got off at the next exit, drifting toward an old Egyptian revival building whose shattered globe lights in the front courtyard made it look like a police precinct fallen on hard times. "She's a bad little bitch," Lee said.

"Who?" Ritchie asked, knowing who, wishing in fact that it had been she instead of Lee who had picked him up. Not that he had anything against Lee Keith.

"I saw her bite into one of those bleach-covered kidneys and start chewing it, and I said 'How the fuck you do that without gagging?' and she told me when she worked at Hooters and wings would go bad, the manager would throw them in a bucket of bleach to make them pass inspection. She said if men can pay to eat that nasty shit, she can get paid to bite it and spit it out." He grunted and turned down a bumpy, potholed road. "You won't catch me eating at one of them places again. I like titties, but not enough to catch hepatitis to look at a pair."

177

"You could order something besides wings," Ritchie said.

That caught Lee off-guard and he cackled. "Yeah, you could be right."

"You got to do something to earn a living."

Lee shrugged, thought about that. "I guess sucking on funky-ass chicken liver beats sucking dick. A lot of people out here doing that to makes ends meet." He glanced at the sun-dappled sidewalk around them, as if he expected to see streetwalkers there. "There's worse things than being a b-actor." He slid his car into a former pocket park, where yellow Matillija poppies flowered in abundance, looking like sunflower patches. "I used to go direct-to-video. These days I'm going straight to DVD." He finally lit his Cuban and said, "Progress."

He wiped the smoke from the cigar from his path. "Let's roll."

Lee started down a rutted dirt road. Black walnuts hovered around them like sentinels, with an open area of grassland stippled with flame-colored chaparral ahead. "Where we going?" Ritchie asked. He'd never thought of joining the Mob, though he'd been around enough Gambino associates and Lucchese goombahs back East to have heard stories about hits, and he was a little worried. Maybe Suhne was really in love with Alecia and he saw Ritchie as a rival, and now he was paying a down-at-heel, direct-to-DVD actor to plant a slug in his brain and leave him in the California woodlands.

"You like Joey?" Lee asked.

Ritchie wiped a bit of sweat from his face with the back of his hand. He was silent as he walked. He wasn't sure what he should say. There was something about Lee he trusted and liked, but not enough to take any chances with the guy. Suhne was their meal ticket, at least for now.

"Sure," Ritchie said, and shrugged. "He's okay."

They reached the open area and the sun hit them with its full force, sending its rays through the latticework of an abandoned trolley bridge a couple hundred feet ahead of them. It was an old Pacific Electric crossing.

"Well, it's too bad you like him," Lee said, "because I killed that motherfucker and cut his head off."

"What?"

Lee smoked his cigar and smiled. "Oh, you want me to say it again." He squared himself to Ritchie. "I said, 'I killed that motherfucker and cut his head off.' Here," he said, tapping Ritchie on the shoulder in a friendly way. "Come see."

"Shit, man." Ritchie didn't want to be an accomplice, but he also didn't want to be a victim, either, so he did as he was told. There was no threatening edge to Lee's voice, but that didn't mean much. Some guys talked a lot of crap and didn't do anything; this guy appeared to be the other type, the kind that did something crazy and then quietly told you about it after the deed was done.

"There," he said, pointing with the glowing coal of his Cuban.

Ritchie walked slowly toward the head. His foot stuck on something below the thin leaf cover. He kicked the dead leaves aside, revealing bits of old Union Pacific roadbed beneath the carpeting of foliage.

It was undeniable after about fifteen more feet. There was the head of Joey Suhne, the eyes closed in a pained rictus as if he had felt the blade, hacksaw, or spade point of a shovel, whatever had his sheared neck and severed through bone to pull the skull free from the body.

The scraggly beard and shoulder-length hair were grimy and the skin showed early signs of decomposition, purpling from the collection of blood flow and rot setting in.

Ritchie felt last night's dinner rushing upward and then a sonic boom blew the head into several pieces. He hit the deck instinctively and heard Lee Keith giggling behind him. The man leaned down to him and helped him up.

"Just fucking with you, kid."

"Shit," Ritchie said, standing and shaking.

"Ritchie Abruzzi," Lee said, "Meet my man Tommy." He held out his hand to the forest, and a layer of witch's hair sphagnum, coastal sage scrub, and chaparral harvested from the clearing they'd passed through trembled and fell free from the sides of a composite steel box. A hand-painted fingerboard done in the trembling hand of a goldminer was staked next to the metal shack that had been camouflaged a moment before.

Tommy Montiligia pointed at the sign. "Cazador Station," he said, and opened the door on what Ritchie saw was a disused trolley car rescued from a scrapheap. "That's the name of the production we're working on out here. It's also what I've dubbed my trailer." He walked forward to shake Ritchie's hand. "I saw you KO Tony Teague a dog's age ago." Tommy wiped sweat from his well-feathered mullet, which was boxed like a coonskin cap. "You're my favorite Italian boxer aside from Vito Antuofermo."

"That's high praise," Ritchie said, giddy from fear. He looked at Lee with a wide smile on his face. He'd played pranks in his day and didn't mind getting got, especially when it was this creative.

"You trying to make the jump from boxing to acting? You could do worse than having Vito as your role model."

"You met him?" Ritchie asked.

"Worked with him," Tommy said, and turned. He waved them in the direction of Casa de Cazador. "Step into my office."

Ritchie got a look at the guy's arms as he waved, the skin visible from wrist to shoulder because Tommy wore a tank top with nothing underneath. His forearms were an unbroken skein of colorful, horror-themed ink. The pièce de résistance had to be the Jason Vorhees hockey mask leaking blood from the eye sockets and mouth holes. The tear-shaped blood trickles spilled onto poor Frankie with the stitches in his forehead and bolts protruding from his green neck. A two-way Motorola crackled from where it was clipped to his hip next to a workman's multi-purpose tool. "Stagecraft, what the hell was that noise?"

Tommy took the walkie-talkie from his hip and spoke into it. "Test. Don't get your bowels in an uproar." He put the Motorola back on the beltline of his acid-washed jeans. He held the door to the trolley car open to the two men. "There's a reason I make sure to keep my trailer far away from the production. I don't want them crawling up my ass every five minutes."

"What about the head?" Ritchie asked, looking back toward the pieces of shattered foam and latex skull.

Tommy waved his hand. "Ain't no thing but a chicken wing."

Ritchie stepped inside the red car. The interior was composite steel and old wood. It was smooth and aerodynamic in shape, like a giant vintage toaster.

Tommy laced his fingers through a brass overhang luggage rack above, exposing the two men to his ample underarm hair and his ripe body odor.

"Goddamn," Lee said, "Looks like you got Buckwheat in a headlock." He pulled the fabric of his moisture-wicking shirt beneath his field jacket to his face, covering his nose. "And you smell like monkey ass."

Tommy dropped his arms, pointed at the stogie. "You might want to kill that, unless you want to blow us all up."

"We'll end up like that prop out there." Ritchie said, sitting on one of the old passenger benches in the car.

"A great magician can always trick the rubes, by which I mean, it only looks like I blew that head up."

"It felt like it," Ritchie said, moving his jaw from side to side to make his ears pop.

"It was just an air-mortar effect, no real explosion. The prop's in seven or eight pieces. I can put that fucker back together faster than your grandma can do a Big Ben puzzle."

Tommy sat down on one of the old passenger benches, beneath an ancient advert featuring a soda jerk with rosy cheeks who looked like a relic from a Rockwell painting. He looked at Lee. "Remember back in the eighties, those headshots I used to do?"

The way the men smiled at each other, Ritchie could tell they had history together. "Won't insure you to do it anymore like that," Lee said, grinding out his stogie on the car floor next to a large cooler.

"Pussies," Tommy said, spitting out the word. "Nothing blows a prop head up like a shotgun, but Jerry Brown's too busy letting illegals take this great Golden State for all its worth to let a nice Eye-Tie like me even walk around with a shotgun."

"Easy, Mussolini," Lee said.

"If I'm Mussolini, you're Idi Amin."

"I lost that part to Yaphet Kotto."

Ritchie saw he was genuinely despondent, not even joking. "What kind of bullshit they got you doing now?" Lee asked Tommy. Ritchie didn't mind being excluded. It gave him a breather, and a chance to observe.

"Working with a bit more than a shoestring, but only because I kicked in completion funds." He looked around the berth. "We got these fuckers for a song. We're gonna demo a couple tomorrow, but I'm thinking of putting this bad boy on a flatbed and taking it with me back to my studio."

Lee Keith frowned, though it was an expression meant more as somber appraisal than sadness. "A lot of people pay top dollar for this antique stuff."

"Yeah, well, demand's about to shoot up, because two thirds of the cars out here are going up in flames tomorrow. You gonna watch the fireworks?"

Lee looked over at Ritchie. "We might have a meeting with Suhne in the morning if it don't happen later today. I'm waiting on the call."

"He got a treatment ready?"

"It's ghostwritten, but he's going to play it off as his own."

Tommy looked over at Ritchie. "What kind of asshole wants a 'A Film By' credit in a porno? Dude's ego's bigger than the Sierra Madres."

Ritchie didn't want to knock his boss, and he changed the subject. "The Teague fight wasn't on TV, was it?"

Tommy ignored the static crackle coming from his walkie-talkie. "No, I was live in the flesh for that one, baby." They shared a contagious smile. Tommy reminded him of any number of Strong Island types who drove I-Rocs, wore gold chains, and lifted weights while staring in the mirror.

"The fuck were you doing at the National Guard Armory in Chelsea, Rhode Island?"

"Shooting a low-budget flick with an Italian giallo crew. They were big fight fans and I got dragged along. I caught the bug that night, though, after I saw you put Tony on his ass." He looked at Lee Keith and nodded at Ritchie. "Don't fuck with this guy too much. You eat one of his one-twos and it's Goodnight, Irene."

A voice came through the static of the Motorola. Tommy made a face like a persistent bluebottle fly was ruining his picnic by swan-diving for the potato salad. "Did you have a mistake over there?" someone on the radio asked.

"Excuse me," Tommy said, and took up the radio in hand. "If I had a mistake, I'd hit the fire with my extinguisher, and I'd put some Neosporin on my burns. Now an accident is a different matter. That's third-degree burns or better. If that happened, I wouldn't even be answering this damn thing. I'd be on my way to the hospital." He stood up and continued speaking into the walkie-talkie. "Furthermore, I've got a zero-percent accident rate, a perfect track record over the course of two decades. You let me do my job, just like I let you do yours." He turned the radio off and sat down, massaging his temples and closing his eyes. "If I do buy this thing, I'm putting in an AC unit."

"Don't fuck around and get heatstroke out here."

Tommy looked at Ritchie. The sweat had caused the FX man's long mullet to curl in Ronny James Dio coils. "How about it, paisan? Let's find us a little commune in Pescara."

"Where's that?" Ritchie asked.

Ritchie could tell his question was a faux pas, that his stock had just dropped in the eyes of the FX man. "Where's that? It's in your namesake homeland, the Abruzzo."

"My father's been, but I didn't go with him."

"You've never been home?"

He shook his head. It was a bit of a sore point with him. "I tried to get my manager Don to get me a fight there, but we could never pull it off."

"Well you and me will go together," Tommy said. "We'll catch fish in the Adriatic and let the Mexicans have California. It was theirs before Cortes took it from them."

Lee pointed his unlit stogie at Tommy. "If you talk about me going back to Africa, you can go head on with that bullshit. I been there once for a shoot, and all I can say is that my black ass needs to thank whoever threw my ancestors on a boat and got us up out of there."

Tommy held up his hands. "Shit, come with us to Italy. Marvin Hagler's black and he moved over there, didn't he?"

"Yeah, first Milan, then Pioltello," Ritchie said.

Both men looked at Ritchie as if they hadn't expected him to know much of anything. He wasn't offended. A small cohort of boxers was whip-smart, and the rest were dumb by design.

Tommy leaned forward, dragged the blue and white cooler toward him, and pulled the top off. Inside were several cans of Pabst Blue Ribbon floating in a half-melted bath of ice. Tommy fished one out, and pointed to the remaining brews drifting inside the cooler. "Help yourselves, boys." He cracked his open, took a slurp, and spoke to Ritchie. "Super Suhne's ratio of projects started to finished is like ten-to-one. A lot get bogged down in pre-production. Money gets wasted for no reason, but Joey's got it to waste."

Ritchie didn't want to blurt out that he knew exactly how much the guy had to waste, but it was tempting and he had to bite his lip. Tommy burped and said, "The guy fronted me a grand to do some work with you, so we need to set a date and do the work on that day. When are you free next week?"

"Whenever," Ritchie said, shifting on the hardwood of the trolley bench. "My son's in town, but we can work around your schedule."

"Bring him if you want. Maybe he's curious and he wants to break into the industry."

"I might," Ritchie said, thinking Matt might find it exciting to be around a film, even a low budget one that might not make it past the preproduction stage.

Lee fished a beer for himself from the cooler, lifted his can to Tommy's, and touched aluminum to aluminum. "Cheers, big ears," Lee said.

Tommy smiled at Lee and then turned back to Ritchie. "What we'd do is I would take an impression of your teeth."

"I've had that done before."

"For gumshields?"

Ritchie nodded.

"We'd do it with dental alginate. After that, we do a life cast of your head. I'm supposed to just give you a lump sum of two-hundred dollars for the day. Everything Suhne is non-union and some of the shit is under the table. No SAG, no per diem. Keep that quiet as kept." Tommy tipped his head back and shook his mullet from side-to-side as he finished the beer in two or three large gulps. He burped, crumpled the empty, and threw the can to the floor.

"The good news is you get paid whether your work or not on any given day, once the shoot starts."

"That is good," Ritchie said, but he knew Tommy had more to say.

"The bad news is you got to live on-set to avoid legal complications from the SAG people. Once shooting starts, you live wherever you shoot."

Keith said, "That could be good or bad, depending on where you shoot."

"Like here," Tommy said, leaning forward into the cooler to snag another beer. He grabbed one up with the quickness of a black bear snagging a salmon going upstream to spawn. "Cazador Station's about the ghost of a train conductor who wants to get even with those who wronged him, so we're shooting in some old train cars." Tommy popped the top and slurped a bit of foam. A shiver went through him and this time he stifled the burp. "You're gonna be a zombie boxer. We might get lucky and get the greenlight to shoot on-location, in an Indian Casino where they've got a boxing ring." Tommy pointed toward the cooler, where now only three beers bobbed. "You sure you don't want one?"

Ritchie shook his head. Tommy continued. "I've worked on fight flicks before. If your set design department's good, they can make one venue look like ten different places, just by decorating it different from day to day."

"Sounds good," Ritchie said. He knew guys who got eaten alive by those green-felt tables, by the red die and the roulette wheel, dudes dying from the vigorish imposed by thumb-breaking and knee-hobbling shylocks. Casinos had never been his thing though, at least not the gaming action. He could do with seeing cocktail waitresses in stockings, black corsets, and red silk bustier though, and it would be nice to get paid to pretend to be punched rather than to absorb some real blows.

There was also something burning in his chest, as if he'd chugged one of the beers rather than standing fast as a teetotaler. It was a force melting his resolve like a candle reduced by flame to a fatty pile of mush. He'd always promised himself he would never be a dirty old man, that whoever he fucked there would be less than a decade of daylight between him and the woman in question. Now, though, he was smitten with a girl who was only a couple of years older than his son. Maybe she was even as young as Matt and just walking around with a fake ID to make her booty-shaking bones at the Fantasy Reign Lounge.

Whatever the case, he felt like a creep, but couldn't stop from hoping, sacrilegiously praying that whenever or wherever they ended up on-set, they got put up in hotel rooms and his was near the room where Star Bella lay.

Another uncouth burp from Tommy brought him out of his reverie. Lee Keith helped himself to another beer. It might come to blows if the supply dwindled further and there was no other alcohol hidden aboard the trolley car.

A light snakelike wisp of smoke was trailing from the shards of the Suhne prosthetic head laid in the dead leaves outside the trailer. "Shit," Tommy said, standing. He reached into the overhead area of the streetcar and produced a small fire extinguisher. "This is why you don't drink and demo on the same day."

Lee laughed and sipped his brew at a leisurely pace. Ritchie wanted to join the actor in laughing, but he had a hard time seeing the joke, since he could feel the volcano erupting in his chest, the flames licking as high as his mind. The fire whispered that a few mil would carry him and Bella away from here, out of Venice and its rusted shopping carts and strip clubs, floating in a yacht or at least a sailboat on the blue waters of the Adriatic, far away from this desert and its oases that didn't have enough water to go around, not by a longshot.

Chapter Seventeen: Monkey Brain in a Box

Their phones went off at the same time and they scrambled to answer their cells in the confines of the Benz.

"Do you care if I go to the skate park?" Matt asked.

Ritchie cupped the phone close to his ear while Lee steered and spoke into his own cellphone. "I thought you didn't skate."

"I don't," Matt said. "I just want to see it."

"Okay."

"Can I take your car?"

Ritchie thought about it. He didn't have insurance for an additional driver, but the alternative was letting the naïve hardhead walk through Oakwood. "Sure, there's a spare key on the counter in the kitchen."

"Thanks. I love you."

"All right." Ritchie hung up. He looked over at Lee, who had finished with his call and was snapping his phone shut.

"What's up?"

Lee stuffed the phone in a pocket on his field jacket. "Suhne's got the treatment ready, and he wants the principals at his house."

"Principals?"

Lee searched his person for the remains of the stogie, realized he'd left it on the film set. "Shit," he said. Then, "Principles means me, you, and Star."

Ritchie blinked from the brightness of the sun. It was so strong now that it was bleaching the Los Angeles Basin monochrome, like the whole world was denaturing of color and they might soon be living in a black and white movie. He made a mental note to pick up some cheapie glasses from one of the carousels at the Korean lady's hut on the boardwalk tomorrow. He'd lost his pair with the bamboo frame.

"Here we go," Lee said, watching from his perch in the parking lot of Fantasy Reign.

The back door opened, two women walking out of the pebbledash stucco side of the building. One had sandy blonde hair and a zebra-print headband, dressed in yoga pants and a t-shirt that rode up and exposed her eight-pack abs and the sides of her tanned, round breasts. The other woman was Bella.

"That's too much for me," Lee said. "I like a woman with a little belly, not a washboard stomach. I mean, it's her body but goddamn."

He stopped speaking as Bella approached. She carried a mocha-colored leather handbag, with a gold chain and buckle on it. Her skin was glowing from a coat of lotion she'd just applied, and the sun doubled her radiance and made her look like an Egyptian goddess. Ritchie thought it was a good thing that Mr. Kramb was already an old man when he glanced out the window of his trailer and got a look at her. If the poet had been in his prime and going through his romantic phase, her existence might have been grounds to open a vein after she inspired him to scrawl some pages of immortal verse. "Hey, boys."

Lee grunted. Ritchie looked out at the street, wondering why his heart was thudding like he was fifteen. He'd figured he was too cynical to be thrown for this loop again.

"You in?" Lee asked, turning in his seat.

"Hit it, daddy!"

"You got it, girl." He pulled out and headed for the hills.

Bella let her legs snake over the headrest again and Ritchie pinched his sinuses.

"Fuck, what is it with guys asking for my number and my real name? They think because they stuff a dollar in your coochie they own you. The place has 'Fantasy' in the name, not 'reality.' It shouldn't be that confusing."

"Men are stupid when it comes to sex," Lee said.

"Everyone gets horny," she said, "but you don't have to be gross or disrespectful." She dropped her right leg on Ritchie's shoulder to get his attention and said, "Did you guys enjoy yourself the other night?"

"Thank you," he said. Her legs smelled like aloe and there were small razor bumps from when she'd shaved.

Lee said, "I just showed him Tommy."

"That guy's a trip."

Ritchie watched her in the side-view mirror as she put on a pair of red sunglasses with heart-shaped frames. They were as bulky as view-masters and they may as well have been. She smiled at the world around her as if it were just a series of pretty images scrolling by in a slideshow arranged for her entertainment.

Ritchie looked at Lee, told himself that he had to prank him at some point to get even with him for what he pulled out there in the woods. At least he hadn't pissed his pants, and Lee wasn't telling Star about how bad Ritchie had been spooked. "You sure that Tommy guy knows what he's doing?"

"Shit," Lee said. "Tommy's the best FX man in the business. I don't mind an incompetent director, but you won't catch me going near someone in charge of pyro or demolition unless I trust him. Tommy's squibbed me up many a time. I trust him with my life."

"Okay." That was good enough for Ritchie.

"As long as it stays between stunt and special effects coordinators, you're golden." Lee fixed Ritchie with his eyes and they achieved a dead, grave quality for a moment. "Now, if Joey tries to cut corners and does some effect himself, you tell him to wait for Danny. Ain't worth it to lose a finger over fifty grand."

"Or your life," Bella said from the backseat. "Lee, what was that one movie where the guy got killed?"

"What you talking about?"

"The helicopter thing."

"Oh, yeah. The Twilight Zone. I actually met Eddie Murphy a couple times and he told me about that shit."

"You know Eddie Murphy?" Ritchie asked, impressed.

"Through his brother," Lee said. "We was road dogs way back in the day."

"He wasn't in that movie," Bella said. "It was Jennifer Jason Leigh's dad."

"Vic Morrow," Lee said, nodding.

"From Combat," Ritchie said. He only knew that because his dad liked the show, and during Bam-Bam's years as world champ he'd been on some of those dumb series like Land of the Lost and Adam-12, and the one they shot in Hawaii. Now he was following in the old man's footsteps again, first in boxing and now in Hollywood, or at least at the very fringes of Tinsel Town.

"Eddie wasn't in the movie," Lee said, "but he worked with that director before, John Landis. The dude wanted him to testify on his behalf and my man said 'Fuck all that noise.'"

"Joey dangerous on-set?" Ritchie asked.

"Motherfucker thinks he's Sam Fuller, shooting a gun instead of yelling action."

"Compensating," Bella said, "for his tiny penis."

"That's what the ladies say," Lee said.

Bella dropped that leg on Ritchie's shoulder again. "My friend at Fantasy says you're packing."

Lee pulled the last remaining clove from his pack and pointed it at Ritchie before lighting it. "You need to thank the Moors for giving y'all a bit of swagger."

"What are you talking about?" Ritchie asked.

"Italians," Lee said, smoking. "Y'all got black in you."

"I've heard that from some boxers," Ritchie said. It might have been true, but Matt had to get it through his head that he wasn't going to be Roy Jones or Floyd Mayweather. He'd be lucky to be Roger Mayweather. Ritchie feared for the boy, but stopped thinking about him as they approached Casa De Suhne, although this time from the back of the palace.

Two gaslight carriage lamps stood to the side of the entry. Lee hit a button on the garage-door opener that was clipped to the driver's side sun visor. The gate buzzed and rolled open. Lee drove at five miles an hour over the gravel as they approached the circular driveway. Giant Moreton figs were spread out around them, trees planted probably a hundred years ago by men who'd bit the dust back when Bam-Bam Abruzzi was still a young prospect. Ritchie half-expected Tarzan clad in a loincloth to come swinging down from a vine and shouting at the top of his lungs.

The grounds didn't look quite so large from the front of the house, but "sprawling" didn't begin to cover it as seen from this angle. They parked and as they walked toward the backdoors, Ritchie couldn't help but thinking the acreage was ample enough for the yard to have end zones.

He wondered how often Suhne left the place. Probably rarely, as there was no need to. He had his own village, a little Xanadu hemmed off from the rest of the world.

"Ladies first," Lee said, holding the door open for Bella.

"Thank you."

He snubbed his clove on one of the colonnaded Moorish arches around the palace, and walked in. Ritchie went in behind him.

"Greetings!" A voice echoed through the marble atrium. The ground beneath their feet was checkered Vitruvian marble, as if they were walking on a giant chessboard. "I am Charles Foster Kane!"

Ritchie looked up toward the voice. Joey Suhne sported a grey Homburg. He wore highwater pants bloused into rubber hip waders. He looked a bit like an archeologist back from sabbatical. He stood above them on a prairie-style pulpit balcony. It looked like a Gothic misericord with a mermaid carved into its wainscoted panels, done in something like cedar or oak. A floor below Suhne was an unlighted fireplace with a tiled hearth, and next to that a giant crate stamped "Fragile" nesting in an inglenook.

"Don't come up," he said. "I'll come down." He pressed a button and a hydraulic lift noise sounded. The landing he stood on descended until he was at their level. He hopped off the secret lift and Ritchie noticed he had a crowbar in his hands. Joey passed it to him, and nodded toward the crate.

Ritchie gripped the cold, curved piece of steel in his hands. "Well," Joey said. "Go ahead and open it." The director-producer tapped Lee and Bella, who stood back with him at a respectful distance, as if some jungle creature might be stowed in the box and ready to spring from its hiding.

Ritchie stuck the grooved teeth of the crowbar between two panels of the unfinished wood, and pulled outward. The box gave like a soggy wooden pallet, straw spilling everywhere, revealing something that looked like a giant refrigerator, only covered in biohazard decals.

"It's not hazardous," Joey said, going to stand beside it. He kicked aside the wooden boards and strands of straw that hadn't already fallen off. "But they didn't know that at Customs. Hence the delay." He stroked the thing like a big game hunter posing with a felled elephant on safari.

"What is it?" Bella asked.

"Let me set the scene," Joey said. He pulled a black viewfinder tool from a necklace below his shirt, and framed Ritchie between his fingers as if getting ready to film him in the square he made of his digits. "A boxer suffers a brutal knockout in the ring, similar to the real TKO you endured against Giachetti."

Ritchie winced from the memory. Joey continued. "The boxer is told never to box again. He is deemed medically unfit after a CAT scan reveals an abnormality." Joey paced as his creative juices flowed. "Our beautiful loser seeks a second opinion. He goes to another doctor, having no idea that this man is a mad scientist, who has fitted his own CAT scan machine with a radioactive rod." Joey pointed at Ritchie, who presumed he was to be the beautiful loser in question. "This is all of course unbeknownst to you, who steps into the doctor's contraption. At first the atomic machine gives you new strength and temporarily cures you of your brain abnormality."

Ritchie nodded. Joey continued. "You slowly become more powerful. You box better than ever. But the radioactive treatments leave you with a craving for human flesh, which takes over by night." Joey pointed at Lee Keith. "You play the detective who grows suspicious in the wake of the slew of murders, and your sights eventually settle on Mr. Abruzzi, the Zombie Boxer."

Lee Keith had to struggle not to sigh or roll his eyes. He'd lost count of the number of times he played a cop. There was even an ironic website run by film buffs who kept a counter and tracked how many times he'd been killed in low-budget flicks, and the manner of his death and time he died. He wondered how he would die in this one. He stifled the urge to do a Hattie McDaniel impression. *I don't know nothin' about no zombie boxers, Mr. Suhne.*

"What am I doing?" Bella asked.

"You," Joey said. He walked toward her, reached for her hair and stroked its shining, glossy strands. Bella struggled not to give in to the desire to pull away from him. "You love the beast." He pointed at Ritchie. "Like Fay Wray and King Kong. You were his wife before he became the zombie, and even after you discover his secret, you can't leave his side, or turn him in to the police." He pointed at Lee, the cop in question. "We play with the typical zombie logic in this one, use werewolf logic instead. That means Ritchie is normal when he goes into the ring and only turns into a roving revenant at night."

He leaned against his machine, smiling as if he expected a standing ovation.

"Not bad," Lee said, but it was like pulling teeth and it sapped all his energy to force the false compliment he knew his boss needed to hear.

Joey Suhne tapped the fiberglass casing of his white machine. "We had this thing special ordered from a medical supply chain. It's just the hull, but it gives the project some credibility. I paid someone to add the stickers, but that might have been a mistake. Or, at least that's what caused the delay."

"What delay?" Lee asked. He walked toward the thing, now that he knew the biohazard stickers were just for show.

It looked a bit like a hyperbaric chamber, some kind of new-age sarcophagus. "Post 9-11 Customs is suspicious of any oversized packages. When Homeland Security saw it, they busted it open. When they saw all the stickers on it, they got scared and held it in a cell and called me. I had to go down there and pick the thing up from the entry point and explain it all to them, show them the paperwork." He sanded his hands together. "It was all very cloak and dagger."

He made six-shooters of his fingers and blasted them at Lee and Ritchie. "Have you two been working together on getting him to do his zombie shuffle?"

The men looked at each other like students who hadn't done their homework. "We've been working with Tommy," Lee said, hoping that would suffice. It didn't. A dark glow suddenly animated Joey Suhne. He turned to

Ritchie, walked until he was a bit too close to him for the boxer's comfort.

"I need you to study monkeys. Go to the botanical gardens."

"Why monkeys?" Ritchie asked.

Lee and Bella shifted nervously where they stood. "I've been researching punch-drunk boxers," Joey said. "And when they vivisected one of these old bareknuckle prizefighters, they found out his brain had shrunken to the size of a monkey's. I need you to learn to mimic their moves."

Ritchie slowly inhaled through his nostrils and exhaled through his mouth. "I can help him," Lee said. "I told him to study some pre-talkies with Lon Chaney. He'll learn to lurk and slink and skulk." He smiled a queasy, uneasy smile.

"Forget that rubbish," Joey said. "Study monkeys." He was honed in totally on Ritchie now. "Do you know any punch-drunk boxers?"

Ritchie grinded his molars until it felt like the enamel would sand off. Bella saw his jaw pulsing. Lee may have noticed. Joey didn't. The director said. "What about your father? The great 'Bam-Bam' Abruzzi? I hired a detective to investigate him, and he reported back that he's barely coherent. I think the more time you spend with your father-"

Ritchie's right came out before he knew what was happening. His clenched fist connected with only half-force but still cracked flush on the kid's cheekbone, knocking him backwards so that he tipped over the brass pokers in a stand next to the fireplace. Joey Suhne landed flat on his back, unconscious.

"Oh fuck!" Bella shouted. "What did you just do? Ritchie ..."

Ritchie held up his hands. Lee Keith walked forward, kneeled before Suhne's prone and sleeping form.

"Ritchie," she said, walking up to him. She put her hands to his cheeks, where tears were falling. She felt them with her fingers before she saw them, and her own eyes watered. He looked away from her, because he didn't want her to see him cry, or to make her cry with his sudden tears.

"I'm sorry," he said.

"He's still breathing," Lee said, his black hand hovering over the director's bleeding nose. "I feel the air."

"Shit," Ritchie said, threw a left for the hearth. His knuckles hit the stone with a splat and the echo of a meaty thud. He drew back the hand with bone exposed and surrounded by a fistula-shaped tear, blood and white fat shining along with something yellow and greasy. He thought maybe it was lumen or marrow.

"Stop it, you dumbass!" Bella shouted and held Ritchie's arms to keep him from punching again. "Lee," she said, "help me with him."

Lee stood, dragged Joey Suhne through the room. He looked at Bella, flicked his head toward Ritchie. "You get him out of here. I'll try to fix this shit."

"Come on," she said, and pulled him away from the room. Its giant, steeply-pitched ceiling along with the pulpit gave Ritchie the eerie feeling that he had just performed some kind of blood sacrifice, that by slaying the old priest he was now the new one.

"Oh, fuck," he said, and staggered outside. He braced himself against a column, his hand leaking a strong drizzle of blood as he walked. Crickets chirped from the shadowy woods around them. It was just about twilight, and the clouds were tinged pale pink. "What did I just do?"

"I think you just ended your movie career." She kept her hand at his back, walking with him slowly like a nurse helping an elderly man down a hall.

"I'm sorry," he said.

"He probably deserved it," she said. "He's had it coming for a while." He noticed she was sobbing. "But you can't just go around hitting people."

"That's what I'm paid to do."

She sighed. She knew men, and knew which ones were beyond hope or helping. Thus she let it drop, and said, "We'll take the Benz back. Try not to spill too much blood in it."

"Okay."

She opened the passenger door and Ritchie carefully lowered himself onto the leather, wincing as he tried to keep from using the hand. He dangled it outside of the ride. A form rushed down the stairs in the darkness toward them, and Ritchie thought for a moment that maybe Suhne kept a couple goons on retainer and now one was coming for his head.

It was only Lee. He passed the keys to the car to Bella. "How is he?" she asked.

"Still asleep," Lee said. "Maybe he has a concussion." He looked past her to Ritchie, who was also on his way to the netherworld of sleep. "How's he doing?"

"He's crazy," she said, sniffling and popping a snot bubble on her nose.

"Get him out of here. Hopefully that little shit don't press charges. I'll let you know. Maybe he hit him so hard when he wakes up he won't remember shit. I can try to trick him into thinking we all got hammered to celebrate the arrival of his package." Lee turned back to ascend the steps and go in the house.

Bella walked around the car to the driver's side. She turned the keys in the ignition. Her hands trembled as she pulled a pack of Camels from her Gucci bag and lit one. "I know I'm not supposed to smoke in here. I don't give a shit. Fuck him."

She pulled out and dragged her cigarette. "What was that stuff about your father?"

"Bam-Bam," Ritchie said, fading in and out of consciousness. He closed his eyes. The night air felt good as it rushed toward them in the convertible. He smiled as the lights of L.A. flickered to life around them.

"What?"

"Is that real?" Ritchie asked.

"Is what real?" She looked over at him, the sympathy now tempered by a bit of anger. She had her own problems and he may have screwed her over with Suhne.

"The handbag," he said. "Is it real?" For some reason it mattered a great deal to him, whether it was an authentic Gucci or a counterfeit.

"This?" She lifted the Gucci bag. "Don't be ridiculous. I can't afford the real thing. It's a sweatshop knockoff. They make them in South L.A. You think I'm grinding my pussy on old men to buy designer handbags? I'm going to be a marine biologist. I just need ten more grand to pay for the undergrad program. No way am I doing what everyone else does with student loans."

"I can get it," Ritchie said. "I can get you ten grand."

"You're talking like an idiot," Bella said. She reached into the purse for another cigarette and lit it with the cherry of the one she was smoking. "You just fucked yourself out of fifty grand. Worry about yourself right now, not me. Speaking of which …" She glanced at his swelling and bleeding hand. "You want to go to the hospital?" She tossed her mostly-smoked cigarette to the roadside and worked on smoking the fresh one down to the filter.

"No," he said, and sat up, suddenly sober. He was almost pain-free from shock, adrenaline, and another wave of rage coursing through him. "I want to see my son, have a talk with him. We also need to make a pit stop or two for some medical supplies, and that includes alcohol."

"Okay," she said, "but please call me if you need a ride to the hospital later."

He nodded faintly, and she said, "If Joey decides to press charges and I find out about it in time, I'll call you and give you a heads-up, so you know what to expect."

That brought another nod, although this one was a bit more forceful. He may have been losing blood, but his resolve was building as night was falling. The plan was taking shape.

Chapter Eighteen: A Son in the Spider Web

It was turning out be one of those nights where everyone in the city seemed to be acting crazy as he was, and he wondered if maybe there was a full moon. He staggered into Ralphs to get an Ace bandage, as well as some meat. The manager barely noticed his hand because he was shouting at a homeless man attempting to jimmy open the bathroom door rather than pay the quarter to use the restroom.

"You fucking useless Squatemalan!"

Someone noticed Ritchie staggering as they came out of the all-night Washateria. The man helpfully offered, "You're leaking everywhere, man" before returning to his drying load of whites. It took a little bit of coaxing but Bella finally relented and drove him to the Liquor Locker, where he picked up some MD 20/20.

He didn't wait to get home to open the grape-flavored, fortified wine. He drank a gulp, struggled to hold down the poisonous brew. "It tastes like storm drain runoff from the Venice Canal."

Bella drove twice as fast, not wanting to get slapped with an open container violation. The night had been bad enough. "You're gonna scare your son," she said.

Ritchie shook his head, said, "He's probably already asleep." He rubbed his functioning hand through his black hair. "I got to find a way to talk him out of being a boxer."

She looked over at him from the driver's side of the Benz. "He wants to box?"

"Unfortunately. His mom will blame me, but I never suggested it."

"Holy shit!" she shouted, and Ritchie braced for a car wreck, wishing he'd worn a seatbelt. He saw a moment later that she was just grooving on a microbus driving past them in the other lane. The hippy ride had a mirror shine and psychedelic sunflowers painted on its sides. Yellow surfboards that looked like giant bananas were strapped down to the luggage rack.

"I want one," she said.

"My buddy's got a nice Airstream that he usually keeps parked in front of my place."

"Oh, the old poet?" She smiled. "He's cute." She pulled a cigarette from the pack. She'd lost count of how many she smoked on the drive so far. Bella lit the Camel and said, "So you think it's really possible that when Joey wakes up he won't have remembered anything?"

"I know it's more than possible. I've seen it happen in fights."

"Did you ever get knocked out?"

"Never," he said, and the pride sent some blood flowing to the aching, wounded limb. "But I know guys who went out there and got KO'd so hard that when they woke up in their dressing rooms, they thought they'd just taken a pre-fight nap. They didn't even know they'd fought, let alone lost."

"Hopefully you hit him hard enough to make him forget you hit him."

She gripped the woodgrain of the steering wheel, then she pointed at Kramb's Globetrotter sitting on the corner. "There he is." Her button nose scrunched up as if she was about to sneeze. "It smells like he's cooking fish."

"Hopefully it's nothing local," Ritchie said. He could smell the sea-rotted wood of the neighborhood floating on the air.

"That's why I want to be a marine biologist." She pulled to the curb in front of his house, behind the Interceptor. Ritchie could tell from the park job that his son had taken the car out. "Anything locally fished here is in the red zone. I want to work on the water in Venice until it's as clean as Catalina."

"It's a worthy goal." Ritchie held the car door handle, righted himself, and walked toward the front door with his plastic bag of supplies and his brown paper bag half-concealing his liquor.

"You need help?" She asked.

"I need a bullet in the head." He ascended the cinderblock steps of the porch carefully, turned and gave her a halfhearted wave of the hand. She honked once and was gone.

He fished in his right pocket for his house key, stuck it in the door, and turned the knob. The sound of horsehair gloves slapping his rubber dummy in the basement was muffled, and there was also the sound of Matt grunting as he mixed combos, putting together head and body shots to the latex dummy.

Ritchie plopped down in a chair in the living room, setting his supplies on a threadbare, dusty rug at his feet. "Good luck, Bella, with the manatees and the sea lions." He took a drink from the MD bottle and tipped it in her honor. "I'll see you at Sea World."

He took another tug on the bottle and let it fall to the floor, where it made a glug-glugging sound while the rest of the purple liquid ran onto the floor. He was so numb that he barely felt the cumbersome form of his son's cellphone below his tailbone. He finally shifted in place and took the thing in his hand.

Onscreen was a "Play" button waiting to be swiped to activate a video. He and Glenn Tremblay were frozen in mid-exchange at the Trump Plaza Hotel in Atlantic City. Ritchie was drunk enough that he had a bit of trouble coordinating his thumb as he tried to get it to swipe the "Play" button, but he made it on the third or fourth try.

"Tremblay" Barry Tompkins said, "on unsteady legs now." Al Bernstein spoke up, "And if you're just tuning in to this Showtime extravaganza, we want to welcome you to our undercard, which is shaping up to be a bigger fight than what we're likely to see in the main event."

Ritchie suddenly realized that everything could be worse, that he could be living in Atlantic City. He watched himself swarm Tremblay now, fight a high-pressure, inside fight as the men leaned their heads together like conjoined twins. Ritchie took a half-step back and hooked from midrange to the body, tricking Tremblay into lowering his hands to cover up. "Redrum" Ritchie slipped an uppercut through his opponent's guard and sent him sailing backwards.

The crowd ripped their collective lungs and the ref shoved Ritchie back. "Neutral corner!"

"You got somebody with you?" Ritchie turned toward his son's voice. Matt stood on the room's threshold, his hands sheathed in oversized bronze sparring gloves.

"Nah, just …" Ritchie pointed toward the phone. "Watching a fight."

Matt came forward, Ritchie dropped the phone, and his son struggled to get his gloves off. "Shit, Dad. You're going to get my phone wet."

Matt bit the Velcro and tore the gloves free from his hands. He wiped sweat on his striped burgundy Puma sweats and picked his cellphone up from the ground before the widening pool of purple liquor could swamp the phone. "You're drunk as hell, man. Shit, this is a mess."

"Show me," Ritchie said, and stood on wobbling legs. The hobo wine moved through him like liquid Novocain, numbing him.

"Show you what?" Matt blotted up the liquor with one of Ritchie's terrycloth towels.

"Christ, why don't you just use my old ring-walk robe if you're going to use one of my good Turkish towels."

"That should do," Matt said, watching the cloth absorb the alcohol.

For some reason Ritchie couldn't stand being ignored now, nor the indignity of his son seeing him in this state. The more responsibly the kid behaved, the more it felt like Matt was judging him. And maybe he would even tell Anna about seeing his dad drunk. It would confirm her worst fears about him not being adult enough to handle the kid, even for a week or two.

"Show me," Ritchie said.

"Show you what?" Matt looked at his father with nothing but rage and contempt in his eyes. Ritchie knew the look, because he had eventually faced his father with the same eyes, after the old man slapped his mother too many times and then kicked his dog. He'd heard Manny Pacquiao had fled home in General Santos City to become a boxer after his father killed, cooked, and ate his favorite dog. There was always ultimately someone with a harder sob story. Still, this kid didn't know what pain was, and Ritchie didn't like the tone he was taking.

Ritchie's right hand came out, slapped Matt with a cuffing, open hand to the ear. "Show me the fucking bloody boxer thing that comes up on Google," Ritchie said. "I want to see what the world sees when they decide to laugh at me."

"Dad, you can't hit me."

"Call the cops on me, then." Ritchie waved at the cellphone.

Matt's eyes shimmered like jewels. The tears were in chrysalis form, ready to break free and bloom across his cheeks. "I'm not calling the cops on you."

Ritchie gritted his teeth. "Then if you're not gonna use the phone to call the cops, use it to show me the pictures of the 'bloody boxer.' I want to see him. I want to see the loser."

Matt shook his head and lowered his eyes so his father wouldn't see the tears. Ritchie didn't bother to conceal his own crying. He was an overdramatic Italian mama's boy who'd wept after fights several times. If his son had gone through his whole career on YouTube and seen his fights, then Ritchie wasn't showing him anything he hadn't already seen.

"Show me."

"Okay." Matt worked his fingers and thumbs over the numerical pad like the millennial he was, digits texting with the speed of a hummingbird's wings. "There!" Matt turned the screen toward him. He gritted his teeth now and Ritchie was scared to see his own anger growing in the boy, like grandfather like grandson. They were doomed. Maybe the kid was meant to be a boxer after all.

Ritchie looked at the screen. A watery downpour of orange-tinged blood from a scalp wound mixed with the richer, near-venous purple flow that pumped from his nose. His eyes were swollen and a subdural hematoma grew as if someone had stuck a bicycle pump beneath his forehead and was slowly inflating it from the inside.

Sober he would have felt like he'd subjected himself to enough. Drunk he was just getting started. He turned the phone toward Matt. "That's your future."

"I want to box," Matt said, and stood firm. He looked Ritchie in the eyes now, despite the tears that coursed down his cheeks and caused him as much shame as Ritchie's bloody mug archived forever on the internet caused him. A reddish handprint was stained on Matt's face, but he didn't seem to care about that either.

"You got heart," Ritchie said, "but that scares me."

"Why?"

"Because heart doesn't help you in this world. It hurts you. You need money."

Ritchie found himself pulling his son into headlock, and tightening the vice as Matt struggled to get out. Ritchie held the phone in his left hand, which was so swollen from pain that it felt like a catcher's mitt drenched in liniment oil. "Look at it. You want to be a monkey, have a monkey brain!" Ritchie threw the phone across the room.

Matt squirmed, started throwing punches to his father's body. "What the hell are you talking about?"

"Zombie!" Ritchie said, hearing his voice as if underwater and watching his actions as if in a nightmare. "A monkey for some fat fuck who sits ringside and watches you get punched, then takes all your money."

Matt was sobbing now, and because his body shots were hurting his hands more than they were hurting the rock-hard backboard of Ritchie's ribs, he relented in his attack. "You broke my phone!"

Ritchie released his son from the headlock, dug in his pocket, and removed five one-hundred dollar bills from his wallet. He flung them at his son so that they danced like green confetti in the air before settling to the ground. Matt cried without looking at his father, collected the money, and muttered, "Fuck you, you asshole." He was out the door.

The face of the phone was broken, the LCD screen cracked and fissured like a busted windshield, but the voices of the commentators on Showtime were still coming through. In all their tussling, the browser had been swiped back to the fight Matt had been watching earlier, his hero worship of what his father once was interrupted by these ghostly remains.

"Fighting in a phone booth here," Al Bernstein said.

"And Tremblay's mouthpiece goes flying into press row."

"You know, this is one of those nights where the drycleaners wonder what we do for a living, I tell you."

Ritchie walked back over in the direction of the chair where he had previously been sitting. He kicked at the terrycloth towel soaked in purple wine, reached down with his right hand stinging from the slap he'd given his son.

"Shit." There was at least one good slug of fortified wine left in the bottle of MD 20/20. He turned his head upward like a wolf baying at the full moon and drank what was there. The empty glass bottle fell from his hand, hit the ground, and spun as if searching for a girl in a game of spin the bottle.

"Okay," Ritchie said. He dug into the plastic bag. "Time for the cut-man to go to work."

He opened the Ace bandage box with his right hand that shivered as if he had the DTs. He tore the elastic and cotton from the package with his teeth, and held one end of the dressing in his mouth while wrapping the gauze above and below the most painful point of his hand, winding in a figure-eight motion and creating a soft cradle for the eggshell-fragile mitt.

Tropical-flavored bile rushed through his stomach, churned and pummeled through the organs soft and sore from the bodywork his son had done. The kid had power.

A knock came at the door. He figured it was the pigs. "We don't need no stinking badges." The knocking continued. "Go fight some other crime." He lifted up his wrapped hand, inspected the dressing. It was pretty good, snug and supporting.

The door opened, and he leaned down to the empty glass bottle, ready to hurl it at the head of the first cop who came for him with the cuffs.

It was Lawrence Kramb. "Everything okay, my friend? Your son ran up the street, crying. He shouldn't be on foot in this neighborhood at this hour."

"I know it," Ritchie said.

"Do you want me to go after him in the Airstream, make sure he's okay?"

"Would you?" Ritchie said, and winced. "I could pay you to keep him for the night."

"Nonsense," Kramb said. "Mi casa, su."

"That's kind."

"You hurt your hand?" the old man asked.

Ritchie held up the left. "Yeah, I think I'm going to go to the ER and find out what's what."

"You need a ride?

"I can drive myself, though I appreciate it. I only need one hand for the steering-wheel." He held up the right, flat palm held toward the old poet with fingers together, as if he were about to perform a benediction or stigmata blood might flow.

"What happened?" Kramb walked until he came to his side. He looked at the mess on the floor and stepped cautiously.

"Sparring accident," Ritchie said. "It might be awhile until I know anything. Radiographs don't show soft tissue problems, but an x-ray should tell me if a bone's broken. I'll have to wait awhile before I can get an MRI probably."

"You should have been a doctor," Lawrence said, leaning down to Ritchie and helping him to his feet.

"I could a been a contender," Ritchie said, speaking from the throat and trying to do his Brando.

"You know, I had the privilege to meet Budd Schulberg once, many, many moons ago."

"Who's that?" Ritchie asked. He compressed the bandage on his sore left hand, holding it with his right. He wanted to go back to the kitchen to get the icepack from the freezer, but it looked like they were on their way out the door.

"The author of the screenplay for that film. I interviewed him at Stillman's Gym in New York City."

"I know where Stillman's was," Ritchie said. Kramb ignored the hostile edge in his voice, understood it was the booze and not the boxer speaking.

"I was a cub reporter, and I did a little feature on the movie they made about Rocky Graziano."

Ritchie elevated his left hand, cradling the left forearm in his right palm, lifting the bandaged paw above his heart. He recalled something his father said, and shared the tidbit as the two men staggered out of the bungalow and onto the creaking wooden planks of the porch. There were no flashing red and blue lights, which was good, but his son wasn't in sight, which was bad. "You know Brando broke his nose sparring and said that before he got his beak broken the ladies didn't really notice him. He was almost too pretty before he took those lumps."

Kramb walked Ritchie carefully down the cinderblock steps. "We neglected to bring up Mr. Schulberg in our discussion the other day of scribes who turned their talents to the fistic arts."

"I'm too drunk to understand what you just said, but it sounded beautiful."

Three gunshots echoed in the distance, pops from a small caliber handgun that cracked like a cross between a Chinese M80 and backfire from an ancient car starting to life. "The City of Los Angeles is certainly red of tooth and nail," Lawrence said. "But Hobbes forgot to factor in steel. I believe in the days when he wrote Leviathan, perhaps only the blunderbuss and a handful of other projectiles like the petard ..."

Ritchie finally gave up some of the ghost, but not all of it, drifting into a place between the sleep of exhaustion and the total shutdown of shock.

Things rarely ever went according to plan, but despite that it somehow hurt even more when events did a total one-eighty from the hoped-for outcome. He regretted not being able to tell Matt that he loved him, and knew that he would not be able to say it in the future, that certain things about him couldn't be changed.

The next time they went to Azteca, or perhaps even when they were down in the spider-web, Ritchie wanted to teach him how to move inside the other guy's punching range, smother, and clinch to spoil the guy's momentum if he was on a roll or he had him hurt. That way he would teach Matt a valuable lesson about how to keep an opponent from getting off his shots at the right distance, sapping power and leverage from the thwarted man in front of him. Imparting this knowledge would have also given him the chance to hug his son without the boy knowing that was his intent.

Lawrence Kramb pulled open the steel door of the Airstream trailer, which was riveted with bolts and spot-welded like the bulkhead of a submarine. Ritchie personally wouldn't have minded being submerged deep underwater now. If there was enough oxygen and food, he could have stayed on the ocean's floor forever, observing the striped tropical fish and purple coral castles with Bella at his side. The marine biologist in his fantasy conjured by blood loss was wearing a set of tortoise-shell glasses and looking sexy and intelligent while making notations on her clipboard.

"She's a mermaid," he said, staggering for the tartan plaid couch. He checked his hand to make sure that the blood, which was pooling on the gauze, was not actually spilling out.

"Yes," Lawrence said.

"Bella," Ritchie wailed.

A hangover headache was already settling on him, a hum and vibration like a tuning fork carrying through his skull. "I left the liver in the bag from Ralphs. If it doesn't get in the fridge soon, it's going to stink to high heaven."

Lawrence situated himself on the double-strung bead cushion draped over the driver's side seat of his car. "I wouldn't worry about it now. Priority one is getting you to the hospital. After that, we need to find Matt."

"You're right," Ritchie said, stretching out on the couch. His tongue was thick in his mouth like a sticky caterpillar, tasting of saccharine food dye and strychnine. "But I need to practice biting raw meat or I'll never be a good zombie."

Lawrence tilted the rearview as he started the caravan, shaking his head. "That's not drunk talk. That's acid or PCP talk." He kept his eye on Ritchie in the rearview as he drove, sporadically checking to make sure the boxer wasn't bleeding out or vomiting. The poet saw that he neither bled nor puked for the duration of the trip, though he was still more than a bit disconcerted because the tears didn't abate for even a moment once they were on the road.

Chapter Nineteen: Marina Dreaming

There was a lead clipped to his finger when he woke up in a small room surrounded by a curtain partition. He knew immediately that he was in a hospital, but he didn't know which one. When he checked the edge of the bed, he saw that he wasn't handcuffed, for which he was grateful.

Machines beeped around him, and the low chatter of nurses and doctors conferring came from beyond the curtain. Ritchie sat up in bed, bracing himself on his right hand, which smelled faintly of iodine. His left arm was in a trauma brace made of blue foam and aluminum. Someone had cut off the half-assed splint he'd done himself. That was probably a good thing, he decided. He didn't know what he was doing and had probably only succeeded in cutting off much-needed circulation.

"Water," he heard himself say.

"Coming."

The curtain was pulled open, and an RN in scrubs and paint-splatter-patterned crocs came in with a Dixie cup. "Here." She seemed putout with him and he wondered what he'd done or said while half-conscious. Remorse was settling into his aching bones.

He took the cup and killed it quickly. It wasn't enough, and only made him more parched, but he feared asking her for anything else.

"Do you know where you are?"

"The hospital."

"Do you know which hospital?" she snapped.

"No." He tried to add an edge to his voice, return fire to her, but she was too focused on the clipboard before her. "USC? LA County?"

"Good guess, but no." She flipped a page on the clipboard and marked something with a pen. "You're at Marina Del Rey. You were brought here by a Lawrence Kramb, who left shortly after dropping you off."

"He's looking for my boy." Ritchie suddenly felt dizzy.

She didn't know what to make of his statement, looked at him askance, then flipped through some more of the sheets before her. "Do you want to tell me what happened?"

Ritchie held up his injured left. "Yeah, I was sparring with a friend, real hardhead, and punched him on the top of the skull. I think I may have sprained my wrist."

"Hardhead?" She asked. If she'd been a bit angry with him before, she looked ready to club him with the clipboard now.

Ritchie leaned over the bed, felt booties on his toes. "Yeah," Ritchie said. "It's just a boxing injury." He stood and tried out his legs. They worked.

"Did this guy have a metal plate in his head?"

He laughed uneasily. "Why do you ask?"

"Because I remember once when I was working during a Rams game, some guy took issue with a Redskins fan in the crowd and threw a punch that missed and hit a metal stair railing." She pointed her ballpoint pen at his injured left. "It looked quite a bit like that."

"What do you want from me?" Ritchie asked.

"Let's start with the truth."

"You know I don't have insurance?"

She looked down at the paperwork before her. "Your emergency point of contact is a one Donatello Perillo?"

"Yes."

Ritchie walked back to the gurney and sat back down on its crinkly sheet.

"He just saved you a trip to our financial services department."

"Shit, he paid my bill?"

She nodded.

"All right," Ritchie said. "Can I go?"

The nurse looked at him with wide, disbelieving eyes. "You don't want to know what's wrong? One of your knuckles was displaced and there was bone showing through the injury site."

"I'm sure you've seen worse. Just give me my script for whatever meds I've got coming and I'll take them when it hurts."

"You came in here with a blood-alcohol level well over the legal limit."

"And? I didn't drive."

"We got the edema under control with cryotherapy. That took care of the swelling, so the doctor could come examine you."

Ritchie ignored her, asked, "You're not going to give me some Percocet, or at least some Vicodin?"

"We couldn't do an intake eval and there was nothing about drug abuse on your file, but the doctor got a look at you and decided you probably have a substance abuse problem. We had no choice but to give you something when you came in, but we're not giving you anything oxycodone-based when you leave." She pulled two sheets from a prescription pad from where they were clipped to the corkboard. "Naproxen and indomethacin is the best we could do. They're nonsteroidal, anti-inflammatories."

Ritchie took the two pieces of paper in hand, walked across the room to the trashcan activated by foot treadle, and threw them in. "I'll go to Oakwood Park and get right there, cop a bag of something to stop the pain."

She sighed heavily and slapped the clipboard against her thighs. "Mr. Abruzzi, you have myositis ossificans traumatica. Even if you were to take conservative care seriously, you still probably need a contrast dye exam, and then surgery."

"It feels okay." He lifted up his splinted and braced left.

"It should. You've had quite a bit of morphine. You might feel a bit differently when it wears off."

"What's wrong with it?" he asked, and walked over to the cubby where a key on a polyurethane pigtail dangled. He turned the key and saw his clothes and effects in a clear plastic bag inside.

"You have a grade three strain."

"I've had sprains before." He started unbuttoning his shirt one-handed, exposing his chest and muscled pectorals.

She snuck a glance, but then regained her bearing and said, "Can you wait until I'm out of the room before you change?"

"Sure." He stopped unbuttoning the shirt and waited.

"I said 'strain' not 'sprain.'"

He thought she should cut him a break. He was doing pretty well for a non-hobo who downed a pint of fortified wine in thirty minutes.

"You've had a complete rupture of the musculotendinous junction. Best case scenario, you'll need at least four to six weeks to heal."

He could heal when he was resting on the deck of his sailboat with Bella and a cool mil or two in the bank. "Anything else?" he asked.

"Yes."

"What?"

"You have multiple bone fragments that need to be taken out. It's called comminuted fractures. They showed up on the x-ray, and based on their position, if you don't let the doctor go in, those shards could slide around and do major damage. If you throw another punch, you may sever something that can't be put back together again, at least not without permanent loss of mobility and function."

217

"Thank you," Ritchie said. He looked at the locker where his stuff was. His tone softened a bit. "Seriously, thank you. I apologize for being an asshole."

Her look softened just as his tone did. "You're going to leave against medical advice?"

"Yes, ma'am."

She turned through the papers on her clipboard. "You know, the longer you delay this operation, the more expensive it will be to repair the damage."

"I might have some real money soon." He didn't feel the need to elaborate, and the nurse didn't press him. She held out the "Against Advice" form and he signed it with his right and handed it back.

She filled in the date on the form, stood, and said, "I'll let you get dressed now." The nurse left the room and pulled the curtain with a deft tug that left the sheet billowing on its runners. Someone paged a doctor over the intercom, and the voice on the PA system echoed down the hall.

Ritchie struggled into his shirt, fidgeted with the buttons. The nurse somehow sensed he was having problems, and her shadowy form spoke from the other side of the curtain. "Do you want a male orderly to come in there and help you?"

"I got this."

He shimmed into his jeans, squirming until they were high enough on his thighs for him to button and zipper them one-handed. He slipped into his loafers. When he opened the curtain, the RN was standing there with an old-fashioned wheelchair. He studied her for a second. She wore a bouffant that was thick and brown, impenetrable like a bird's nest or a helmet. She had sweet blue eyes guarded by long lashes. Her age barely showed in the crows' feet tugging at the corners of her eyes.

"I know you can walk," she said. "This is just a legal formality."

"Is a legal formality a law?"

"I'm not going to call the police on you if you walk out on your own two, but it would help if you could at least try to surprise me and everyone else here by being at least a little compliant."

"All right."

He sat against the thin leather-backed wheelchair and closed his eyes as the fluorescent light fixtures flicked by and the spokes of the unoiled wheels squeaked. He held his chin in his right hand while she pushed him along.

"Sorry," he said. He wasn't sure if he'd said that yet.

"You already apologized once," she said, setting him straight on that count.

"I just don't like to go to the hospital. It's been awhile since I've been here."

He tried to recall through the haze of the waning morphine the last time he was in one of these places for anything more than post-fight routine. A sinking feeling settled on his stomach, the fear of unwanted memory coming to the surface causing him to grip the handrails of the wheelchair. If they were wood instead of steel, he would have ripped them free from their screws and moorings.

"After the Kroekel fight," he said, under his breath.

"I'm sorry?" She leaned down to him as she pushed him down the hall.

"I was in Russia. I beat this guy into a coma. Right after the fight I went to the hospital. I sat there and waited while he went under the knife."

"I think maybe you should stay, Mr. Abruzzi." She halted the wheelchair. "You can get a lot of help here. Not just for your hand."

An Indian doctor doing his residency walked past them, wearing a salmon-colored shirt and a paisley tie. Ritchie waved his hand. "Andale, puede usted," he said, and she knew enough Spanglish to keep pushing. "They were trying to relieve the intracranial pressure," Ritchie said. "He had a severe concussion. He died a couple hours later. His father spit at me."

"I'm sure you've heard this before," the nurse said, "but he was trying to hurt you, too, in your boxing match, wasn't he?"

Ritchie shook his head. "He didn't have it in him to hurt me. I could have gone for the body, instead of headhunting. I was going through some shit with my wife and my management and I tried to make him suffer in the ring." He looked down at his hands, the one braced and splinted in foam and metal, the other naked and still dangerous. "I'm a murderer."

"That's not murder," she said, pushing him along. "It was a fight."

"His mother called me a murderer. You try telling her I didn't murder her boy."

"You can't blame her."

"I don't blame her," Ritchie said. "I blame me." He stood up out of the chair while it was in motion and kept walking.

"Mr. Abruzzi."

He walked down the corridor, away from the voice behind him, toward the automatic doors of the exit. He pulled his phone from his pants pocket, saw the cell was powered down. Either he'd turned it off or the battery died. Only one way to find out. He held down the button and the thing came to life, the lithium green battery icon filled with about eight-percent power on its bar.

The scent of flowers and clean seawater carried on the morning breeze. The sun was a mellow, subdued lemon-yellow ball painting the postcard-worthy palms lining the streets and warming Ritchie's raw nerves, soothing him and his rage with its rays like a natural heroin drip leaking from the sky.

In the center of the roundabout was a grassland island where birds of paradise sprouted, the heads of the flowers perfect as origami cranes done in red tissue paper. He saw he had two missed calls, the first from Don and the second from Bella. He called Don first.

The line rang twice. "Kid, you okay?"

"Never better," Ritchie said, though he could feel the dope wearing off. "I want to thank you for paying my nut."

"Nah," Don said, embarrassed, uncomfortable with the gratitude.

"How much was it?" Ritchie asked.

"Rich, don't fucking worry about it. Okay?"

"Listen, Don." He paused. "You still got pawnshops, and you got connections for jewelry and gold and whatnot?"

"Don't play yourself like that. You want to be like all these other fucking ex-boxers who get caught pulling robberies? You know Cliff Etienne is doing something like two-hundred years, breaking rocks in Angola. You want that for you?"

"I think Cliff shot at a couple of cops. You think I'm that out of it?"

"I don't know. You've been acting real dumb of late. And I say that out of love and concern. I see someone I love fucking up, I'm going to tell them." Don huffed so that his wheezing caused a scraping sound in the phone. Ritchie wondered about his angina.

"How's your heart holding out?"

"It'd be better if I didn't get calls from the ER saying my friends were breaking their fucking hands. What'd you punch, by the way?"

Ritchie knew there was no use in trying to BS him. If it didn't work with a nurse, it wasn't going to work with a guy who had more years in the hurt business than Ritchie had on earth. He decided to not even bother with a lie, changed the subject instead. "Can I get ten per on a haul? I mean, if I get you something, like something really nice, like Crown Jewels nice, can you move it for the going rate?"

"You think I want to fucking die in prison? I got the best Jew doctors taking care of me at Cedars-Sinai, and you want me cooling my heels in fucking Quentin, lining up for morning meds while worrying about some moolie putting a sharpened toothbrush in my back."

"I don't think you want to die in jail," Ritchie said. "I think you want to die in Acapulco, drinking rum from a coconut with a little umbrella in it, knowing your grandkids got their college covered."

"Don't get yourself killed over some dumb shit, Ritchie."

"Keep your phone on. If I'm still alive in a couple of days, you may want to hear what I have to say. No pressure. It's just an offer."

"Ritch …"

"Enough with this 'Ritch' shit," Ritchie said, and hung up. His heart thumped like a war drum as his right thumb drifted over the missed call from Bella. All he would have to do to lay it all on the line, to make the big move, was flick that little name on the face of his phone with his thumb.

He didn't get the chance. Another call from someone else was incoming. He accepted it. "Hello?"

"How are you?" It was Lawrence.

"Mr. Kramb, I want to thank you for driving me here, and I want to apologize for anything I did or said on the drive in. I was really drunk, you know. I was belligerent, obnoxious."

"No need for thanks, or to apologize. Also no need for this 'Mr.' formality. Even when I taught at the Naropa Institute I didn't ask anyone to call me 'Mr.'"

"I don't want to call you Kerouac," Ritchie said. He didn't like the way people cynically shit on the poet just because he was chasing birds and the muse rather than dope and money like everyone else.

"'Lawrence' will suffice."

"Okay, Lawrence it is." Now that that was settled he asked, "Any word on the Matty front?"

"Your son?"

"Yes."

"No," Lawrence said. "It's needle in a haystack time. I don't think I need to tell you with the transient nature of Venice, and with the number of runaways currently there, it's nigh-on impossible to find someone who doesn't want to be found. If I see him, however, you will be the first to know. Any specific message you would like me to relay to him?"

"Yes," Ritchie said, although even as he said it he didn't know what he had in mind. His son definitely deserved an apology. He didn't want to apologize to anyone ever again, no matter how warranted. Apologies almost always had a begging, pathetic quality to them, and they rarely resolved anything. They bred contempt. "Tell him I love him," Ritchie said, and hung up.

The phone vibrated in his hand, and Bella's name danced on the screen. Ritchie wondered if the rumbling in his chest was anything like what it felt like when Don Perillo's pacemaker kicked in.

"Hello?" He winced, bit his lip. He'd picked up on the first ring. That smacked of desperation, need. He was needy and desperate, but it was best to disguise those emotions with a woman. Such tells were suicide in this sexual equivalent of poker.

"Are you okay?" she asked.

"Yes. How's Suhne?"

"He's pissed," she said, "but I don't think he's pressing charges."

"So he remembers?"

"He does." Her voice was tinged with sadness. He thought it was possible that she had wanted to work with him, and was disappointed now that he was out of the picture. Apparently, he hadn't hit the kid hard enough to give him amnesia. "Will you come pick me up?" Ritchie asked.

"Yes." She spoke fast enough for him to suspect that maybe she had been hoping he'd make such a move. "Where are you?" There was undisguised need in her voice, so he didn't feel the need to conceal his own hunger anymore.

"Marina Del Rey emergency entrance."

"Okay," she said. "I have to work tonight, but we can hang out before and after I go on stage."

"That's good," Ritchie said, "because we need to talk."

They hung up at the same time. An ambulance with lights flashing pulled into the roundabout, and Ritchie stepped aside to let the wounded man or woman be carried inside on the stretcher by the EMTs.

He wished he was in Manhattan right now, on Mulberry Street near Broome in Little Italy. Hell, he would have even considered Glenwood Houses in Canarsie on an overcast day an improvement over L.A. at its sunniest and most seductive. This city was a fucking snake, the streets nothing but a forked tongue branching in many directions, all roads ultimately leading to hell.

He knew he'd get there soon enough.

Chapter Twenty: A Bed beneath the Steer Skull

Hunger and limited funds conspired to send them careening toward Jack-in-the-Box. He'd had half a grand on his person last night, but that was before he'd thrown his wad of money at his son to repay him for destroying his cellphone. He lied to Bella on their drive downtown. "I paid out of pocket for my ER treatment back there." He waved toward the hospital with his braced arm and winced. It felt better when he didn't move it.

"What's wrong?" she asked.

"Hairline fracture," he said, lying again. He shifted in the contours of the Honda's bucket seat. "Where's the Benz?" It wasn't that he minded riding in the hatchback, but this ride didn't look like it belonged to a near-billionaire. It was tricked out with an aftermarket spoiler and all kinds of kits. It looked and felt like it belonged to a go-nowhere boyfriend who was in a band and always borrowing money for new parts.

"I'm on punishment with Joey," she said, "so I'm driving my roommate's car."

The fast food restaurant was near an old film studio that had been remodeled and sliced into lofts, condos, and artist studios. Some sort of exhibit inside the building was drawing a crowd toward the old loading dock entrance, where paintings were hung on the white walls. The young women were in legwarmers and denim skirts, and the men wore striped ties, vintage hats, and thick sideburns.

"Want to try to sneak in with them?" Ritchie asked. "Free wine and cheese inside, maybe."

"I could pull it off," she said, "but you might stand out."

"You're probably right." They pulled into the drive-thru behind a blue Kia four-door.

"Do you know what you want?" she asked.

"Just get me some kind of breakfast sandwich, and a coffee."

The engine rumbled and a whiff of carbon monoxide strong enough to come from a school bus wafted upwards. Bella coughed and waved her hand. "Shit, Ashley doesn't have the money for repairs right now, and I don't have the cash to help her either. This sucks."

Ritchie had had enough. "Listen," he said, and the change in his tone of voice caused her to turn down the radio and look over at him. "Do you know how much Suhne is worth?"

Her eyes went wide and she shook her head. "Huh-uh. A few mil?"

"Try a few hundred million. Like five-hundred million."

"Holy shit," she whispered. Her lips remained puckered in a severely cute shape. He couldn't bear to look at her anymore.

"I know he's got a few million worth of jewelry in the house," Ritchie said.

"But if he sees you, he's going to call the police immediately."

"He won't see me," Ritchie said. He looked toward the back of the car. "I can duck down in the backseat underneath a blanket or something. You get us inside, and let me do the rest."

Bella shook her head, not as if she wasn't thinking about it, but as if she had but had already talked herself out of it before, seeing some angle still not obvious to him. "I don't want to be an accomplice."

A car honked behind them and caused them both to jump in their seats. A man in a Toyota compact leaned out of the driver's side of the car. "Let's go, assholes! Some of us have to go to work."

226

Ritchie leaned out of the passenger side and flipped the guy off with his unbandaged right. "Fuck you, motherfucker!"

"Ritchie ..." She put her right hand on him. It calmed him immediately, like he was a lion and she his tamer. "It's okay." She pulled forward and spoke into the intercom nestled in the cube from which the antenna ball sprung. The mascot smiled with the sugar cone turned upside-down on its head. Smiley didn't know he and the restaurant were slated for demolition, and would soon succumb to the devouring orbit of the gastropubs and boutiques spreading over the neighborhood.

"One large coffee, a bacon and egg chicken sandwich, and a cranberry muffin."

A Hispanic female voice spoke their total through the intercom and they drove forward. "You won't be an accomplice," Ritchie said. "I'll make it look like I snuck in and you didn't know it. Something goes wrong, and you can testify in court. I'll back up your claim."

"You're crazy," she said.

"I might be, but I'm not a liar. My word is my bond. If this shit goes south, it's all on me." He looked out the passenger-side window, at a low wooden fence on the other side of which was a McDonald's. The golden arch rose on a pylon arm into the air where it got lost in among the power lines and overarching mercury vapor lamps. Ritchie watched a bird fly by and said, "I've got a gun. It's just for show, though. I'll unload it, use it to put the fear of God in him. We'll get the jewels and I'll sell them and that's that."

She pulled up to the window and paid the woman, who handed them out their paper bag and the roasted coffee. "Thank you," Bella said to the woman at the window. She drove to an empty spot facing the fence beyond which was the McDonald's. She blew steam from the lip of the coffee cup lid. "Can we split the coffee?"

"Sure," Ritchie said, and reached inside the bag for his sandwich. He took a bite of the greasy fried thing and forced himself to swallow it. He had a cast-iron stomach when it came to absorbing punches, but fast food was a different story.

Bella took a tentative sip of the coffee, found it was too hot still, and handed it off to him. He took the plastic cup by the cardboard sleeve.

"How do you know that he keeps jewels in the house?"

"I've got connections." Ritchie didn't mention that his connection was literally his son's internet connection, or that he didn't know anything for sure.

"And where are you going to unload this stuff without getting busted?"

"Connections again," he said, and this time he wasn't lying, assuming Don Perillo came through. He figured the old man might protest over the phone, but once Ritchie had the shiny metal and glittering stones in hand, Don would go along, whether out of greed, loyalty, or some combination of the two. Somehow Ritchie would get him across the finish line.

Bella took a bite of her cranberry muffin, halving the top in one healthy bite. She spoke through a mouthful of sugary crumbs. "We'd have to kill him."

"I'm not a murderer," Ritchie said, even though he thought he not only could kill a man over money, but that he had done that when he beat Vasily Kroekel to death. "We don't have to kill him."

She held the muffin up in her right hand by its paper baking cup. "You think he's just going to let us rob him without reporting it to the police?"

Ritchie turned so that he was facing her in the rubber racing seat. "You think we don't have something we can hang over his head, to keep him from going to the police?" He tried the coffee. It was hot but drinkable.

"Like what?"

"You know like what," he said. He didn't want to sound too forceful, but he didn't want to play all day either.

Her honey-brown eyes narrowed to pinpoints.

"Your girlfriend who gave me a lap dance," Ritchie said, "What did he have her doing, or what did he try to get her to do that got her so upset?"

Bella took a smoke from the crumpled soft pack sitting in the cup holder. "I need a cigarette."

She lit the smoke, crumpled up the remains of the muffin, and threw it into the paper bag. She'd eaten less than half of the muffin, but he didn't suspect an eating disorder. Her goddess booty was ample and he found her hourglass form to be all soft and round curves on those few lucky occasions when she accidentally brushed her brown body up against his.

"I don't know if he still does it," she said, pulling out, "but Joey would pay a caballero to bring a donkey out to his stables. Sometimes he'd go to the shows across the border and pay girls to get it on with the burros there."

Ritchie took one of the cigarettes and watched her as she drove. She paused in her story and her smoking and looked at him, taking her eyes from the road for a moment as she drove. "I didn't know you smoke."

"Rarely." This was one of those rare occasions. She flicked the flame on the lighter for him and he moved his face closer to the fire, puffing and coughing slightly as he inhaled.

"Anyway, he showed her some of the photos, and offered her a grand to fuck a donkey. Jewel told me he bragged that one of the girls he'd gotten to do it died of internal bleeding later."

"Jewel is the girl-"

"Who gave you the lap dance?"

Ritchie took another drag of the cigarette, tried not to cough, and failed. Bella also tried not to laugh at him smoking like a novice and failed in her endeavor, too. He didn't mind being comic relief. Any kind of relief was welcome at this point.

"See?" Ritchie said.

"See what?" she asked.

"You think he wants that getting out? That he's involved in that stuff, that he got a girl killed?"

Bella paused, flicked her ash out of the driver's side window, and turned right. She gazed at the horizon and shook her head. "I don't know. You ever been to Juarez?"

"Nah," he said. "I've been to Mexico, but never there."

"I can't see the police getting too worked up about it. Girls get murdered there every day. My roommate told me about it."

"The one whose car we're in?"

"It's her boyfriend's car, but yes. She did work for an NGO. She still does. Ashley's her name. She's out of town for a few days. They call them maquiladoras."

"They call what maquiladoras?" Ritchie knew Azteca beer and Julio Caesar Chavez's famed bodywork. Outside of beer and boxing he didn't know much about what went on in Mexico.

"The factories the girls work at, the sweatshops. They take busses to and from work early in the morning and late at night. A lot of them never make it home. Hundreds of them have died and turned up all cut to pieces Jack the Ripper-style." She shook her head, finished her cigarette, and tossed it out the window. "No one gives a shit."

"We've got enough leverage to make him keep his fool mouth shut," Ritchie said. "Everybody loves their lives, especially cowards. He's got five-hundred mil. He can kick down a few mil to us."

"All right," she said.

"All right?"

She hunched her shoulders as she gripped the steering wheel and drove. A strand of her brown hair fell before her eyes, looking like intertwined bits of Rapunzel's gold-spun straw. "I don't want to work at a strip club anymore."

"This thing goes according to plan, you might not have to work at all for a while, maybe ever."

She slowed down as they pulled down a residential block of midcentury modern houses. The five-fingered ferns at either side of the road were drooping from an uncommonly heavy rain that must have fallen while he was unconscious in the hospital, and the spines of the prickly pear cactuses erupted from their green pads like blowfish spoiling for a fight with a shark.

"I can believe that a couple mil might keep us from working for a while, but a million dollars isn't what is used to be."

"You're right," he said, "but I know people who can turn a few hundred grand into a few million. Like my manager, Don Perillo. You get your hands on a decent amount of paper, and you can be a silent partner in a trucking line, or just sit back and collect rents from properties you buy. We just need that nest egg and then we can lay in the cut and watch our paper stack." He was so worked up that he forgot his left hand was hurt and pounded it into his right, wincing. "Goddamn!"

"Careful," she said. She parked on a concrete pad below her friend's house. The home sat on reinforced stilt columns that threw them into shadow. She touched the fingers protruding from the brace on his hand and he pulled her hair away from her eyes. "Come on," she said, nodding in the direction of the house and tucking her hair behind her ear. Her voice was a husky whisper, deep but feminine, in contrast to the girlish tone she usually spoke in. He didn't know why or how the woman had awakened in her and he was afraid to ask, because he feared it was only the talk of money that had made her pussy so wet. Not that he would blame her.

He watched her ass cheeks as she moved up the bamboo stairs ahead of him, the rounded scimitar-crescent shapes sprouting from beneath the white stretch yoga pants she wore. Her bikini bottoms were straining under the thin fabric of the revealing hose, gauze skintight over tan glutes and a white thong nestled in her ass crack.

Ritchie couldn't help himself, and bit her ass as he walked up the stairs behind her. He clutched the material of the bikini bottoms through the nylon fabric of her leggings, hanging on like a dog locking on a chew toy. She laughed a triumphant laugh she'd earned. It was the cackle of a chambermaid who secretly knew the king was her fool beneath her feet in the antechamber.

He'd smelled her pussy, the wild ripened fruit scent of it, and his cock grew with such force that the blood rushed until he couldn't even feel his hands, let alone the pain in his left paw. They staggered through the lanai shaded by rubber trees, and she kept her dark eyes fixed on him with her head turned as she pulled the torn screen door open and maneuvered the key in the door.

"I have to get ready in less than an hour, but we can fool around for a little while."

"Is she here?" Ritchie asked. A moment later he was afraid that his question would sound piggish, like Bella alone wouldn't be enough and he wanted to involve a third girl. Bella was all he needed, though, and two girls or a harem of twenty women would have detracted from her and what he wanted from her alone.

"It's just us," she said. "Like I said, Ashley's out of town."

He lost it, running toward her, picking her up in his strong arms and rushing her to the nearest bedroom. "This isn't my room," she said.

"So?" He dropped her on the edge of the bed, on the folded square of a rough turquoise saddle blanket.

"She'll be able to smell it," she said.

"What?"

"The sex. She'll smell it."

He pulled her yoga pants and bikini bottoms off as quickly as if they were dead skin on a snake ready to reveal its new colored markings. The warmth of her womb hit him in humid, sticky overpowering waves. Her pussy was L.A., the promise, the riches, and the beautiful lies of Hollywood and Beverly Hills concentrated in a couple inches of wet, perfect pink flesh dripping with nectar. He placed his nose against the bone above her pussy, which was shelved with a perfectly contoured layer of soft fat that enveloped his nose and mouth as he pushed his face forward. He wanted to hide, disappear in her flesh and hair and as he nuzzled against her he hoped she didn't interpret this as the cowardice of a man seeking a place to shield himself from the world and trying to disappear between her legs.

"I don't know," she whispered.

"What?" He remained on his knees at the foot of the bed, while she squirmed on the edge. He saw the well-pedicured nails of her toes, a slight crack in the otherwise uniform red coat of paint. He kissed her toes, licked the bottom of her right foot.

She giggled, closed her eyes, and threw her hand over her face. "You're so hot but you fucking scare me. Also, I'm not sure you want to eat me out."

It was a little late for that. He rubbed his cheek against the hair above the wrinkled slick pink lips inviting his mouth into her body. "Why?" he said, although he wasn't sure she understood his question because his tongue was planted on the pearl of her clit and he couldn't pronounce his words well.

Catholic guilt left from childhood in upstate New York made the cunnilingus better, as he imagined himself as the asp in the garden teaching Eve about herself. He lashed the pussy with his tongue as if it were forked and he were a serpent imparting ultimate knowledge, letting the goddess know that she was greater than the god at her feet.

"I usually like to wash first. Also, I think my period is going to start soon." The excuses tapered as he made her breathless with the circular licking motions of his tongue, the patters without pattern, the very soft touch of his tongue that tortured her until her ass cheeks clenched and pulled the fabric of her roommate's blanket into her quaking ass. "I'm worried I smell," she finally said. "I'm always worried about my smell."

He removed his wet face from her pussy, kept his nose an inch away from it, as if in a faceoff with an opponent in a press conference. He breathed as deeply as he could, tasting her scent totally with his nose, intoxicating himself and breathing until he felt enslaved to her musk. He jerked off furiously with the hand that he didn't use to spread her pussy lips, and as she heard his perverse and exaggerated inhalation of her that deep sound of womanhood came again, rumbling from her core like an earthquake.

"Smell me," she said. "Smell my pussy and lick it." She closed her eyes, opened them, stared once at the steer skull hanging over the doorway of her friend's bedroom. The pale horned skull gazed at her with its eye hollows, looking like some damned inversion of a mistletoe that had drawn them here together. She felt the orgasm coming in warm waves working its way over her. She had trouble believing that such a big, violent man could forego using the cock she'd already heard about and instead barely touched her with a tongue that moved with the sensitivity of a feather gracing an alchemist's quill.

"Eat me, daddy," she said, and held his head in her hands, pulling his hair and then digging her nails into his neck while fanning her brown legs. He obeyed like a puppet

234

who had no use but to dangle on the threads she manipulated from her perch above him. Bella closed her eyes again, imagined the boxer Ritchie Abruzzi and the director Joey Suhne stabbing each other to death with daggers on a heap of jewels that she would inherit after the men had expended themselves over a pile of treasure and her pussy, both of which would be hers to keep after it was all said and done. And she felt no guilt.

Chapter Twenty-One: The Winner and New Champion

The map of the house was drawn in crayon on the back of a placemat from the Burbank Big Bite Diner. An arrow pointed at the side of the house. Bella tapped her one-hitter on the map. "You've been to the front and to the back. You haven't been to the side entrance." She handed him her purse and the one-hitter. "Pack it up for me," she said. Her hands were shaking.

She looked at the dark road ahead, gripped the custom wheel cover made of scaled leather covered in red racing stripes. Ritchie dug in her Gucci knockoff for the orange prescription bottle. He uncapped the childproof top and the car filled with the lush scent of Humboldt hydroponic weed.

"Smells good," he said, thinking that it smelled a bit like her vagina and her hair but keeping the thought to himself. Maybe smoking it caused it to get deep into the pores where it was then secreted out in sweat and in her squirting. He packed the gooey bud inside the aluminum faux cigarette's mouth.

"The weed's too good to waste in a one-hitter, but if we're really hitting a major lick tonight I figure I can splurge."

"We're going to come out smelling like roses," Ritchie said.

Bella turned left. Ritchie looked out the window and noticed neon was glowing from the undercarriage of the Honda Civic. "Here," Ritchie said.

She took back the one-hitter and sparked it with a butane torch lighter shaped like a revolver. It was fitting for the night's work, he thought. "So I'll go in," she said, holding a volume of smoke in her lungs. "You wait about twenty minutes. Then you get out of the car, and just follow the sound in the house."

"He keeps the TV that loud?" Ritchie asked.

She blew out a stream of smoke and coughed a bit. She hammered her chest and spoke as if she had bronchitis. "It's not a TV. He watches old movies on a screen in his bedroom, which is also where I'm going to keep him busy for twenty minutes or so." She held out the one-hitter to him. "That's why I'm trying to get a buzz-on first. I don't want to tell you what I have to do to get him hot, but it will keep him distracted long enough for you to come in through the side entrance." She stopped the car. He noticed they were at the curb in Oakwood, parked behind his Interceptor. "It won't be hard for me to persuade him to keep the doors open to the courtyard. The weather's beautiful." She sniffled, took another hit. Her face glowed in the torchlight. She spouted out a cloud of smoke and said, "Who doesn't love a summer breeze?"

Ritchie grabbed his door handle, looked at her glazed and serene eyes, the syrupy pools of warm brown watching him. A slight smile played across her lips and they were on each other, mouths open and panting. He reached inside of her black bra, touching her nipple until it grew hard as Indian rubber. Her tongue snaked in his mouth and he pulled back. He'd never thought that he would love the smell and taste of stale weed on his lips.

"Be right back." He stumbled with his erection toward the front door. He looked around as he walked up the front steps of his bungalow. A distant part of him feared she would drive off, leave him, betray him, do something drastic and sadistic now that she knew he needed her, or at least that he wanted her.

A more practical part of him was scanning for the usual assortment of lowlifes, stickup kids and strong-arm robbers, the homeless who might waylay him, or maybe a private head buster that Suhne had hired because he didn't have the stones to do his own dirty work.

Everything was silent, though, save for the faraway call of the surf and the thump of bass from a house party in another cottage up the block. He opened the front door to his place and held his breath against the comingled smells of muscatel and rotgut, the science experiment gone-awry scent of the rotted liver he'd bought on a whim and the liquor he'd spilled while shitfaced. He saw no evidence that Matt had been back here, and he couldn't say that he blamed him.

He went into the basement, walked past the spider-web in front of his rubber dummy. He walked to the massive safe in the corner, worked the combination with his right hand, and opened the heavy metal plate concealing the trinkets of his past, as well as everything he would need tonight.

Ritchie hefted the Colt Python in his hand. He pulled the extractor rod, opened the cylinder and spun it, counting six rounds. He snapped the cylinder back into place, pulled up his blue Polo shirt, and stuck the gun against his waistband. Then he pulled the shirt over that.

Next came the question of how much money to take. He grabbed the crumpled wad of bills from his poor man's bank. Like most boxers, he'd never trusted credit or even understood things like annuities and compound interest or concepts like equity. There was a reason that Don King could get further with a BMW and a gold chain than someone else could get with a piece of paper promising ten times as much money in the future. Fighters understood now. Ritchie knew damn well he wasn't immune to the instant jolt that cash could transfuse into a man. He felt it at this moment as he counted out twenty thousand dollars. He broke the pile into two stacks of ten grand. He wrapped a band around one stack and then banded the second one. He put the rest of the money back into the safe and then headed outside.

The lights were off in Kramb's Globetrotter. The poet was slumbering.

Bella was leaning against the side of the Honda hatchback. She smiled, showing that enchanting gap between her teeth and the slight chip to her one tooth that drove him crazy. He kissed her lips and she responded, biting him as she brought his bottom lip between her teeth and held it until he was sure he would come in his pants or bleed from the lip or both. He pushed her off.

She reached down, touched his cock. "You got it?" She whispered.

"I got it," he said, and though he wanted her hand to stay where it was, he pulled her palm up until it was touching the body of the Python.

"Ew," she said, moaning slightly. "It's big."

"Knock it off," he said, and pulled her hand away.

"It's unloaded, right?" She batted her eyelashes and he didn't know if she was setting him up for something or just melting him with the doe eyes because she could.

"Yeah," he said. He didn't want to lie but he didn't want to scare her either.

"Okay," she said, and pulled the passenger seat up to expose a cramped backseat, piled high with so many blankets it looked like they'd done a daytrip to a Fort Mojave trading post. "You hide under those," she said.

"All right." He readied to get in, stopped. "Wait."

"Wait, what?"

"Here." He passed her one of the ten stacks before he could think about what he was doing or chastise himself for being a fool.

The money seemed to either rouse her out of her high or make her more stoned, but something in her face changed. "What's this?"

"Money," he said, struggling into the backseat. He wished again that they still had the Benz.

He lay prone and let her cover him up with the blankets, one on another, until her voice came to him as if from a distance. He fought the thought that he was being buried alive and he ignored the dread swelling in his belly already heavy with tumult.

"I know it's money. What for?"

"Just take it," he said, hearing his muffled voice from beneath the blanket. "In case we get separated and you need to get a hotel, or hop the border to Mexico."

She put the passenger seat back in place and walked around to the front of the car. He heard a door close and another one open. The engine started, and she said, "Ten grand will go a long way in Old Mexico."

Bella started singing Doors tunes, adding a flamenco inflection as she drove while shout-serenading him with poems about whiskey bars and Spanish caravans. After chambering a few more tokes of the Black Widow strain of dispensary dope, she no longer sounded like she was doing karaoke. By the time she got to People are Strange her crooning took on an eerie and pitch-perfect quality that had Ritchie gripping the checkered butt of the Colt and praying the night would hurry up and be over, and that they would be rich when the sun dawned. Ultimately, he prayed more than anything else to Mother Mary that Joey Suhne didn't try anything stupid. Ritchie didn't like the little worm, but he didn't want to have to grease him if it could be avoided.

"You were right," Bella said, halting in her playlist of sixties standards.

"How so?" Ritchie lifted the blanket off his sweating head. He wasn't sure which blanket was the one they had fucked on in her roommate's bedroom, but Bella's passion fruit tang was too strong on the wool for that cover not to be in among the other ones she piled on him.

"How rich he was," she said. "I checked it out online."

"You don't trust me."

"I trust you," she said, putting her pipe back in the purse. "I was just curious." She tilted the rearview to him and watched him with her hazel eyes. Her hair framed her face into an oval shape. The sun had streaked her hair with natural highlights, burning it sienna.

"We don't have to get greedy," Ritchie said. "Let's just get a few mil and then get the hell out of California."

"You don't like L.A?"

"I'm a New York boy."

"You're gonna be a Bahamas Boy soon," she said. "Maybe Cancun. Maybe, we can do both."

"That's the spirit."

She took her eyes off the rearview and he covered his head with the blanket again, sensing they were getting close. He ran his sweat-slicked right hand over the gold inlays of the gun, the scrollwork, rubbing the cameo carving of the Madonna as if praying the rosary, knowing it was blasphemy but praying also for millions of dollars.

"Okay," she whispered, as the car slowed. "Keep quiet. Whatever you do, don't make a move or a sound."

He didn't respond, didn't twitch. The car stopped. He heard her speak into her cellphone. "Hey Joey, I got the jackrabbit with me."

The gate opened and Ritchie wondered what the hell that meant. He'd felt a pang of conscience over not telling her he'd loaded the piece. Now, though, he suspected maybe this "jackrabbit" horseshit was code to let Joey know the trap had been sprung and he was glad the Python had rounds in it just in case.

Gravel crunched beneath the wheels as the car circled the roundabout before the house. "Okay," she whispered as she pulled the Honda to a stop. "Try to wait a few minutes, then walk around the right side of the house. Just let the sounds guide you."

He didn't say anything, didn't mention that he would use the lock screen on his cellphone to keep perfect track of time. If something went wrong tonight, it wouldn't be because of him.

"Don't take too long," she said. "The longer I stay with him, the weirder it's going to get."

He didn't know what that meant, but figured he would learn soon enough. She got out of the car and closed the door. He heard her heels scraping the gravel of the driveway and then all was silent for a moment as her feet walked over the soft, wet grass. He slowly pulled the Python from the elastic band of his underwear, where it had become cinched on the ride over here.

Ritchie pressed the face of his phone, figured about three or four minutes had elapsed since she had left the car. Some sort of tinny ragtime music came from inside of the house, an off-key pianoforte roll that must have been all the rage about ninety years ago.

He slowly peeled off three layers of blankets, growing instantly cooler. Still wearing a couple of blankets over him like a sniper's ghillie suit, he blindly felt for the catch that would release the front passenger seat and allow his cramped legs some mercy.

He fumbled a few tries and then latched onto it with his right hand, sliding the seat forward. His left hand was throbbing as if it had been slammed in a doorjamb.

The phone said he had a few more minutes to wait. He ran through the lyrics to a couple of Doors songs in his head, thought of Jim Morrison's deep and untrained baritone, his blue-eyed soul growl. He tossed in the backseat like an insomniac, looked at the phone again and figured he'd waited long enough.

He kept crouched down as he opened the passenger door and walked low with the Python in his right hand. His adrenaline pumped like an orgasm was imminent, and he felt almost as good as he had this afternoon fucking Bella.

Ritchie did as she told him to do, walked along the side of the house. He followed the sound of music counterpointed by a mechanical hum like a lift in action, along with a male groan of either pain or ecstasy or both. He wondered if maybe something had already gone askew and she was stabbing or strangling Suhne. He hoped not. He had to find out where the jewels were.

An arabesque curtain billowed out from the side of the house, inviting Ritchie in. He walked slowly forward, turned around the corner with the gun held in front of him, ready to pull the trigger if it came to that, maybe even wanting to pull the trigger. There was no one there, though the sound of the ivory being tickled by a long-dead pit player and the motor hum continued to grow in volume, along with the moaning. He stepped forward, into a Pompeian loggia with travertine marble lain in a honeycomb pattern at his feet. He watched his hushpuppies skitter quietly over the stone. The floor of a heated lagoon-shaped blue pool cast rippling gold and blue shadows against the walls and against his sweating skin, throwing him and his gun into long shadow as he moved through the grotto that was moist as a sauna.

There was a breezeway connecting the room he was in to the source of the sound and light ahead, where he knew Suhne and Bella were engaged in perhaps a life-and-death struggle of some kind. He didn't want to give up the element of surprise, and he had to struggle not to break out in a run as he double-timed it through the breezeway. The ceiling was half-timbered in Tudor wood, creating a smell that made the sauna comparison twice as apt as the sweat continued to coat his face, stream down his eyes until it was a hindrance like blood in a fight.

This connecting room was actually larger than his bungalow, he realized, large enough to be the longhouse of a Western character actor who'd saved his money and retired to a ranch.

He came into the room where Bella was on a canopy bed surrounded by parted mosquito netting, with

Joey Suhne lain on Egyptian sheets before her. A silent film ran on a projector against a screen on the opposite wall, showing a scene of a prospector with a handlebar mustache and a ten-gallon hat crying beside his dead horse in Death Valley. It reminded Ritchie a bit of an episode of the Twilight Zone he'd watched with his old man about some guy in a desert with a bunch of gold bars who kept trading his precious metal for sips of water.

"Ugh," Joey moaned. His eyes were closed and Ritchie noticed he didn't see him. He was spread eagle with his bony, hair-covered legs wide apart while Bella sat there with a look of disgust on her face. Ritchie froze, admired her for a moment while her eyes held an urgent appeal for him to save her from this fucking guy. She was wearing only a black molded bra with gold underwire accenting her plunging neckline, along with black panties speckled with peacock feathers.

He looked at her right hand, which was manipulating a purple silicon ten-speed dildo in the director's ass. It was slicked with milky prostate fluid and water-based lube that had a strawberry scent to it.

Ritchie pointed the gun at the twosome. "All right, bitch. Put the jackrabbit down and get on the ground. You," he said to Suhne, "put your hands where my eyes can see or I'm going to start shooting."

Suhne jolted with fear so hard that he pulled two-thirds of the purple latex inside of his flaccid and pimply ass. Its humming quieted some and Bella bit her lip to keep from laughing. Ritchie tried to keep the smile out of his voice and said, "Now!"

She fell to the floor, and Joey Suhne slowly lifted his left arm. He glanced over at Bella. "You set this shit up, you fucking whore!"

"Baby," she purred.

"How did he know what it was called?" Suhne tilted his head toward the dildo trapped in his ass. "He called it a 'jackrabbit.'"

"Don't worry about that," Ritchie said, cursing himself for not just calling it a dildo or a toy. "Let me see the right or I'll start shooting." He was worried. This asshole had seen a lot of movies and not all of them were silent.

"Okay," Suhne said. Ritchie heard a click, knew what it was, and pulled the trigger.

Eiderdown and feathers flew from the bed and Bella screamed.

"Action!" Suhne shouted and pulled the trigger on his own piece he'd brought from beneath his pillow. Ritchie flinched but kept his cool, raising the piece he'd never bothered to zero at the range.

Both men squeezed, Ritchie at Suhne and Suhne at Bella. Suhne's blued piece of small steel flashed and spit fire, throwing the girl against a mantelpiece on top of which was a Ming vase and a clock gilded in gold leaf.

Two more of Ritchie's shots missed, but the third connected with Suhne's knee and caused him to drop his Rohrbaugh 9mm and wail out like he was undergoing surgery without anesthetic.

Suhne's kneecap exploded like a balloon. Blood and bone filled the air in a wet combination that dissolved quickly into a red mist that spilled over the bed and caused the director to blink his eyes in disbelief.

"Shit," Suhne moaned, and reached with his right hand for the gun he'd dropped when he got shot. His pistol was right next to Bella's head. She was dead, motionless, a streak of blood thick as paint flowing from her mouth onto her left cheek.

Ritchie took his time aiming, squeezed and watched the man's other knee explode in misted spray, followed by that tortured whine that soothed Ritchie's soul. This man's pain was exactly what he needed to hear and see right now. There was no amount of agony he could impose as a sentence that would satisfy him.

Ritchie walked until he was standing over Suhne, who squirmed and gagged. The dildo still softly hummed in his ass.

"Looks like the monkey-brained boxer pulled a fast one on you."

"Let me …"

Ritchie dropped the butt of the Colt on the man's right cheek, heard a crunch like peanut-brittle giving way to a ballpeen hammer. Several teeth fell out and half the man's face was pulled into a permanent grin that exposed bloody gum tissue. A couple of teeth had impacted into the gums, sharp enamel stabbing into flesh after the gun unseated teeth and dislodged jawbone that now shifted unhinged.

"Help," Suhne said.

"Money," Ritchie said. "Jewels, then help. I'll call nine-one-one for you."

Suhne held up his trembling hands. He spoke with his newly-rearranged mouth and his tongue made a kind of watery farting sound as he tried to learn to express himself sans so many teeth. "Don't shoot. I'll show you."

"Show me." Ritchie grabbed him with his left hand and ignored his own agony. He knew not to look at Bella dead on the ground again, because if he did he would shoot Suhne before he got the money or jewels, or whatever it was he came here to get. If the guy had another gun hidden somewhere and this was his plan to get to it, Ritchie was going to smash each one of the knuckles in his hands individually and beat off to the screams coming from his mangled mouth.

"There." Suhne pointed across the hall, to a room filled with mirrors that had gold backings, with gold brocade curtains and even carpets fringed in what looked like gold tassels edging a threadbare, room-length oriental rug. It was a Georgian salon of some sort, stately enough to pass for the room where some treaty to end a world conflict could have been signed.

Ritchie let go of Suhne, who choked on his blood and lay on the floor on his back. The director tried to grab at the shredded openings where his kneecaps hung by threads like the skull crowns of cowboys who got scalped by Indians before the cavalry could arrive.

Ritchie kicked the guy's hands so he couldn't nurse his wounds. He stepped on the left hand until he heard another crunch, which made him feel a little bit better. He thought of dead Bella and leaned, stomped, listening to the screams that came as dependably from his kicks as purrs would have come from a correctly stroked cat.

"Where?" Ritchie said.

Suhne lifted his right hand to a framed photograph in the center of the room. This house had evidently been open to tours at one point, since there was a golden plaque screwed into place next to the black and white photograph on the wall of a white man in an Australian bush hat who was holding a wooden walking stick

The white man in the photo stood with several shirtless Asian women, whose breasts sagged and whose faces were hard from sun and work. The golden plaque said, "Ama pearl divers were known to hold their breath for two minutes and could dive to twenty-five meters in freezing water."

"Pearls?" Ritchie asked.

"No," Joey gasped and spit up a mouthful of blood on which a couple of teeth swam. "That's just the photo. Diamonds."

He fell backwards on the Oriental rug. Ritchie was confident enough that he'd maimed the kid into being too timid and crippled to try anything, so he turned his back on him without much worry. He pulled the photo from the wireframe on which it was mounted, and exposed a hidden cubbyhole in which a black satin pouch sat. The velvet bag was tied with a brocaded drawstring as long and intricately braided as a Chinese queue ponytail.

Suhne sputtered out his sentences now. "They're dead, so I can tell you. They smuggled Golconda diamonds out of India. They had someone mule them. The mule died from an infection. She caught something over there, so they didn't even have to give her a commission. They kept going back and they eventually got sick, too."

He laughed, surprising Ritchie as he gazed now into the fires of his own past. "My mom and dad were viewed as upright citizens, Chamber-of-Commerce types, self-made. They've got a wing in the Getty Museum named in their honor." He shook his head and laughed as the blood continued to leak out of him. "They were thieves and forgers. They changed karat designations on all kinds of jewelry, sold the shit and kept the good stuff for themselves."

Ritchie held a satchel-full of the kid's inheritance in his hand. He listened to the diamonds clatter together, making a sound like a snake's rattler. "How much is this worth?"

Suhne coughed, said, "Fifteen to twenty million. We could never afford to have the Golconda haul publicly appraised. It wasn't the kind of thing you could take to Christie's or Kahn's." He smiled that grotesque grin that pulled his face into the shape of a torn mask.

"There's more in the house. I'm worth much more than that." He glanced with the functioning side of his face at the sack. "Just call nine-one-one and leave. I'll write it off as a robbery."

Joey Suhne made it to his knees and Ritchie walked toward him. "Please," Suhne said. "I just gave you dirt on my family. I wouldn't risk besmirching my family's good name to take you down and have all of this became known in a trial." He looked around the confines of the Georgian salon. That grin returned to the portion of his face that wasn't paralyzed or shattered. "I can even get a good insurance haul out of all this."

Ritchie planted his foot in Suhne's chest and flipped him over onto his stomach. The dildo had slipped deep enough inside him now to look like a purple butt plug vibrating against his prostate.

"What are you doing?"

"Don't know yet," Ritchie said, "If I'm to be perfectly honest, I have to admit I'm thinking on the fly." He wanted to test himself, find out if there were limits to the sadistic abyss that this mansion put between him and the world. The house was big and the acreage around it was endless and heavily wooded. He knew he could do whatever he wanted and no one would know, or even find the decomposing body for quite some time. That excited him, which bothered him. He knew there was nothing left of Ritchie Abruzzi, that the sixteen mil or ten per from the fence wouldn't cover what he had done to himself nor what he had exposed that beautiful girl to. She'd been little more than a child. As for Suhne, the sack of shit before him …

He pressed the barrel of his gun to the covered plastic battery slot of the dildo vibrating in the man's body. Liquid feces leaked from Suhne's rear. Ritchie pushed and heard the man moan into the carpet.

"That feel good?"

The moaning continued. It was an animal noise of rage, a smidgen of humiliation, followed by an impotent wail. It was everything Ritchie needed and wanted to hear from the sniveler bleeding out on the carpet before him.

"Tell me," Suhne said, panting, turning his head to the side.

"Tell you what?"

"Was she in on it?"

Ritchie pulled back the hammer of the Python. On the one hand, he wanted to tell Suhne that Bella had played him, that she didn't even like to use her real name around him, that he was unworthy of her love. But he also wanted to preserve her memory, and her innocence. Why or for whom were questions that didn't interest him now. He was defending her character to someone who was about to be killed, so it shouldn't have mattered. But it did.

"No," Ritchie said. "She wasn't in on it. She was innocent. She did however smoke a couple of cigarettes in your car, and either me or Lee Keith took the blame. Her real name was Alecia Powell and she was stripping and shoving dildoes up your ass so she could get enough money to become a marine biologist. Fucked up world we live in, isn't it?"

Ritchie pressed the long nose of the revolver hard against the dildo in Joey Suhne's ass.

"Wait!"

Ritchie didn't wait. He pulled the trigger and the round broke through the plastic and latex of the dildo, shattering the batteries inside Suhne's colon and ripping his intestines like slickened suet as the round mushroomed and traveled through his body and charted a path out through the top of his head.

The gun leaked smoke from its barrel, and Ritchie held the heavy Colt over his head and shouted so that his voice carried through the mansion's empty halls. "The winner, and new champion of the world. Ritchie 'Redrum' Abruzzi!"

Chapter Twenty-Two: Fire in the Hills

The plan had been to lay hands on a few million and ride off into the sunset with his princess. Half the plan still had a chance of coming off, the rest of it was in the shitter. Ritchie closed Bella's brown eyes, pushed her hair back from her head, and kissed her on her still-warm scalp.

He rummaged through her purse. He found some spare batteries for the vibrator, the ten grand he'd given her, and the pewter-sheathed butane lighter shaped like a revolver. He took the money and the torch, and pocketed them. After that he fished through the Gucci knockoff purse, found the keys to the Honda, and walked out of the house the same way he came in.

The stars were visible this far from the city, winking from the purple canvas of the sky. Ritchie opened the side door on the Honda and grabbed up several of the blankets in his hands. He tried not to breathe too deeply, but still managed to catch a whiff of Bella. A vision flitted through his head, days of sugary sands turned blinding white by the sun in a summer without end. He saw them drinking expensive red wine in a seafood restaurant floating in the marina, or halving the blue waters into white foam as they cruised in his speedboat.

It just wasn't meant to be.

He studied the hand-loomed Navajo blankets in his arms. They were patterned with arrowhead shapes and little satyr-like fertility gods with gorgon hair coils, playing their flutes to make the wives of the warriors fruitful. He saw the blanket they had screwed on and moved it to the bottom of the pile.

He wrapped Bella's body first, creating a sort of massive papoose for her and then carrying her shrouded corpse down the hall until he saw the prairie pulpit from which Joey Suhne had descended to unveil the bold outlines for Zombie Boxer. It didn't look like that flick was getting produced anytime soon.

He left Bella's body in the wooden box jutting out from the balcony, and carried out the same process with Joey Suhne's corpse, although without the same reverence. Where Ritchie had shrouded her body, haloing it into a kind of pear-shaped mandorla, he slipped Suhne into the blankets like garbage that had to be hauled to the curb. Once both bodies were on the lift, he searched around until he found the toggle switch hidden on the woodwork of the raised wooden box.

The lift hummed and he waited until it touched the ground floor. He carefully cradled Bella' s body and set it down in front of the fireplace, and then flipped Suhne's body and kicked it a couple of times. For a moment, he considered spitting on Suhne or pissing on him, but knew that if he did that it would make Forensics' job easier if they recovered anything from the ashes.

He'd heard from someone that Jimmy Hoffa's body had been incinerated in a crematorium, but he wasn't sure if a bonfire could reach the same temperature as an incinerator. This friend of his had worked at a mob-associated funeral home, and while he'd listened with interest as he talked about disposing of inconvenient problems, he never thought the day would come when he would need to know the exact degree at which bone burned.

His phone vibrated in his pocket, next to where the lighter shaped like a gun sat. He looked at the face of his cellphone's lock screen. It was Don Perillo.

"Hey, Don."

"Just checking in with you, kid. You okay?"

"Yeah." Ritchie wandered into an untouched part of the house that had a ghostly chill to it. The walls were unpainted here. The rooms were mostly unfurnished, and the few chairs and tables were covered in white cloths that caused the wooden relics to assume the bulky dimensions of children dressed as ghosts.

"You still thinking of getting that stuff for me?" Don asked.

"Why?" Ritchie followed the light of a vintage Sputnik wall sconce, the only electric glow in this part of the house, toward a room where a pump organ with bodywork like a wooden Bavarian cuckoo clock sat. The thing was so beautiful that whoever had gone through the house covering things in white cloth had elected not to shroud it.

"I don't think you should pull something like that." Don paused to cough. "If you need money, just ask."

Ritchie opened the door to a walk-in closet filled with clothes on hangers and a wooden shelf above that. "It's too late," Ritchie said. "I did the thing we were talking about."

He pulled a suit from the closest at random, a charcoal bespoke piece that was a bit musty and mothballed, with shoulders a little too boxy for him. It looked and smelled like it had last been worn for some gala function or funeral three decades ago. He held it up against the bloody clothes he wore and tried to imagine it on his body. A highly-starched beige dress shirt and striped tie knotted in a wrinkled half-Windsor were tucked underneath the jacket, as if the entire ensemble had just been picked up from the drycleaner's. It would work.

"Ritchie," Don said. There was fear in his voice.

"No sweat," Ritchie said. "No one got hurt." He selected a pair of coffee-colored dress shoes from the shelf above the hanging clothes and dropped them onto the floor. Their soles slapped the hardwood with a thunderous clap.

"Was that a gunshot?" Don asked.

"New shoes," Ritchie said. "I'm buying a new wardrobe. I'm with a tailor around Santee in the Garment District. He's making sure I look my best when we meet."

"If you're getting fitted with a wire and I'm walking into some kind of sting …"

"Don't come to my house, then," Ritchie said, walking down the hall. He glanced in each of the many rooms lining the corridor, looking quickly into each like a doctor searching out a specific patient in the cells of a labyrinthine hospital. "I'll get rid of my box of chocolates abroad. Maybe I'll hit Golconda."

Don wheezed like he'd just made it up twelve flights of stairs. "Now I know it's a setup."

"Why?"

Ritchie finally found a bathroom, adjacent to a billiard room. "You forget," Don said. "I know a couple things about diamonds. I ain't got a yarmulke but I didn't just fall off the fucking turnip truck, either. And there ain't no way someone like you laid hands on something like that, not without bringing the wrath of God down on your head."

"My hands are clean," Ritchie said. He looked at the bloodstains on his palms that made it look like he'd been using berries to dye clothes.

"When and where you want to meet?"

"My place," Ritchie said, shimmying out of his jeans. "Noon. Bring your gem loop."

He hung up and set the phone down on the edge of a sink shining like a polished pearl. The room had glass walls and a skylight. It still felt private and it was protected by boughs heavy with peaches growing from a dense orchard on this side of the house. Ritchie took off the rest of his clothes and stepped into the walk-in shower, gripped the Umbria tiles with his toes, and turned on the water.

Hot nettles from the shower washed the blood away into pools where it collected at his feet and swirled down the drain. The glass of the shower's sliding door misted over with fog. He ignored the seaweed exfoliant and the pumice stone sitting in a golden wall-mounted tray, and cleaned himself with the hot drops that fell from the showerhead like rainwater.

Afterward, he turned off the taps and stepped out, air-drying as he grabbed his cell phone from the sink and everything he needed from his bloody discarded pants. He changed into his new, tightly-fitting suit, and then walked into the billiard room next door. A TV sprouted from one of the walls finished in mission white, and two well-worn and chalked cue sticks sat on the billiard table, next to a pile of white papers.

It was too late to blackmail Suhne, but he was curious to see what was written on the papers laid on the table. He laughed as he read. It was a pile of test screen cards for Sexy Zombie Sluts. Some of the cards were empty and others filled out with demographic info like age, sex, how often the viewer went to the movies, and so on. The "Extra Page for Additional Comments" was the funniest. Someone had scrawled in big letters, under the paragraph's worth of lined space: "NEEDS MORE BOOBS."

Ritchie picked up the two billiard cues, gripped them like a couple of wooden fasces broken loose from a bundle. He snapped them down into kindling and set them in a teepee shape on the table. He then shredded the stack of comment cards into tiny piles of white scrap paper and passed those underneath the wooden teepee he'd constructed.

Those years as a boy scout spent camping in the Catskills were paying off finally. He pulled out Bella's gun-shaped torch and pulled the trigger. Flame spurted onto the paper, which curled on itself in flashes of orange and yellow, licking at the wood and causing cinders to spit out. He could hear the wood crackling as he went back into the bathroom and studied the new him.

He glanced at himself in the mirror, tugged the lapels of the suit jacket, and turned around. He thought at best he looked like a mortician whose good suit was being mended.

His phone buzzed from texts that had come in that he'd missed. The first was from Alpo and stated simply, "Get at me." The second was from Lee Keith and was a question: "Have you seen Star or Suhne?" The last was a message from Matt. It said "Fuck you."

He put the phone away, walked down the hall back in the direction of the room where Bella's body lay bundled next to Joey Suhne's corpse. He leaned down to pull Bella toward the room where the flames had started their dance, and as he did so he saw the hull of the faux radioactive CAT scan machine that was supposed to explain his transformation from has-been fighter to zombie avenger.

If he didn't know what flame did to bone, he definitely didn't know what the growing rages of the fire would do to the carbon fiber shell covered in biohazard stickers. He hoped only that it would be reduced to ashes, or that if it remained, it at least lived out its half-life as some charred relic whose purpose was rendered inexplicable after the screen treatment for Zombie Boxer went up in flames. A lot of the mansion was rock, and would respond to flame like adobe clay in a kiln, but whatever was timber was getting eaten by fire, and whatever was glass was getting shattered by pressure.

Best case scenario was that by the time the cops and fire units got there, the place had collapsed on itself and looked like a miniature version of the Northridge Earthquake had struck the grounds of Case De Suhne and swallowed it away into some sinkhole, dragging it toward the earth's core.

He searched through the kitchen as the black smoke started to creep from the hallway, not sure now if the crackling sound was bone or wood popping. The keys to the various cars in the driveway were on a wooden pegboard next to a Casbah lantern fixed in the wall of the kitchen. The light was electric, but it cast a glow convincing enough to be wax burning a golden circuit down to the wick in some corner of a Marrakech trader's opium-hazed dream.

The fire must have eaten through electrical wiring a few seconds later, for, after a quick shower of sparks and another pop, everything in the mansion went dark. The only light left came from the risen moon.

Ritchie whistled Sinatra on his way to the Benz. He started the car, fondled the diamonds in their velvet pouch, and drove to the front gate of the house. A quick press of the little black box clipped to the sun visor opened the wrought-iron gate, and invited him to leave behind the memory and enjoy the glittering jeweled lights of L.A. The neon from the restaurants, shops, bars and strip clubs seemed to be in on the conspiracy with him, along with the stars, all of which shined and pulsed in a subtle strobing wink to let him know he was the new owner of the diamonds, at least for a while.

Ritchie drove to a Fatburger in the eleven-thousand block of Venice. He ordered a triple XL burger and devoured it. Grease from the burger seeped onto his fingers, and when he licked his digits, he wasn't sure if some human blood was mixed in there with the juice from the meat. Moreover, he didn't care.

A part of him expected the sobering red and blue lights to puncture the muted neons that turned Los Angeles into his midnight aquarium, but none of the squad cars rushing through the night were meant for him. He played it safe, however, and after scarfing down the most satisfying burger he'd had in his life he left the keys in the Benz in the parking lot, tuned the radio to a hip-hop station, and adjusted the volume until it was at full blast.

He had faith that the car would work as bait for a jacker, who would at least add their prints to his if they didn't chop down the car for parts and permanently erase the problem of the dead man's luxury auto. Suhne wouldn't be able to collect any insurance payout, but Ritchie had faith that wouldn't much trouble the director now.

The walk home was time alone he needed to get his head straight before meeting with Don. He walked on medians and concrete islands with his hands in the pockets of his new dress pants, his feet sore from the pinching sensation that came whenever one of his feet touched down and he could feel each of the cobbler's hobnails pounding into his arches.

His left hand still throbbed as if it were undergoing some inflammation that might cost him the arm, and Bella's sultry voice came to him in waves of uninvited and unwanted whispers. Her smell was on the wind on the walk home, and each time his hands clutched empty air he wished it was the soft ample contours of her bubble-shaped ass.

He'd always been an ass man, and though he was a lapsed Catholic, he hoped there was a God or some kind of afterlife, and that whatever Bella had coming it was better than a strip club. Maybe Heaven was even a giant ocean.

Ritchie wasn't too keen on extending his own pity party. He had twenty grand in his wallet, a pocketful of diamonds, and he was still a free man breathing in lungsful of cool night air.

Chapter Twenty-Three: Goodbye, Golconda

All the windows in the bungalow were open as he swept the house. The smell of rotted meat was nearly gone, replaced now by the scent of flowers blooming alongside the house and crawling over the cement walls surrounding the yard. Ritchie sneezed from the milkweed struggling to grow in between the twining strands of white morning glory and yellow primrose shining in the sun.

He was still in his shirt and tie from last night, but had stripped down to boxers and black socks at some point. A knock came at the door while he was sweeping. He pulled the door open and saw Don Perillo standing there in a burnt orange thermal running suit.

"You trying to lose weight?" Ritchie held the door open for his old promoter and set the willow broom down.

"You know me," Don said, his hands in his pockets. "I'm always trying to shed those last one-hundred and fifty pounds." His old trainer pointed a finger at him, stubby as the remnants of a smoked Cuban. "And you're trying to give me a myocardial infarction with this shit." He shook his head, and replaced his hand in the right pocket of his sweat suit after pointing at Ritchie.

"How the hell can you accuse me of trying to give you something I can't even pronounce?"

"It's a fancy way of saying 'heart attack,'" Don said.

"I figured as much." Ritchie went into the kitchen, grabbed up the diamonds, and handed the black velvet sack to Don.

"Polpette," Don said, gasping. He walked the diamonds to the counter, moving like he had a hot dish in his hands.

"What?" Ritchie followed him.

"Meatballs," Don said. He pulled what looked like a small black pistol from his pocket, and Ritchie braced for the gunshot. It didn't come. The old man took the gun-looking thing and set it on the counter next to the diamonds. He then reached into one of the many zippered pouches of his suit and pulled out a small tray with little steel divots in it. He looked over his shoulder at Ritchie and the gesture turned his waddle of fat into a shelf of several chins. "You didn't tell me these mothers weren't in settings, but I came prepared anyway."

Ritchie stood behind Don and didn't say anything. Don took one of the diamonds at random and settled it in the tray. He pointed the gun-shaped tool at the diamond, and light refracted through it. "Not too bright or clear."

"Is that good?" Ritchie asked.

"It's no fugace, that's for sure." He took his finger off the trigger of the tester tool, and set it on the counter. He turned around.

"So, they're not cubic zirconia?"

"Nah." The old man wagged his head from side to side and Ritchie thought he still might have a heart attack, although more from joy than shock or stress. Don licked his upper lip and said, "Level with me. I don't want to know where you got them or how you got them." He paused. "But how hot are they?"

"En fuego," Ritchie said. He couldn't keep up with Don's Italian but he could match it with his smattering of Spanish. "But I'll tell you what." He pointed at the shiny pile of stones behind Don. "They're worth at least ten million, which means my end should be a million flat. I just want a hundred grand, today, and then I'll give you the keys to this place and let you sell her out to whoever you want."

"I definitely ain't selling it to Delgado, like I maybe planned to do."

"Who?" Ritchie's brow furrowed.

"Kid of mine up for a title shot that would have netted us a few mil next month," Don said. "I had him in one of my rental properties, went by unexpected and saw needles and bloody cotton balls all over the place."

"Heroin?"

Don shook his head. "He's juicing, steroids, y'know? He was a bolo on his last VADA test but he said he got a false positive from eating beef when he was in TJ."

"You bought that?"

Don shrugged. "We all did. They use different hormones for their beef down there in Mexico. Anything's possible." He glanced once at the diamonds behind him. "All right, I got a quarter-mil in the Jew canoe out there." Don pointed the hand on which he wore his Rolex toward the Lincoln Town Car at the curb. "I was planning on giving you that as down payment, and giving you the other seven-fifty this week."

"I don't want it," Ritchie said. "I want a hundred grand, and instead of the other nine-hundred, I want something else."

"Name it," Don said.

"I want in on whatever kind of nest egg you got ready for your retirement. In a couple of years, I'll be old enough for my first prostate exam. I want to invest. I want to collect rents. Let someone else worry about how they're going to make their nut every month."

"Done," Don said, and walked toward the front of the bungalow. "Wait here one minute. I'm going to hook you up good."

Ritchie nodded, stood in the kitchen, and thought that now it was his turn to wait it out. He'd seen the SWAT in action in Oakwood several times, and if Don was setting him up, they would rappel in and do an extraction with their shields and tear gas before he could even manage to cuss the old snake out.

He sweated for a couple of minutes, wishing he hadn't left his piece in the director's mansion, wondering if the fire had smelted the Colt Python down to a pile of melted iron. He hadn't heard a word about either the Benz or a massacre at the millionaire's house, but he hadn't had the balls to check the news, either.

"Okay," Don said. "You want to be a silent partner, I'll let you in on the ground floor." The old man threw some papers on the linoleum counter. One piece was a folded pamphlet for a wholesale foundation supplier back east, with an Egg Harbor address in New Jersey, and the other sheet was some kind of blueprint schematic for a house.

"What's this?" Ritchie asked.

Don went from left to right, pointing with his stubby finger. "My boys there make concrete slabs like Van Camp's makes pork 'n beans." Don shifted his attention to the other piece of paper. "They're going to supply me with cut-rate concrete and I'm going to get this architect and his developer friend to build some of these domino houses."

"What's that?"

Don's right hand shot out and pinched Ritchie's right cheek, reducing him to a teenager in his benefactor's arms again. "You ain't got no culture, no class. It's a Le Corbusier design for open floor plan houses. It's 'minimalist.' That means we don't have to do much work or waste too much reinforced concrete, but the artsy fartsy types will pay top dollar. Less is always less for you and me, but less is more to them. It works out to the mutual satisfaction of all parties involved." Don gave another one of his patented what-are-you-gonna-do shrugs.

"How many of these you planning on building?"

"That all depended on how well you played high-low today. I was going to talk you down from one-point six mil on the haul to a flat mil."

"And now that I'm only asking for a hundred large?"

"Your lack of greed probably means that, with a little patience, you'll make out better than you would if you would have if you'd played hardball for the short money.

You didn't kill the goose so you should get a little golden egg whenever she lays." Don took up the pamphlet and the blueprints, put them in the main pocket of his windbreaker suit. "I ain't got much more time left on this Earth, but I figure with a development of ten to fifteen units, we can be making money clean and free in two, three years tops." He winked at Ritchie. "I already got the tract picked out."

"What's my end?"

Don clucked his tongue, had to think about it. "I was thinking twenty-five percent of rentals and sales, whichever way we decide to go, and in return I set you up with a UBS bank account in Basel so you don't have to worry about getting pinched when you get your monthly ducats. I'll cover the laundry surcharge out of my end. Don't ask me any questions about how I clean the money, and I won't get curious about these diamonds."

"Basel?" Ritchie frowned. "That in Italy?"

"It's in Switzerland, you fucking momo."

Ritchie held up his hands. "Just asking, fucking sue me."

Don dug a Nordstrom cowhide money clip from his pocket, bulging with creamy stacks of hundreds. "You might think of going there if you got a passport still."

"I still got the one I used when I was boxing."

"No way that's still up-to-date." Don shook his head. "Get your passport renewed and check out Switzerland if you can."

"What's there?" Ritchie asked. "I mean, aside from banks?"

"Not American cops, or feds for one. I haven't talked with my shyster for a while but they might find it hard to extradite you if you're leaving behind a trail of bodies here."

"Just a couple bodies," Ritchie said, smiling and hoping the reverse psychology worked. It didn't. Don didn't even smile.

The ancient Italian man's voice was barely audible. "Pop smoke, Ritchie. Get the fuck out of Dodge and stay gone." He handed over the money.

"I'm ghosting," Ritchie said. He walked toward the diamonds and the testing unit and handed both over to Don, who concealed them in the endless silken folds and billows of his suit. "Just one other thing."

"What?" Don asked.

"What are you going to call this place? All these Domino houses? You can't call it Domino's. They've already got a pizza franchise."

"Wise guy," Don muttered, thinking about it. "How about we name it after a boxer?"

"How about 'Abruzzi Heights'?" Ritchie waved his hands, picturing it as if he were Bugsy Siegel dreaming big of that little desert trap Vegas and what it might one day become, after the Flamingo planted its flag.

"You fucking retarded, kid? A silent partner ain't supposed to put his name on the sign in front of the business."

Ritchie shook his head. "Not Ritchie 'Redrum' Abruzzi. It's for Bam-Bam. My father."

Don's look softened. "You got it." He raised his hand as if there was a highball glass clutched there with which he could toast a Salud. Ritchie patted him on the shoulder and opened the door for him.

"Vaya con dios."

"I always do," Don said, which was true in a way. Where Ritchie had his little Golden Gloves trinket dangling from a beaded chain on the Crown Vic's rearview, Don kept a rosary he'd gotten from the gift shop in Vatican City on one of his trips to the mother country. Ritchie wondered why the bank account couldn't be in Florence or Milan. He asked himself again what the hell was in Switzerland, anyway, aside from those girls with the blonde pigtails, some mountains, and good chocolate. He wouldn't fit in there any better than he had here.

Don got into his champagne-colored sedan, stabbing a finger through the rolled-down car window at Ritchie one more time before leaving. "Put some fucking pants on, kid. Venice ain't as laidback as it used to be."

"Don't I know it."

The horn of the Lincoln honked once and Don was gone. Ritchie had a feeling he'd never see the old man again. Either age would get Don or the cops would get Ritchie before too long. A cruiser slowly drove by, and though its lights were off and it wasn't on the hunt, he took it as a sign and walked back in the house, heading down into the spider web. The space now only reminded him of his son.

"Don't let the kid be a boxer," he said to God, but he wasn't sure if the man upstairs had any interest in fielding his petitions.

The safe was waiting for him in the corner, near the exposed rock wall on the far side of the room. He leaned down to it, hit the combo, and opened the face. He took out the rest of the sweaty stacks of cash inside, as well as his old NABF belt to hold as a keepsake.

He felt the green body of the belt, which had started to crack and wear a bit, and he wondered if the leather itself was fake. There was a slight chemical smell to the belt, as if it were treated pleather.

He bet the cheap pricks at the commission skimped on that, too. All those sanctioning fees went to line their pockets and make sure they kept those cushy sinecures forever. Boxing judges and officials made union no-show gigs look like honest labor. The alleged gold plates on the bauble looked and felt to be made of the same enamel as the button-shaped flags of the USA, Canada, and Mexico that had been lain into the belt. The luster of the three flags and of the gold itself was gone, the polish no longer glinting in the light as he held up the belt and studied it. He kept the cash in his hands, both that in the money clip and the rubber-banded dough. It all added up to a bit more than one-hundred and fifty large.

He settled the belt around his waist, above his exposed boxer shorts and over the dress shirt he'd snatched from the walk-in closet at Suhne's mansion in the hills. Yesterday he'd felt like a challenger who'd gone into another fighter's hometown and beat him convincingly in his backyard. The dulcet sound of Michael Buffer's voice in his head had announced, "The winner and new champion, Ritchie 'Redrum' Abruzzi!"

That same voice was still there now, only its tune had changed and was backed by the plangent ringing of the timekeeper hitting his gong. The new voice said, "The winner and still champion …"

No one stayed undefeated forever and he didn't want to tempt fate further. He ran up the stairs of the basement with the belt cinched around his waist like the buckle piece of the orneriest Texan in the world. He spread everything out on the ground in the living room before him and got ready to get cleaned up and dressed for his final day as a Californian.

He meant to take Don's advice, but there were still also a couple more things to take care of before he headed back East, away from the sun and surf and the many betrayals of the golden coast that had turned out to be a pyrite sham.

Chapter Twenty-Four: Globetrotting Again

It was only right to stop by the old poet's Globetrotter and wish him well before leaving town. Ritchie knocked with his right hand, his left now so swollen and painful that it felt like a bowling ball had been permanently affixed in his grip.

"Good day," Lawrence Kramb said, holding the door open for his guest. Mr. Kramb let the door go after Ritchie was in. He then continued stroking his beard with Amish balm while studying his reflection in a piece of glass small even by prison tier standards. "How goes it?"

"Think I need to get in touch with that kid of Don's who's juicing," Ritchie said.

"What?" Lawrence Kramb had primped his Van Dyke until he looked like Czar Nicholas II.

"Nothing," Ritchie lifted his left arm. "Thank you for taking me to the hospital."

"No need to mention it. How is the arm?"

Ritchie walked over to the tartan plaid couch and sagged into its well-worn cushions. "I need some Piroxicam, something maybe veterinary-strength." He knew Alpo had contacts in the dogfighting game who had backdoor channels for animal dope. That was an option. If he didn't do something soon, gangrene would set it.

"I used to make the odd jaunt over the border to get things for my friends from the Peaceful Pill group. Phenobarbital could be had over-the-counter if you ducked into the right shop."

"What's Peaceful Pill?" Ritchie set his left arm on the couch's armrest.

"It's the inheritor to the Hemlock Society's mantle. They believe that for those who are in palliative care and suffering, with little or no chance of recovery, death with dignity should remain an option."

"I know a couple fighters who checked out early." He shrugged. "Can't say I blame them."

The poet stopped combing his beard. He stood and walked into the kitchen. "I saw you loading up your car. Are you leaving?"

"I'm gone," Ritchie said. "For good."

"I'm sorry to hear that," Lawrence said. He shook his head as he returned to the room with a salvaged antique of some kind in his hands. "You brought a bit of character to Oakwood, adding a dash of spice to our collective Californian goulash."

"The City of Dreams isn't for me." He dug a rubber-banded stack of ten-thousand dollars from his pocket, and reached toward Lawrence, whose eyes bugged.

"How much is that?" His face puckered up in surprise, and grew a bit jowly around the edges of the beard, giving him a latter-day Orson Welles look.

"Ten large," Ritchie said. He realized he wasn't speaking with Don and adjusted code. "Ten thousand dollars. Five is for you, for all the trouble you've taken to make sure things stay quiet here around Oakwood, in your unofficial capacity as captain of neighborhood watch."

"That's a bit exorbitant," Lawrence said, pausing with his hand just shy of gripping the money.

"No, it's not." Ritchie shook his head. "The other five is for if you see my kid, Matty. Make sure to help him out. I don't want him trying to earn money in the streets out here."

"I have seen him." Lawrence lifted the object on his lap, an old radio with an ivory case. There was a small cardboard card that was vaguely familiar to Ritchie jutting from the vintage thing's vacuum tubing.

"Where?" Ritchie sat up. "When?" He wanted to be pissed with Kramb for not letting him know, but the old man was a luddite who only used payphones in absolute emergencies and wouldn't buy a cellphone even if it was required by federal law.

"He came by last night for a little while. He said he's going back home, to his mother in New York."

Ritchie made a mental note to avoid upstate if he drove back East. He didn't want to bother his son, or run into Anna ever again. He didn't even want word getting out that he was home. L.A. had beaten him but he wanted people to think the fight had come off a draw.

"Keep the other five large," Ritchie said, wincing as he cursed himself as an uncouth guinea for the second time. "Five thousand, I mean."

"I will give it to the Socialist Poets' Collective."

"Good idea," Ritchie said, and, at the risk of sounding dumb, he asked, "I thought you guys were against money?"

Kramb shook his head, pocketed the money, and held up his hand. This talk galvanized him more than the ten-thousand dollars. Ritchie wished more people were so cavalier about material goods. "Communism died with Trotsky."

"Yeah, he got an icepick in the back of the neck or something like that, right?" That kind of thing Ritchie understood.

"Exactly. Both Lenin and Stalin recognized that for world-revolution to succeed, acquiescence had to be made to certain features of the capitalist system."

"Such as?"

"Concessions had to be granted to industrialists, for instance. Henry Ford, the supposed beau ideal of capitalist enterprise recognized this sine qua non as well as the Russians."

"That's a lot of Greek to me."

"Latin," Lawrence said, wincing a bit from his friend's ignorance. "Ford recognized, due to the virtual annihilation of draft animals during the Great War, that his Fordson machine could prove essential to the agricultural-"

The radio rescued Ritchie. It crackled to life, some sort of signal carrying through the copper wire used as a makeshift antenna on the apparatus. "Where'd you get that?" Ritchie asked.

"From the same resourceful fellow who provided you with that massive tire for your backyard."

Lawrence proudly stroked the ivory case of the old GE appliance. Ritchie would have offered him money for it, but the man already seemed attached to his salvaged toy.

"Does it work?"

"Yes, although I try to ignore the local news and listen only to classical music on it."

Ritchie tried to make his next question sound offhand. "Anything interesting going on in the news?"

A despondent look washed over Lawrence. "Depends how you define 'interesting,' I suppose." He fondled the cardboard wedge that was nestled in between the ribs of the radio's face like a baseball card stuck in the spokes of a bicycle. "A young Hispanic male was shot and killed near Venice High School. Suspect is an African-American teenager." Kramb stroked the radio. "I shan't kill the messenger."

"What model is that?"

"It's a Musophonic, rebuilt. I much prefer the solid states, but I pick from the shore whatever the tide washes up."

"Musophobic?"

"No," Lawrence said, patience tried twice thus far today. "That is fear of mice. Musophonic."

Kramb turned the thing on. A reporter spoke. "Firefighters think they have finally contained a blaze over twenty acres in scope, believed to have been started by an electrical wire malfunction in the filmmaker's Holmby

Hacienda. A water-dispatching helicopter in tandem with over one-hundred first-responders ..."

Ritchie was grateful when the old man turned the radio off. "I guess even the rich get it sometimes in LA," he said absently, hoping that Kramb couldn't parse his words for any trace of personal involvement in the news item.

"Indeed," Kramb said.

The air was thick, awkward with a pressing silence that Ritchie couldn't stand for much longer. He latched onto the card stuck in the face of the radio. "Do you mind if I look at that?"

Kramb slapped the sides of the radio loud enough to send a hollow thud through the body of the thing. "That's why I brought this over here." He pulled the card free from its place and handed it to Ritchie.

His stomach swam with a bundle of emotions interwoven too tightly to be called happiness or sadness, just some joining of whatever essence made childhood what it was. The cardboard edges of the Kellogg's card were frayed. On the front of the card was a boxer, a pale white man in a tiger crouch with pomaded hair and glinting eyes that would have been colorless even if the photo hadn't been black and white.

"The Man of Steel," Ritchie said. "Tony Zale." He flipped the card over. "My dad got one of these out of a cornflakes box and then he started boxing. He never stopped collecting them either." Ritchie held the thing precariously in his right hand. He didn't know much about the secondary market for the cards, but he thought the thing should have been sleeved in Mylar.

The back of the card said, "Won the title from Al Hostak and Georgie Abrams in 1942. Named 'Fighter of the Year' in 1946 after knocking out Rocky Graziano." He handed the card back to Kramb, not wanting to smudge it further with his greasy fingerprints. "My pops had a bunch of those."

The old poet took the card and stuck it back in its secured place on the face of the radio. "Your son gave it to me. He said he got it from your father when he went to visit him."

What felt like the first real smile he'd shown in a decade slipped across Ritchie's face. He couldn't control it.

It was infectious and Lawrence Kramb smiled, happy in the presence of another's happiness. "What?"

"The old man lost those cards and a bunch of memorabilia years ago to some thief of a promoter. The boxing game's crawling with them." That wiped the smile from Ritchie's face, but at least it had been there for a moment, however fleeting.

"It looks like he reclaimed at least some of his lost booty, and perhaps this is how Matthew wanted to convey that message to you, through the card he gave to me."

Ritchie nodded solemnly. It looked like maybe Denise had gotten a good attorney, or just fired off a letter or email to Bam-Bam's old promoter that had put the fear of god into the shyster. In any event, Ritchie still intended to set up direct-deposit monthly wire transfers from his UBS account to Denise. That way the original Abruzzi patriarch could live out his last days in peace, comfort, and, rarest of all for an ex-pug, dignity.

Tony Zale's eyes in that card followed Ritchie's gaze. The "Man of Steel" had gotten his handle from working in a foundry in Gary, Indiana. A young kid like Matt could bullshit himself about boxing and life, because he'd been hiding between Anna's legs these last sixteen years or so, narcotized by Ritalin and the internet and whatever other gadgets the kids kept themselves preoccupied with. It was much harder to bullshit a man about the nature of the beast when he worked at a steel foundry in Gary, Indiana.

"He got hosed," Ritchie said, voicing his thoughts now. He had no choice, releasing the words as if the pressure of thinking them without speaking was killing him. It felt like a trephination of sorts, a hole he'd drilled in his head to let the thoughts out and let them enter Mr. Kramb.

"How do you mean?" the poet asked. He didn't know if they were talking about the man gracing the Kellogg's baseball card, Ritchie's father, or his son.

"Zale beat Graziano two out of three, the first one and then their rubber match, but Graziano got all the glory, the TV shows, he got to schmooze with the Rat Pack." Ritchie realized he never would have broached this subject with his father, that he'd kept his secret bitterness over the way the lily-white guy was robbed by fate to himself, because his father wouldn't brook the idea that an Italian getting anything, no matter how he got it, was unfair. Graziano deserved all the glory because he was Italian. It was tribal, grease-ball bullshit, humanity's way.

"Why do you think Zale never got his due?"

"Because our species is fucking lousy," Ritchie said. "Graziano was cocky and he had a big mouth, and Zale had dignity. The fans don't like dignity. The promoters don't like it. The journalists don't like it. Dignity makes them uncomfortable because they don't have any."

Kramb cocked his head as if listening to birdsong, replaying the tenor of Ritchie's words in his head to see if they struck a true chord. They passed muster with the poet, who stood with his radio and said, "You know, you may not be the most eloquent man I've ever known, but in your way, you are wise."

Ritchie sloughed off the compliment like a punch that came up short. "Wisdom's nothing but knowledge you can't use, or even explain. People got to get wise for themselves. I hope Matt makes it." He felt he'd taken up enough of the beatnik's time, and stood.

"Happy trails, my friend."

"You too," Ritchie said.

He stepped out of the trailer and saw a homeless man in an unseasonably warm burglar black skullcap peering in through the passenger-side window at the seat of the parked Crown Vic. The big money was in the trunk, in a Samsonite case that had a combo lock on it, but Ritchie wasn't in the mood for games.

"Hey, motherfucker!" Ritchie walked toward him, kept his arms loose at his sides. Using the left was out of the question, but if the guy didn't step off he might catch an errant chicken wing elbow, a right-armed strike to the nose that might teach him the value of private property.

"I'm just admiring the belt," the man said. His teeth were soft and conical, like candy corn, causing him to slur his speech whether he was drunk or not. "They gonna give me a belt here in a week or two. They're having it made for me in Orange County."

This sounded like the schizoid talk of a refugee from the Reagan administration's mass-release, America's own Marielito mess, only this time on the West Coast rather than in Florida. "What are you talking about?" Ritchie asked.

"Look up Brutal Bums online, man. I fight other homeless dudes for some white cat who lives in Orange County. He films it, gives the winner a hundred bucks, some canned heat to drink, and a blowjob from this chick he brings down from Skid Row." The man lowered his voice, and leaned in to whisper, but the strength of his fetid breath was too much for Ritchie to join in whatever conspiracy he was inviting him into. Nevertheless, he listened. "Keep this shit quiet as kept, but I used to be nice with my hands."

The luster of the man's eyes was faded by drink, dope, and time, and his skin was burnished to a ruddy clay mask, but he summoned up some fiery gaze deep from his forgotten past, dredging it all up just long enough to make eye contact with Ritchie, and force him to remember.

"Oh, shit," Ritchie said.

"You remember now," the bum said.

"I saw you fight back in the day."

"I flatlined Greg Haugen's ass in a gym war a month a Sundays ago. He'll lie about the shit, but it's on a tape that's floating around. I gave Mark Breland a run for his money, too." The homeless man shook his head, and now that his credentials were no longer in question, he seemed calmer, more rational. Ritchie doubted he was crazy. LA and boxing were crazy, and he had responded to their insanity by doing what any rational man with a heart would do, by trying to destroy himself.

"I wish I'd captured that Olympic gold like him," the man said. "I could have pawned that medal for a grip."

Ritchie reached in his right pocket and sanded off a c-note, snaked it to the man. "Here."

"Fucking A!" The man smiled with his mouth of mangled teeth and his eyes closed in bliss. "Jesus is gonna remember this shit when he comes back. Best believe that."

"Let's hope," Ritchie said, walking around his car and getting in on the driver's side. "I got to do something to tip the balance in my favor." He thanked God he was Catholic. Without the allowance of indulgences, he would have been screwed. He'd have no chance if the predestination types were right. He'd seen the way kingmaking worked with selecting who got title shots and rankings, and he knew his chances for being one of the elect were slim to none, and, as Don King once said, Slim was out of town.

He started the car and his cellphone rang. He looked at the face of the phone. It was Alpo. "Talk to me," Ritchie said.

"What's good?"

"Everything," Ritchie said. He drove the speed limit, breathed deeply, and made sure not to California roll at stop signs. No way was he going to go down on a minor technicality.

"You feel like doing a pickup?"

"Nah," Ritchie said, turning left. He looked askance at the radio, frustrated to hear that some Bennett had worked its way onto his burnt CD of Sinatra standards. Not that he didn't like Tony.

"Mad scrilla for you, guap galore, carnalito."

"My man, you can come up with as many names for cash as you want, but I'm set."

"You hit some kind of lick? Armored cars?" Alpo tittered that weirdly feminine laugh of his that was at odds with his nature as a killer.

"Nothing so dramatic," Ritchie said, thinking on his feet as he drove. "I ain't Kreskin with his magic ball, but I got lucky at the track."

"Oh, word? I ain't been to the OTB in a hot minute."

"Trifecta, on Fat Chance, Mighty Atom, and Blood in Your Eye. I'm going North to celebrate." He was heading East, but it wasn't any of Alpo's business.

"Listen," Alpo said. His voice was usually traced with humor, but it now dropped into the dead zone, flat and affectless. "This kid wants it with you bad, money or no. He says he knows you."

Ritchie's blood chilled. "Knows me," he said, so weak with dread that he could only manage the two words.

"Says he needs to thump with you. Says that if you don't fight him, he's going to body you." Alpo was whispering now, leveling with him. "He says he's had you staked out for a while."

Ritchie thought he had a good idea who Alpo had with him now. He listened while the shot-caller laid it all out. "Kid gave me fifty-thousand Euros just to call you. He had an interpreter break the shit down for me. He doesn't hable Ingles. But his man said he ain't gonna give you no reprieve until you knuckle-up …Or knuckle under."

This was it. Pride, stupid, animal pride had him ready to throw away the favor and luck he'd garnered over the last few days. He'd walked through fire, literally, and just as literally stepped over bodies, and now it looked like he was going to be last man standing. But he had balls and they wouldn't let him be, or think, or live. As much as he hated the Suhne kid, he was right. Ritchie was a zombie and a monkey and nothing could change that. He would rather punch a man for a few minutes than spend an eternity in paradise.

"I don't even know how much a Euro's worth. I can tell you about pesos all day."

"It's worth more than a dollar," Ritchie said. "Even I know that."

"Anyway, I'll chop up the purse and give you your bit afterwards. You hit Tom Bradley Terminal at LAX and they'll change that shit to American greenbacks for you."

"I don't want your money," Ritchie said, although he thought he might hit the terminal to trade dollars for Swiss francs at some point.

"So you don't want the fight?" Alpo asked. He didn't understand fighting for free, unless it was to avenge wounded pride, against maybe a friend who'd fucked his girl, or a girlfriend who aborted one of his babies without telling him.

"Yeah, I want the fight," Ritchie said. "For free."

"My man," Alpo said, out of stony-serious mode and snickering again like a hairdresser soaking up gossip. "You want the address?"

"Give it to me," Ritchie said, and as he listened to Alpo speak, he cradled the phone between shoulder and jawbone and started to undo the brace around his purplish left arm. He heard Stitch's croak in his head, as the old-timer adjusted his leather Kangol driver's cap and told him it was time to do the do one last time.

Chapter Twenty-Five: Bodysnatching Season

His last fight was in the flood plain region of LA, in a section of Elysian old enough to still be called Frogtown. Bits of the area's edges had been gentrified, but in the part where Ritchie drove now it looked like gangbangers still outnumbered graphic designers ten-to-one.

He could make out some of the tags, like a neon blockbuster done in glowing bubble letters that announced "RASCALS." There was a burner tag above that which he couldn't read, but the disrespectful scrawl over the hieroglyphs let him know his fight with the Kroekel kid might not be the only war going on around here.

"Mira! Aqui!"

Ritchie heard Alpo shouting to him from his left, and he turned beyond the graffiti-scorched ramparts, driving up the hill toward where an SUV was parked. He stopped the Crown Vic at the crest of the hill, near where several cement blocks the size of boulders stood, giving the overlook the feel of a South LA Stonehenge.

"What's up?" Alpo asked. He wore a white t-shirt and what Ritchie thought at first were suspenders, but closer inspection revealed to be a leather harness with two holsters for twin Ruger handguns.

"Hey," Ritchie said. He carried the NABF trophy with him, although now he slung it over his shoulder rather than wearing it as a belt. He wasn't sure what he was trying to prove by walking around with the thing, but Alpo seemed amused.

"Yo, Dontae!"

Alpo's friend stepped out of the SUV. Dontae was a stocky black man with glaring eyes and a long beard that made him look like a black version of Rasputin. He wore a designer t-shirt with a purple background whose centerpiece was a tiger embossed in some baroque metal fiber, maybe Lamé. Ritchie mused for a second on the eerie convergence between the fashion choices between young black men and old Jewish women. He thought of telling the guy that if he liked Versace, he might want to think of raiding Don's wife's closet.

"Let me peep that right quick." Dontae held out his hand for the belt. Ritchie threw it to him. It landed in the dust and grass at his feet "Keep it."

"Oh, word?" The man picked the belt up and slung it over his shoulder, leaned against his Navigator. The car's sparkling apple clear coat shone in the sun, although at least the gullwing doors kept Dontae half in the shade.

Ritchie took his shirt off and set it on the hood of the Interceptor behind him. He did some neck rolls.

"You good to thump?" Alpo asked. He was wearing his sunglasses but Ritchie could feel the man's scrutiny on his left arm.

"I'm good to go." He knew guys who fought rounds with broken jaws. He could endure a few minutes in the squared circle with the Russian kid, who now shed his own shirt. He was compact where Ritchie was sinewy, and when he took up his boxing stance it only made him smaller. His back hunched until it was a veritable shell of muscle and bone.

Ritchie didn't bother trying to explain anything about that night in Pyatigorsk. He knew a "sorry" didn't mean shit to the man's son.

It felt strangely good to see someone who looked like the man he'd killed, to lay eyes on someone with the same genes as the boxer who appeared in his twice-weekly nightmares. The main difference was that Konstantin's eyes were lighter than his father's, with less of a wolfish quality. He also wore his hair in a stylish Cossack forelock that might allow him to blend with the Abbot-Kinney crowd in Venice if he wasn't also pure ripped muscle. He had the weirdly feminine lips contrasted with hard features that marked a lot of Slavic men, giving him a look that was both sensual and violent rather than just purely hard. His cheekbones were so high that if he squinted they would have touched his eyebrows and thrown his eyes entirely into shadow.

Konstantin started his stretches, and Alpo glanced at his watch studded in diamond bezels. "Y'all got three more minutes to stretch." He held down his thumb with his pinky and shot the kid his three fingers. The slightest nod came from Kroekel.

"Damn, kid …"

Ritchie heard rustling from his side and glanced at Alpo counting his wad of purple and pink cash Konstantin had used to bribe his way into the fight game. "Shit don't even look real." He fanned the money and held the Euros out to the light, exposing the watermarks and holographs to the light. Sunrays pierced the bridges and stars patterned on the bills.

"It's real," Dontae said, from inside of the SUV. He was working on getting the subwoofer synced to the neon tubes on the ride. "Your monkey ass just ain't ever been overseas." He fidgeted with something on the dash and each time the bass hit now the purple lights flashed. The booms bled into each other and formed a constant Ohm sound that mellowed Ritchie even though the rapper was just mumbling a recipe for purple drank. From what he could tell the mixture required some codeine-based prescription cough syrup, Sprite, and Skittles. The emcee didn't specify in which measure. It didn't sound like something Ritchie was likely to try, so he didn't listen too closely.

"Did I tell you my daughter won that contest?" Alpo asked.

"Nope," Ritchie said. "Congratulations, though." He and Kroekel couldn't take their eyes off each other.

"Yep, the city's gonna build my baby's bridge." He stood up off the rock he was on, slapped the concrete boulder. "She's smarter than her old man. She showed me this spot on her little 'Hidden L.A.' tour."

"The fuck is this place, anyway?" Dontae asked.

Alpo drew a flat hand across his throat, the signal to kill the music. Dontae turned down the stereo, and Alpo said, "It was part of the Red Car line way back in the day." He glanced at his watch. "Y'all ready?" He pointed the same flat karate chop hand at Kroekel, who nodded. Then he looked at Ritchie.

"Yeah."

"All right, protect yourselves at all times. Come out swinging at the bell."

Dontae hit the car horn and the men started circling each other, Ritchie drifting left with his right hand up, and the kid moving right.

The two spectators shouted and the two fighters moved toward each other in a magnetic orbit. The pace at which they approached each other was slow but had something inevitable about it. Kroekel threw first, double-jabbing. His guard was high and tight, hands to his chin like an Olympian who'd soaked up his fundamentals from an amateur coach and never abandoned them.

Ritchie threw a decoy left hook to the head to bring the kid's hands out, and when Kroekel reflexively defended himself with the earmuffs, Ritchie threw a straight right that skidded from the kid's mouth to nose to forehead, stopping at each layer of his face like a skipping stone touching down multiple times on the surface of the water.

The kid pulled back and covered his escape with a flurry of shots, but then out of nowhere doubled the work-rate and came forward, bringing Ritchie right into his work-rate like a buzz saw. Ritchie dropped both elbows to cover his body. It worked on the right but before he could throw a counter Kroekel's hand landed solidly against his left arm. Ritchie heard a woman's scream leave his lungs, and the kid might as well have had a knife in his right hand for all the pain his punches caused.

"Cat's out of the bag," Dontae said.

"Bird's working with a broken wing," Alpo said.

Ritchie hid his left arm behind his back as if getting ready to cuff up for the cops. He figured Konstantin would circle left to target the broken arm, and so he moved left first. They plowed into each other, Ritchie wrapping his right hand around the kid's waist and continuing to hide the left behind his back. His assumption was that Kroekel would continue to punch the left arm in the clinch, but instead he started delivering rabbit punches, trying to pound Ritchie's occipital lobe with his knuckles as if the bone were a soft pimple he could make explode into pus. It became clear to Ritchie then what the kid was trying to do. He wasn't trying to fight Ritchie, or hurt him, or tweak his sore and crippled arm to make him suffer. The son of Vasily Kroekel was trying to kill him.

"Hey, hey," Alpo said, clearly enjoying the power high that came with officiating. He pushed the men apart and stood in front of Kroekel. He tapped the back of his own head, the universal gesture employed when a ref and fighter didn't speak the same language to stop with the blows to the back of the head. "Knock that shit off."

Kroekel bowed a bit to Alpo, breaking at the waist to give a little respect. The fighters moved toward each other again. Ritchie threw a short right straight and hooked off it for the kid's chin. Kroekel moved back with the footwork of a tap dancer, and as Ritchie pressed forward Konstantin continued to step back, taking the sting off Ritchie's hooks but not negating their power entirely.

The kid fought well off the backfoot, but decided to press forward again and stung Ritchie with a three-piece combination consisting of a jab to the head, and two hooks to the body. Ritchie felt his kidneys reverberate and took up a southpaw stance, as if he was holding the left in reserve rather than just trying to keep the kid from touching the screaming limb. Kroekel headhunted now, and Ritchie bobbed and countered with his right, snapping the kid's head back, frustrating him, flicking him in the faces with his punches and blinding him with his right fist that snapped from all angles.

He sniped, circling still, keeping Kroekel at the end of his punches and causing blood to flow from his nose and a mouse to appear beneath his eye. "No End-Swell, kid."

Kroekel's hands were kept at home now. He'd been punished too many times for opening up and he was in survival mode. He muttered to Ritchie in Russian, but Ritchie understood as much of what the kid said as what he wrote in the letter.

He was now as angry at Kroekel as the kid was at him, but his was a controlled aggression. It was a rage deep enough for him to bring his left from behind his back and throw it into the mix. He shot a straight and a jab to the face, both of which connected. He felt the kid's orbital socket fracture under one of his knuckles, crumple like an aluminum can in a drunk's hand.

The boy's mouth was open, trying to suck air while filling with blood. Ritchie mixed his attack now, feinted for the chin and went downstairs, repaying the kid for the decent bodywork he'd done earlier. He hoped Konstantin pissed blood in the morning.

Kroekel groaned and hit the ground, found it wasn't as forgiving as the canvas at the gym where he trained. Ritchie did a beeline for Alpo, so fast that the dealer was convinced he was going to sock him, throw a punch at the puppet master and thereby cut the strings. Dontae was shaken enough for the smile to slide from his face, and he stood up from his seat in the car just in case his road dog needed backup.

Ritchie pulled one of the Ruger pieces from the double-holster Alpo wore. He walked with the sun in his eyes back toward the downed kid who moaned and clutched his stomach as if he had food poisoning.

"Don't body him, man!" Alpo said. "Yo, he's just a baby and you ain't a killer. It ain't worth it, cuz."

Ritchie ignored Alpo, and Dontae's commiserating in the background. "These white boys got us fucked up. I can't be fucking with you no more, Alpo."

Kroekel shielded his eyes from the sun, squinting from the pain and swelling that were setting in now that the first flush of adrenaline had washed away. "Here," Ritchie said. He handed the gun to the kid.

"It's like that?" Alpo said.

Possession of the gun gave Kroekel a new burst of energy, and his eyes twinkled as he held the gun in his hand. He struggled to his feet, winced as he regained his footing, still hobbled especially from the body shots. There was nothing he wanted in the world more than to sit back down, aside from to shoot the man who had killed his father.

He pointed the gun at Ritchie's head, tears falling from his eyes as a jackolantern smile pulled up the corners of his mouth. Ritchie looked inside the gun's barrel, the adrenaline from the fight spiking to new, heretofore unknown levels now that the violence of fists was backed by the sterner promise of death brought by the gun. Ritchie figured this must be what cocaine felt like, or since the gun made everything both rush forward and slow down, maybe it was more like a speedball, the coke and heroin intertwining in his heart as he lived harder now than ever while playing with death.

Kroekel pulled the trigger, and the gun jammed. He'd held it sideways, like the gangsters in the movies. He winced, blinked, deflated. The round had done a stovepipe in the chamber.

Ritchie took the gun from the boy's limp hand, thought about pistol-whipping the kid into submission, but then discarded the notion. He walked the gun back over to

Alpo, who, along with his friend, didn't know what to think now.

"Keep the belt," Ritchie said, and walked back to his car beaten, bruised, and bloodied, yet still alive. Maybe.

ABOUT JOSEPH HIRSCH

Joseph Hirsch is the author of several published novels, short stories, novellas, essays and articles. He holds an M.A. in German Studies and has also worked as a sports journalist, covering boxing matches around the globe. He lives in Cincinnati, Ohio, and can be found online at http://www.joeyhirsch.com